# THE TYPING LADY

*And Other Fictions*

ALSO BY RUTH OZEKI

*My Year of Meats*

*All Over Creation*

*A Tale for the Time Being*

*The Face: A Time Code*

*The Book of Form and Emptiness*

# THE TYPING LADY

*And Other Fictions*

Ruth Ozeki

VIKING

VIKING
An imprint of Penguin Random House LLC
1745 Broadway, New York, NY 10019
penguinrandomhouse.com



Page 322 constitutes an extension of this copyright page.

*Designed by Alexis Sulaimani*

LIBRARY OF CONGRESS CATALOGING-IN-PUBLICATION DATA

Names: Ozeki, Ruth, 1956– author
Title: The typing lady : and other fictions / Ruth Ozeki.
Other titles: Typing lady (Compilation)
Description: New York, NY : Viking, 2026.
Identifiers: LCCN 2025047146 (print) | LCCN 2025047147 (ebook) |
ISBN 9780593832714 hardcover | ISBN 9780593832721 ebook
Subjects: LCGFT: Fiction | Short stories
Classification: LCC PS3565.Z45 T97 2026 (print) | LCC PS3565.Z45 (ebook)
LC record available at https://lccn.loc.gov/2025047146
LC ebook record available at https://lccn.loc.gov/2025047147

Published in hardcover in Great Britain by Canongate Books Ltd., Edinburgh, in 2026.
First United States edition published by Viking, 2026.

Printed in the United States of America
1st Printing

The authorized representative in the EU for product safety and compliance is Penguin Random House Ireland, Morrison Chambers, 32 Nassau Street, Dublin D02 YH68, Ireland, https://eu-contact.penguin.ie.

This book was printed in the United States of America on Alternative Book Cream FSC stock, which is manufactured using FSC-certified fiber.

*For you. Who else?*

## One Art

The art of losing isn't hard to master;
so many things seem filled with the intent
to be lost that their loss is no disaster.

Lose something every day. Accept the fluster
of lost door keys, the hour badly spent.
The art of losing isn't hard to master.

Then practice losing farther, losing faster:
places, and names, and where it was you meant
to travel. None of these will bring disaster.

I lost my mother's watch. And look! my last, or
next-to-last, of three loved houses went.
The art of losing isn't hard to master.

I lost two cities, lovely ones. And vaster,
some realms I owned, two rivers, a continent.
I miss them, but it wasn't a disaster.

—Even losing you (the joking voice, a gesture
I love) I shan't have lied. It's evident
the art of losing's not too hard to master
though it may look like (*Write* it!) like disaster.

—*Elizabeth Bishop*

# Contents

# THE TYPING LADY

*And Other Fictions*

# THE TYPING LADY

## *An Author's Note*

I first met the typing lady in a library. "Met" is not the right word. Let's say I noticed her, became aware of her presence, caught sight of her out of the corner of my eye. She was sitting at a carrel, surrounded by books, typing furiously away on her laptop. It was the typing that drew my attention. The woman herself was nondescript: oldish, in her fifties or sixties, Asian-looking, with black-framed glasses and gray-streaked hair. Not the kind of person one would look at twice, were it not for the typing and the way she scanned the room like an automated monitoring device, her head swiveling one way until her neck reached its limit, then reversing to circle back the other way. She rarely glanced at her keyboard or her screen, yet her fingers never stopped moving, as if she were typing rapid, detailed field notes of her observations, determined not to miss anything.

From time to time, she would pause to study a particular patron—a boy reading, a student sleeping—and I found this interesting because I was studying those same people too. (I wondered to what degree her observations correlated with mine. I would have given anything to see those notes of hers.) Whenever her head rotated in my direction, I pretended to be engrossed in the book on my desk. Her eyes never lingered on me for long. I guess she didn't find me as interesting as I found her. But every time her gaze passed over me, like a shadow, I felt my hackles rise.

Her desk, like mine, was always piled high with books for her research. Sometimes, when she stepped away, I would look at the titles. She read nonfiction mostly, books about philosophy and psychopharmacology, visions and dreams, revolution and madness. I remember seeing familiar names like Borges, Benjamin, and the Grimms, and noting that her tastes were not dissimilar to mine, which, for some reason, annoyed me. Week after week I watched her watching, and so the months passed.

And then, one day, she stopped coming. At first I thought that something must have happened to her. She was not young, as I have said, and naturally I suspected the worst. One becomes fearful with age, anticipating disasters from the personal (heart attacks, strokes, cancers, dementias) to the global (wars, plagues, pestilence, pandemics). Had she gotten sick? Tripped and fallen down the stairs? Been hit by a delivery truck? The staff at our branch keep an eye on the regulars, so I went to the information desk and asked the librarian about the typing lady—did he know whom I meant? Older woman, in her fifties or sixties, black glasses, gray hair, part Asian, perhaps? Had he seen her?—but the librarian just gave me an odd look and shook his head. I knew what he was thinking. I have this power—although it's not consistent—to see inside a person's head and read their mind. Some minds, like the librarian's, are transparent. Others, like the typing lady's, are entirely opaque.

I could see that the librarian thought I was imagining things—paranoid, hallucinating, or high on drugs. It did not escape his notice that the typing lady, as I described her, bore some resemblance to me, and as I walked away from the information desk, it occurred to me that perhaps he was right. Maybe I was experiencing some sort of psychic transference, projecting a doppelgänger into an unoccupied hole in the space-time continuum. Or maybe the typing lady was just in my head?

I decided it was best to forget her, so I did, and went on with my life.

But then, one day, about two years later, as I was passing a bookstore, I noticed a poster announcing a book launch for a new collection of short fiction by a local author, who, to my surprise, looked very much like the typing lady. I stopped to study the poster, and as I inspected the face in the photograph, I could see there were differences. For one thing, the author was elegantly made up and well put together. The typing lady, as I recalled, was unkempt and a little scruffy. I decided to attend the book launch and see for myself.

• • •

The owner of our local independent bookstore has a penchant for fantasy and science fiction, which is reflected in the shop's décor and the titles she carries. Strings of crystals hang in the large front window, refracting light and casting ephemeral rainbows onto the shelves in the dark interior. When the door opens, letting in a slight breeze, the crystals begin to spin, causing the rainbows to dance across the books' spines.

There was a good turnout that day. The author, who may or may not have been the typing lady, seemed to have a loyal local readership, many of whom appeared quite familiar with her oeuvre. The bookstore owner introduced her and gave her an effusive welcome as she took her place at the podium. She was dressed entirely in gray. Her hair was more silvery than I remembered (if, indeed, I was remembering and not making her up), and she had traded her square black glasses for roundish, steely ones, presumably to match her hair. She greeted us warmly and then said she would read a story from the new collection. Part of the story was set in a library, and to my delight I recognized the setting as the one we had shared. But to my frustration, she stopped reading before revealing what happened there.

She smiled and told us we'd have to buy the book to find out. Annoying.

She then moved on to talk about writing—what she called her "process"—and finally took questions from the audience. These were what you might expect: questions about where her ideas for stories came from, about the voices of her characters and the political themes in her work. Someone asked why, after writing only novels, she had decided to switch to short fiction. She said she'd always admired the form and wanted a new challenge, and from there segued into a brief rant about time poverty and patience, diminishing attention spans, and the impact of digital technology on reading skills. Someone asked if she had noticed this in her students, and it became clear that two years earlier she had accepted a visiting writer position at a well-known East Coast liberal-arts college. *Aha!* I thought. That explained it, and I knew for certain that, despite her spruced-up appearance, this was the same woman I used to see typing at the library.

She went on about how much she loved her students—these intense, talented, demanding young writers who were freaking out about all the very legitimate things there are to freak out about these days—but she found herself spending too much time on the institutional bureaucracy of higher ed, wrestling with the college's cloud-based, integrated human-resources management platform, and attending emergency departmental meetings about pedagogy in the age of AI. She said she missed the old days when she was just a writer. I was sitting toward the back of the room, but at that moment I could have sworn she looked right at me.

"What are you writing now?" someone asked, and she laughed. "Emails," she said. She was so busy teaching and touring with the new book that she hadn't written a word of fiction since she turned in her copyedits. Whenever she sat down to write, she fell asleep. She closed her eyes and ran her fingers through her silvery hair. The gesture was a bit theatrical.

I bought a copy of her book and waited in line to get it signed. When my turn came and I approached the table where she sat, she glanced up at me, and it was like looking into a mirror. She must have felt it, too, because she gave me a puzzled stare. "You seem familiar," she said. "Have we met?"

I said we hadn't, which was not a lie. I'd noticed her, been aware of her, studied her closely, but we'd never met. She frowned slightly, shook her head, and then opened her book—now my book—to the title page and asked if I'd like her to personalize it. For a moment, I was tempted to say yes, but what if I read it and didn't like it? I didn't want my name lingering inside a book I might sell or give away.

"Just your signature," I said, and she looked slightly offended.

• • •

I started reading it when I got home that night. The title of the first story in the collection—and the collection itself—was "The

Typing Lady," and in case you think this too much of a coincidence to be believed, I should explain that, prior to reading her story, I did not think of her as "the typing lady." When I first noticed her typing at the library, she was just "that woman who is always typing at the library," or simply "that writer." I came to call her by the moniker only later, *after* I learned of her collection and read the eponymous title story that I am now about to recount, whose protagonist is also called "the typing lady."

I'm sorry if this is confusing.

Anyway, as I was saying, I started reading her story when I got home that night and quickly realized, with a frisson of prurient delight, that it had to be autofiction. *At last!* I thought. A chance to peer inside her head, to glimpse that opaque mind.

The typing lady (the protagonist), like the typing lady (the author), was a writer who traveled around giving lectures about her work at fancy East Coast colleges and universities. Driving through a Boston suburb after a lecture at Harvard, she passed an old typewriter store. She almost drove right by it, but at the last second she noticed an empty parking space in front, and on a whim she pulled over. The shop looked closed, but when she tried the door, it opened, and a bell tinkled overhead. The interior was dim, and it took a while for her eyes to adjust, but slowly she began to make out details. Dusty metal shelves lined the walls, upon which rested row after row of old manual typewriters. The typing lady had never seen so many typewriters in one place before, and as she gazed at these handsome old machines, she knew she must have one. The owner, hearing the bell, emerged from the workshop at the rear of the store to greet her. He cleared a space on an old wooden desk, handed her a stack of blank white paper, and told her to feel free to try any of the machines. Her gaze traveled along the rows.

"They're all so beautiful," she said. "I don't know where to start."

"Start anywhere," he said. "Choose one that speaks to you and see how it feels. You'll know the right one when you type on it."

A matte-black 1947 Remington Rand caught her eye. The round, black keys and soft curve of the top cover were familiar and pleasing. Her mother had owned a Remington like this. She lifted it from the shelf, carried it to the desk, slid a sheet of paper into the roller, and began to type.

T he q uic k bro wn f ox jum ped ove r t he laz y d og.

The space bar seemed sticky—the spaces erratic, words splitting, letters drifting—but the clack of the keys and the carriage return sounded exactly as she remembered from her childhood. Her mother used to type sonnets on her Remington Rand, which she submitted to the weekend Poetry Corner in their local newspaper. The typing lady remembered how, during the week after a submission, her mother would chain-smoke cigarettes as she waited to learn whether her poem would be chosen. Her father, a history professor who had published several well-regarded books about the Tudors, laughed at her. "Your mother has great ambitions," he'd say. "She wants to see her name in print. She wants to be immortalized."

The typing lady remembered this. She remembered laughing at her mother too. It seemed funny at the time.

When her mother died, she found the typed carbon copies of her sonnets in a filing cabinet, along with polite submission letters to the editor. In one manila folder lay a single newspaper clipping. It was a limerick, which read:

```
There once was an unhappy wife
Whose heart was tormented by strife.
But with courage and grace,
Her discontent she displaced,
To embrace all the wonders of life.
```

The poet's name was printed underneath the verse, but it was not her mother's name. Was it her mother's poem? Had she published it under a pen name? As far as the typing lady knew, her mother didn't write doggerel, so perhaps the limerick wasn't hers. But then she found a second ditty, typed on the back of an old envelope. At first, it looked like a draft of the published poem, but after reading it, she wondered if her mother had written it later, in response.

There once was an unhappy wife
Who uprooted her strife with a knife.
She carved out her heart,
And took it apart,
And so ended her unfulfilled life.

The typing lady remembered all this as she set the Remington back on the shelf.

The next typewriter she tried was an antique Underwood, circa 1930. It was a heavy machine, upright and cumbersome, and she knew it was wrong as soon as she started typing.

Now is the time for all brave men

The carriage was stiff, and the keys were stubbornly resistant, so she stopped before finishing the sentence. It was a Depression-era machine, and it reminded her of her father, who had always insisted that her mother's death had been an accident.

The next one was a watermelon-pink Olivetti Lettera, made in Italy in 1972. It was sleek and low, light to the touch. The keys were responsive, and so she quickly typed:

*Pack my box zith five dowen liquor jugs.*

The letters were all working, and the italic typeface was nice, but the keyboard had a European QZERTY rather than a

QWERTY layout, which she hadn't noticed at first. She tried again, more slowly:

`Waltz, bad nymph, for quick jigs are vexing,`

before concluding that her fingers would never remember where the *W* and *Z* keys were, and that anyway, the pink was distracting.

It took her almost three hours, but in the end she left the store with a plain gray-green 1956 Royal, with a solid metal body and a double gothic typeface. It was a workmanlike machine, nothing flashy. She took it home and set it on her dining room table. A week later, after a lecture at Columbia, she bought a second one—a 1940 Smith-Corona with a pica typeface—at a typewriter store near Gramercy Park. The third she bought on eBay: a two-toned German Olympia, with a rare senatorial sans-serif typeface. The fourth . . .

Her dining room table was soon covered with old typewriters. Reminded of stories she had read about hoarders, she worried she might be going overboard, but she couldn't help herself. The machines were so beautiful. She liked typing at night, a tumbler of Irish whiskey at hand, after her other work was done. She was enchanted by the physicality of typing, how her fingers had to labor for each letter, and though it was awkward and slow at first, her hands remembered the work. Her ears remembered the clack of the keys, the margin bell, and the carriage return. Her mind remembered how to think slowly enough for her fingers to keep up. She liked how the keys struck the page with letters and words, leaving a tangible impression of her ideas that she could not delete, even the mistaken ones.

As her thoughts slowed, strange things began to happen. Her fingers typed sentences that at first she didn't recognize as hers, and then the sentences turned into characters with desires she couldn't control. It was as if they were germinating *inside* the typewriters themselves, and she began to wonder whether there might be some kind of mechanism—something highly responsive and even interactive, like an organ inside a human body or an algorithm in a large language model—that was producing these texts. Little by little she saw that the characters and stories she was typing were not entirely unknown to her; indeed, the more she typed, the more familiar they became. The typewriters seemed to be *learning* her.

She started to recognize things on the page: random objects from old stories; discarded characters from early drafts; settings, plot points, and symbols she had used in the past and then forgotten. These fictional elements were like ghostly relics—refugees from earlier work that had somehow found their way back, seeking shelter deep inside these antique machines—waiting for the right time to resurface on the page, to resume their old lives or even find new ones.

And this was the astonishing part: these old elements not only found new lives, they were lives unlike any she had ever thought to type before. They were the lives of others. Some of them were small and unremarkable (like her mother's), and these pages she tore from whichever typewriter had produced them and quickly recycled. But other lives were singular and thrilling: the epic lives of men who went to war, or battled bulls, or landed large fishes; the tripped-out lives of Beat poets, trapped inside their fever dreams; the postapocalyptic lives of stoic fathers and sons, struggling to survive in the ruins of a once-great land.

Where could they be coming from? Lying in bed at night, drunk on whiskey and the clamor of words, she remembered that this was how she'd felt when she was starting out as a writer, banging away on an old Smith-Corona into the wee hours, fueled by youthful ambition. As if anything were possible. Now she wondered if her mother had felt this way, too, when she was young and working on her sonnets. Thoughts like these made sleep difficult.

The machines were old, and when a key got stuck or the carriage jammed, all output stopped. She went on Reddit, downloaded PDFs of vintage typewriter repair manuals, and bought tools and parts on eBay. She watched YouTube videos and learned how to take the typewriters apart, and as her knowledge of their inner workings grew, she became obsessed with finding the mechanism of origin—the source of all these lives and stories—but it eluded her, until—

Just then, the sound of someone fumbling with the porch lock interrupted my reading. It was my husband, Oliver, who had arrived on the late train from the city, where he teaches. We see each other on the weekends. Sometimes he comes here, and sometimes I go there. We've been married for a long time, and this arrangement suits us. I put the book down and went to greet him and pour him a beer, and we got to talking. Later, as I was brushing my teeth before bed, I caught sight of my reflection in the mirror and realized I looked nothing like the typing lady after all. Over the long weekend, her short-story collection got buried beneath the stack of unopened mail my husband brought back from the city, and I forgot all about it. When he left and I had time to read again, I remembered the book and went to look for it. I couldn't find it anywhere. Thinking Oliver might have taken it by mistake, I texted him to ask.

"It's called *The Typing Lady*," I typed. "It has a picture of a typewriter on the cover."

"Nope. Not here."

Frustrating. I hate it when things go missing, which may be why I couldn't stop thinking about it. I found myself wondering how the story ended, and whether the typing lady (the protagonist) had found what she was looking for inside her machines. I went online and checked the library database, but there was a two-month wait, so I didn't bother placing a hold. I could have bought another copy, but I couldn't bring myself to spend money on something I already owned. I'm stubborn that way.

And then, a few weeks later, I had a dream. I was in the typing lady's house, though I wasn't sure whether it was the house of the writer or her protagonist. Probably the latter, because her dining room table was covered with typewriters and typewriter parts, as it had been in the story. The light was dim, but I could make out piles of typebars and striker keys, platens and rollers, spool nuts and thumbscrews, assorted knobs and ribbons. There were jars filled with tools: small wrenches, screwdrivers, and needle-nose pliers. There were springs, bands, bells, and hundreds of tiny parts in dishes. There were cleaning supplies too: oil cans, bottles of methylated spirits, stiff brushes, soft brushes, and an assortment of cloths.

Amid all this sat the typing lady. She was hunched over the carapace of a matte-black antique typewriter, but I couldn't see the make. She was wearing an old-fashioned monocular loupe over one eye, the kind a watchmaker or a jeweler might use, and she had a headlamp strapped to her forehead. In her right hand she held a butter knife, and in the left a pair of long surgical forceps. The bright LED beam was aimed at the interior of the machine. Carefully she inserted the forceps into the hollow, followed by the blade of the knife. I took a step closer, aware of a low, liquid throbbing sound, which seemed to emanate from the workspace in front of her, though it might only have been a bass track from some ambient electronica playing in the background. I tried to look over her shoulder, and although I still couldn't get close enough to see what she was doing inside, I did recognize the label identifying the typewriter as a Remington Rand. She seemed to be probing for something with the forceps, and then she must have found it, because she started teasing it out with the butter knife, the way you might winkle a clam from its shell. Slowly she withdrew the forceps, and I could see an object dangling from the tips. It was small, red, and glistening, and it seemed to be squirming, as if alive, though perhaps that was only the trembling of the typing lady's hand. Her breath caught, but then she steadied herself, transferring the object to the flat blade of the knife and bringing it closer to her face to inspect it—and that's when I got a better look at it too. It lay on the blade, bright red against the stainless steel. It was still squirming, and at first I thought it was the tip of a tongue, but looking more closely, I saw it was a tiny living heart.

The typing lady stared at it, and her eyes filled with tears. "Is that you?" she whispered. The tiny heart didn't answer. It looked tired. The typing lady closed her eyes. "I'm sorry," she said, and then, as I watched, she brought the blade to her lips, slid the heart into her mouth, and swallowed.

• • •

It was a creepy, shockingly vivid dream, and the image of that tired heart, beating on the end of the blade, haunted me for days. Have you had dreams like that—ones that linger and cloud your waking hours? Don't you wonder where they come from? What they mean?

Clearly, the image was connected to the typing lady's mother and to her hopeful sonnets and her terrible rhymes, but why, then, did my subconscious create a scenario in which the daughter eats her mother's heart?

Is this what children do?

My mother had dreams. Yours probably did too—dreams and aspirations, ambitions they set aside in order to have us. My mom lived a long life and died just shy of ninety. I think she was happy, or at least happy enough. I know she had moments of happiness. She tried to write a memoir once, but I don't think her heart was in it. She also had a typewriter. I don't remember what kind it was, and neither did she. At the end of her life, she had Alzheimer's, so there was much that she forgot.

I never did find the typing lady's book, so I don't know what befell her or her protagonist. But this author's note is not really about their stories. It's about yours and mine, about how, when we read a story, we bring our own lives to bear on it and make it ours, no matter what the writer might have intended. Stories are like that. They are collaborations between people who read and people who type. They are how we co-create each other and dream ourselves into being.

# THE ANTHROPOLOGIST'S KID

There used to be this joke at Yale that in order to get tenure in the Anthropology Department you had to have an "Oriental" wife. Nowadays, of course, it's not okay to use that word, but this was back in the olden days, when we used language like that, and mostly it was the Oriental wives who told this joke and found it funny. Everyone knew there was truth in it. After the war, many of the tenured anthropologists had married Asian women, and if you included all the graduate students and untenured teaching staff—the assistants, associates, and adjuncts who, by accident or design, had mimicked the marital predilections of the senior faculty—their numbers achieved some statistical significance.

The anthropologists were all white guys.

They were tall white guys with stooped shoulders and sunburned necks they protected from the foreign rays with folded kerchiefs. Their skin, leathery from years in the field, had the crosshatched texture of plucked chickens. Their thin, sand-colored hair was matted with sweat and stuck to their high, receding foreheads when they took off their pith helmets. Some of them worked for the CIA.

I'm just kidding. They didn't really wear pith helmets, at least not at home. At home, in New Haven, our dads wore tweed jackets with fraying cuffs, elbow patches, and missing buttons—buttons that their wives, our moms, deftly repaired with quick, Asian fingers, sucking their teeth and muttering all the while in their various tongues.

Our moms were indeed various. They were Japanese and Korean and Burmese. They were Filipina and Fujianese, Maldivian and Malay. Some of them had been students. Others worked as secretaries or linguistic informants for their husbands. A few had PhDs and taught. All of them knew how to type, catalog, and file. Here is something else they had in common: They were all considerably shorter than their husbands.

Anthropology Department parties were exotic affairs, tribal gatherings much envied by other faculties at Yale. When a political science or mathematics professor was invited to dinner, or graduate students from econ or English lit infiltrated one of our cocktail parties, they stood out like sore thumbs, made instantly conspicuous by their tall, blond wives. In the days before cheap ethnic cuisine—before sushi and pad thai and shawarma and falafel became available on every street corner in New Haven—

these departmental outsiders came to sample our anthropological fare. They came to eat our roasted meat on skewers, to dip their shrimp chips into our strange sauces. Because when an Oriental wife cooked even something as mundane as meat loaf, you could be sure it had a hidden kick to it, something peppery and piquant.

Our mothers were narrow and neat. They wore sheathlike shifts with small stand-up collars and cap sleeves. They wore cat-eye glasses that accentuated the slant of their eyes. They had dark hair that they kept bobbed or cropped or curled with chemical permanent waves in an Occidental style. They held themselves as carefully as they held their drinks, never spilling a drop. They were quick, bright, and birdlike, compared with our slow-moving, long-limbed, observant fathers. We, their dusky, half-breed children, slipped among their adult legs like eels in seagrass. We fed from the circulating trays and ogled our guests, those exotic non-anthropological Others. We snapped up shrimp toast and small dumplings, trying to avoid the sharp eyes and pinching fingers of our mothers, who could scold us in so many languages and never hesitated to do so.

My best friend in the department was a girl named Fatima, who was half Filipina. Her mother was a Moro from Mindanao, and Fatima used to tell people that she was a cannibal. She and I were always trying to one-up each other, shuffling through our ancestors' ethnographic traits and hurling exoticisms down onto the table like baseball cards.

"My grandpa had a samurai sword," I told her once. "He could have cut your grandpa up into little pieces."

She stared at me and shook her head. "Nah," she said. "My grandpa woulda ate your grandpa for breakfast and digested him and pooped him out before lunch."

What could you say to that?

I was named Joji after my Japanese grandfather, but everyone called me Georgie, or Georgie-boy, which I hated. Fatima had an American name, too—Norma—but as the son of an anthropologist, I was drawn to authenticity, so I insisted on using her Muslim name when we were together. She let me, as long as I promised not to call her that in school. She told me that in the Philippines she had always been just Fatima, but when she came here, the kids called her Fatty. She wasn't fat at all—in fact, she was tiny—still, it bothered her just the same. That was before America toughened her up.

Her mom couldn't drive, and my mom had a job at the museum, so after school we hung around the Anthropology Department and waited for our dads to finish teaching so they could drive us home. The department was located at 51 Hillhouse Avenue, next to the president's mansion. It was housed in an old wooden folly of a building, bristling with turrets and arches and pinnacles and dentil moldings. It's brown now, but back then it was painted a dark yellow that always looked faded, and it had a huge, heavy pair of oaken doors that I couldn't open by myself until I was seven.

Inside, a wide staircase rose through the middle of the building, with a swooping banister we could slide down when classes were over and no one was watching. In the winter we played in one of the empty seminar rooms or in my dad's office. The secretaries let us type on their typewriters. They gave us scrap paper to draw on, and sometimes, if we begged them, they let us help run the mimeograph machine. That was our favorite. We loved the smell of the purple ink. You could almost get high on it.

In early summer, when the weather turned hot and the New Haven air grew as thick and muggy as a tropical rainforest, we sat on the splintery wooden steps of the department building and talked. The large casement windows in the downstairs classrooms were kept open in the heat, and we could hear our dads inside, droning on about kinship systems or totemism or sexual taboos. When we got bored, we played hopscotch or bounced our Super Balls on the sidewalk in front. There was one particular spot of pavement that sounded hollow and therefore, we reasoned, must contain something hidden or lost: a vast store of untold treasure; votive statuary in solid gold; jewel-encrusted amulets; exquisite trinkets and baubles. Being anthropologists' kids, we knew all about these things.

"It's right under here," I told Fatima, bouncing. "Can you hear it?"

Beneath the thin skin of the sidewalk, the cavity resounded. If we could only reach it and uncover its riches, we would be so celebrated! Our fathers would run from their classrooms, trailed by their graduate students. They would shake their heads and marvel—*Imagine! A discovery this important, made by mere children!*—while our mothers would smile knowingly.

"Yes," Fatima said. "How are we going to get it out?"

Fatima had an annoying tendency to get mired in practicalities, but she had a point. This, however, was my area of expertise, since my dad was more on the archaeological side of anthropology, whereas hers leaned more toward the cultural.

"We have to launch an expedition," I told her. "We have to secure funding. We'll apply for a grant. We'll hire graduate students to do the digging."

I pictured the moment when the square of pavement would be lifted like a lid to reveal not just the treasure, but an entire ancient world below—a world where boys like me were princes, lying under canopies on silken divans with ropes of gold draped around our necks, while beautiful Egyptian slave girls with palm fronds fanned our languid bodies. It shames me to think of these childhood fantasies now, but back then these images were rife on TV, in the movies, and in our comic books. We never questioned them.

Fatima looked skeptical. "What if there's no treasure?"

"There's treasure. Just listen." I bounced my Super Ball on the adjacent concrete and the sound was solid and dense. Then I tried the spot in question, which gave a hollow echo. "See?"

"What if it's just a hole."

I wanted to hit her. "It's not," I said. I found a stick and crouched to dig into a crumbling patch of cement, uprooting a tuft of grass that had withered in the heat. "It's filled with stuff, I promise."

Fatima watched me. "You know," she said, "even just one diamond, if it was big enough, could be worth millions of dollars."

I considered this possibility. "I'm sure there's at least two," I told her. It was my hole. I could afford to be generous.

"Well, even if there is treasure, we can't keep it," she said.

"We won't. We'll sell it."

And I knew exactly how I would spend my millions. I would buy the Adventures in Chemistry! set that I'd seen in the toy department at Malley's. The deluxe edition had a picture on the box of an earnest-looking, blue-eyed boy in shorts with a blond cowlick. I wanted to be him, and if I couldn't be him, then I wanted his chemistry set. It came with forty-nine different chemicals, test tubes you could display on a rack, and a booklet with more than 1,500 experiments that would teach the young chemist everything from nuclear physics and atomic energy to glassblowing. I was going to turn my bedroom into a lab and learn how to blow things up. I was going to make a fortune inventing enormous Super Balls that would bounce me to the moon. I was going to concoct a special potion that would make me as fair as the chemistry boy, or as dark and beautiful as Fatima.

She shook her head. "You can't," she said.

"Why not?"

"'Cause you have to make the treasure available to science, so that other people can study it and benefit. You have to donate it to a museum or something."

She was right, of course, but her high-minded principles were cramping my infinite chemical potentiality, and I resented her for that. Without the sale of at least one large diamond I would never be able to buy the deluxe edition of Adventures in Chemistry!, and without it, my world contracted abruptly.

"We won't tell them," I said. "We'll turn over most of the stuff but just keep one gem each . . ."

Fatima frowned and pushed forward her lower lip, which I admired for its plumpness and purplish tinge. "It's wrong to keep secrets," she said. Fatima was a bit square, which could get on a person's nerves. "They'd find out, and then we'd be in trouble."

"So what? We'd be rich. It wouldn't matter."

I was always the bold one. I was the boy, after all, and almost eleven, a full year older than she was. And my dad was the chairman of the department, and her dad didn't even have tenure. Usually I could make Fatima do what I said, but not always.

• • •

The day the two men in suits showed up at the department, we were in the supply room on the second floor, sniffing Magic Markers and stealing chalk. We were going to make a secret map with invisible ink, leading to our treasure, but first we had to mark the spot on the sidewalk with an X, which is why we needed the chalk. The markers had nothing to do with our plan, except that the acrid smell made us lightheaded and kept us in the closet longer than we needed to be. Just as we were about to step out, we heard the creak of the staircase and the sound of footsteps on the treads. We ducked back inside, leaving the door open just a crack. Crouched in the dark, we saw the close-cropped tops of two men's heads rise into view as they climbed. Then, a moment later, we noticed the suits.

Suits like these were signifiers. With the exception of some of the younger faculty who had taken to wearing turtlenecks because it was 1969, most of the anthropologists wore jackets and collared shirts and neckties to the office. These ensembles of our fathers could hardly be called suits, however, since their jackets and trousers rarely matched. But these two men were different. They matched. Nobody in our tribe dressed like this.

It was a subtle thing, the semiotics of these suits that enabled Fatima and me to read danger. Most conspicuous was the color and texture of the fabric, a sleek, gunmetal gray, with a brand-new sheen that was decidedly not anthropological. Then there was the condition of the clothing, the conspicuous absence of fraying on the jacket cuffs and the equally significant presence of freshly pressed creases in the trousers.

There were other telltale signs, too, which marked these men as outsiders as clearly as ritual scarification or a facial tattoo: the bristling military crew cuts; the subdued, monochrome neckties, neatly tucked inside their jackets; the jackets that were properly buttoned. They carried folded raincoats over their arms and slim briefcases that shut properly and weren't spilling over with ungraded papers. They did not wear cardigan sweaters. They hadn't forgotten to shave.

"They must be spies!" I whispered to Fatima, as they passed our closet. "Or assassins. Come on!"

Fatima clung to my shirt. "We can't!"

"We can," I told her, gravely. "We must."

I slipped out of the closet and followed, staying close to the wall where the worn floorboards were less likely to creak and give away our position. I could hear the men moving down the hallway toward my father's office, and even their footsteps sounded different—not the distracted, professorial shuffle, but a purposeful stride.

Fatima, my shadow, was right behind me. We ducked behind a filing cabinet in the small conference room adjacent to my father's office and watched as the men came to a full stop in front of his door. They glanced at each other and nodded, and then they knocked. I heard my dad's muffled voice answer, and I knew they had caught him in the bathroom. My dad hated being chairman of the department because people were always catching him in the bathroom. People were always dropping into his office right before classes were about to start, or phoning him at home just as we were about to sit down for dinner. And sure enough, when he came to the door, he was wiping his hands on his handkerchief, and his necktie was crooked. I wanted to tell him to straighten it, but one of the men had started talking in a low voice that I couldn't hear, and then my dad stepped back, and I heard him sigh and say, "Of course. Come in. But I have a class starting in a few minutes."

I watched those two neat men cross in front of my rumpled father. The door clicked shut behind them, and the sound made me shiver. Just then Dorothy, the department secretary, came up the stairs with a stack of mail. She spotted us lurking and shooed us downstairs and out the door.

• • •

"G-men!" my mother said that night. Her lip curled, and she expelled the two syllables as though they were something horribly bitter. She deposited a loaded dinner plate in front of my dad.

"Well, yes," my dad said, looking up at her. "So you see why I couldn't exactly send them packing . . ."

My mom didn't reply, just turned her back, which meant she certainly did not see at all.

Dinner that night was beef teriyaki, which was one of my favorites. I waited until she finished serving and sat down. "What's a geemen?" I asked her.

"Eat," she told me, picking up her chopsticks.

I took a bite and swallowed, and then turned to my dad. "What's a geemen?"

My dad cleared his throat. "Government men," he said. "*G* stands for government."

My mother snorted. "Gangster, more like it."

"Michi . . ."

"It's true," she said.

I waited, but she didn't continue. "Are they really gangsters?" I asked.

"Of course not," my dad said. "They work for the Central Intelligence Agency, which is part of the federal government."

"Intelligence?" my mother said, but it wasn't a question. She put down her chopsticks. "They steal," she said. "They kidnap. Just like gangsters."

My father didn't reply. Married to an Oriental, he had learned a thing or two about silence.

"You know it's true," my mother told him, then she turned to me. "They stole Grandpa Joji's store. They kidnapped us and took us to the desert. They made us live in a horse stall. All of us Japanese. We lost everything."

I knew the story. I'd heard it a million times. She turned back to my father. "I hope you told them to get lost."

"Well," my dad said, clearing his throat. "In a manner of speaking . . ."

My mother pursed her lips and made a sound with her nose,

which indicated how she felt about my father's manner of speaking.

"It's not that simple, Michi," my dad said, defensively. "You know I'm opposed to this kind of thing. I told them I was certain none of our men would be interested. I can only hope they got the message."

"Good riddance," my mother said.

My dad hesitated. "They wanted to talk to Manny."

My mom looked up. "Why Manny?"

Manuel Estrada was Fatima's dad. He was a white guy, but different. He was short. And Hispanic. His jackets were just a little bit nattier, like he was trying too hard.

"Did he do something wrong?" I asked.

"Of course not," Dad said. He took another bite of teriyaki and paused to chew. He was a very thorough chewer. I thought the conversation was over, but then he turned to my mom. "Things are heating up again in his part of the world."

The men of anthropology had the world pretty much divided up and covered. Manny's part of the world was the Philippines.

"Are they going to kidnap him?" I asked. If they were going to kidnap him, I had to warn Fatima.

"Of course not."

"Are they going to assassinate him?" It wasn't such a far-fetched idea. Martin Luther King Jr. and Robert F. Kennedy had both been assassinated the previous year.

"Don't be silly, Georgie," my father said.

"Poor Manny," my mother said. "Are you going to give him tenure or not?"

"It's not just up to me, Michi. You know that."

"Poor Samira," my mom said.

• • •

The Peabody Museum of Natural History is the big neo-Gothic building with steep pinnacles and vaulted windows on Whitney Avenue, right around the corner from the Anthropology Department. My mom worked there, cataloging for the curator, and Fatima and I liked to hang out in the gift shop, where they sold small, polished stones that we would slip into our pockets when the cashier wasn't looking. There were two matching silver rings inlaid with mother-of-pearl that we coveted, too, but they were locked in the display case by the register. I decided that once I sold my diamond, I would buy us those rings, and then maybe Fatima would marry me—not immediately, of course, but someday.

I had grown up in the museum. The Great Hall of Dinosaurs was as familiar to me as my own living room, and I had even helped paint the base under the towering brontosaurus skeleton. Now that I was older, I was colonizing less-populated corners of the cavernous old building. Cutting through the Ages of Man, I would lead Fatima past the dioramas where Native Americans crouched in perpetuity next to teepees, weaving baskets and skinning elk with crude stone tools. We climbed the stairs, ignoring the Birds of the Connecticut Valley, and headed instead for the live reptiles. There are no live animals at the Peabody now, but back then they kept a few, tucked away on the very top floor. There, amid the snake tanks, I taught Fatima how to fox-trot.

I was taking ballroom dancing at the Lawn Club once a week. It was my mother's idea. She thought boys needed to be civilized and that dance classes would do the trick. Although I sensed he didn't quite agree, my father kept quiet. I didn't mind. Unlike my dad, I liked dancing, and I was good at it. The teacher, Mr. Porter, was tall and probably gay, although we didn't know it at the time. He was so tall that when he demonstrated a dance step with the girls, they would have to stretch their arms way over their heads to reach his shoulder, lifting their minidresses up the backs of their thighs until sometimes you could even see their underpants. The boys liked that. They sat on the sidelines and laughed and tried to push each other off the folding chairs. I wasn't that interested in girls, except for Fatima, but I liked the boxes of cream-filled chocolates that you could win if you did the steps right. I would save my chocolates and share them with Fatima at the museum. We would stick our tongues right into the creamy centers. Fatima didn't take dance lessons. She said she didn't want to, but I think she wasn't allowed. Dark people didn't go to the Lawn Club. It was that kind of place in those days.

Box-stepping Fatima past the asps and the thick constrictors, I would tell her about dance class and who'd had to waltz with Mr. Porter. We would circle the cobra that hung from its stump, then tango down to Minerals and Gems, where the halls were narrow and black lights made the hard crystals glitter. There, in the darkness, next to the long shafts of tourmaline, I shared my chocolates with her and showed her how to do things. In front of the feldspar, I taught her to suck the inside of her arm hard enough to leave a hickey. I was always amazed, holding her wrist and turning it over, to see how pale the underside of her arm was. In the dim ultraviolet light, she glowed like alabaster, and in my childish, inchoate way, I wanted to bring blood to the surface of her skin, to mark her with my lips. Maybe we're all a little cannibal at heart.

The day after the dinner conversation with my parents, I met Fatima in the Peabody gift shop after school. We didn't linger. I grabbed her hand and dragged her up the old stone stairs to the deserted top floor. Without so much as a curtsy or a bow, I took her in my arms and danced her down the Hall of Gems and told her what I'd heard about the G-men.

"They want to kidnap your dad," I whispered in her ear. "Things are heating up in his part of the world."

I felt Fatima stumble. I pressed my palm to the small of her back and held her tighter.

"They may even want to assassinate him."

I was sure she would argue with me, but to my surprise she

whimpered, as if she might cry. I gave her a gentle push, steering her deeper into the darkness.

"We have to save him."

My breath tangled in her hair and felt hot against my lips. Her small fingers tightened on my shoulder as I danced her toward the wall. We came to a stop against the glass of a display case. Backlit by ultraviolet, with the rocks and minerals sparkling behind her, she looked beautiful and mysterious. Her black hair veiled her face. Her eyes filled with tears and glinted like agates. I lifted a wing of her hair and kissed her. Her mouth was soft and wet and strangely compliant, and somehow that confused and maddened me. She wasn't doing it right. Girls should resist, I thought, and so I kissed her again, harder, aware now of the edge of her tooth, the ridgeline of her jaw. My tongue was a primitive tool, a blunt rock or a sharpened stick, meant to pry her open. She started to struggle, so I clamped my hands on her narrow skull to hold her in place. I heard a strangled noise—her voice, a cry of protest—but I ignored it. Part of me knew I was pushing too far. I should have stopped. I should have listened to her. I should have respected her wishes. But I didn't, so she bit off my tongue.

Only the tip was severed, but the pain was blinding, a searing whiteness that exploded inside my head like shrapnel. I staggered back, shoving her away. Hot blood filled my mouth. She stared in horror, then her hand flew to her lips. Through the haze of pain, I watched her spit and then look down at the little nub of flesh cupped in her palm. Not knowing what to do with it, she held it out to me.

"Here," she said.

It looked like a small piece of bloody chewing gum. Speechless, I reached for it, and she tipped my tongue into the palm of my hand, and that was when I fainted.

• • •

Fatima never told anyone what really happened, and neither did I. Later I learned that she had run downstairs to the basement and the museum archives, where my mother was doing some filing. Fatima's mouth was red with blood, so of course my mom, having no way of knowing that the blood was mine, thought she had been horribly injured. Somehow Fatima convinced her otherwise, and then she led my mom in a mad dash up the many flights of stairs because the ancient elevator was too slow. They found me on the floor beside the tourmalines and crystals, deathly pale beneath the black light that had drained all color from my face. The gemstones glittered. The blood spilled from my mouth, inky under the ultraviolet. My mother must have screamed then, because I came to and opened my eyes. An image of her face, as white as a vampire, fluttered briefly into my consciousness before I passed out again.

The next thing I remember was lying on a bed in the hospital, under the bright light, with my mouth prised open, jaw clamped, and a doctor leaning over me, attempting to stitch the tip of my tongue back onto its root. They had found the little nub, clutched in my fist on the way to the emergency room. Once again, Fatima had led them to it. In the midst of all the chaos and commotion, she reached over and took my wrist and pried open my fingers, one by one. Then she tugged on my mom's sleeve to show her.

"It's his tongue," she whispered.

They say that mouth wounds heal quickly, but it still took several weeks. My mother let me stay home from school for the first little while, and she fed me rice puddings, Japanese egg custard, and bright cherry Jell-O with discs of pale banana suspended inside. It soon became clear that the damage to the anterior portion of my tongue was permanent, although not terribly severe. I lost some of my ability to taste sweetness, and I still speak with a slight lisp. But I shouldn't complain. What I did was wrong, and the fact that I have a tongue at all is due to Fatima's kindness. That I almost lost it was certainly not her fault.

My mother never questioned the explanation I provided. At first, on account of the injury, I couldn't say much of anything at all, and by the time I could talk again, I'd concocted a story about tripping and falling and knocking my jaw against the display case. But I could tell by the way my mother looked at me askance from behind her cat-eye glasses that she had her suspicions. She was wondering how my blood had ended up on Fatima. In Fatima's mouth. She never confided her suspicions to my father, however. These were matters that our mothers handled on their own.

"Where's your little friend?" my dad would ask me in the months that followed, when he noticed me skulking around the Anthropology Department corridors alone. I would shrug and play dumb, and he would pat my head absentmindedly and shamble off. That's one thing about anthropologists—they never notice what is happening right beneath their noses.

When I could eat again, I returned to school and quickly realized that Fatima was avoiding me. She wouldn't talk to me. She wouldn't even meet my eye. Our mothers had apparently come to a decision, either by direct consultation or some other form of inscrutable, telepathic consensus, to end our friendship. Samira was very strict, and I knew Fatima would obey the maternal dictum without protest. I tried to convince myself that this was the only reason she wasn't talking to me, but I suspected our estrangement reflected her preference as well.

Desperate to win her back, I considered my options and finally came up with a plan. If her father was in danger, I would protect him. I would keep an eye on him, shadow his every move, and when the G-men jumped him, I would be there to save his life. There would be a fight of some sort—this part was still hazy in my mind—but in the end, due to my cleverness, the righteousness of my cause, and the power of my love, I would prevail. My father would clap my shoulder and shake my hand and give Manny tenure. Samira would weep with gratitude at my bravery, and my mother would, too, and together they would humbly apologize for their sly interferences and aspersions. But best of all, Fatima would be mine again.

The minute school was out, I ran down to Hillhouse Avenue and began the stakeout. Mostly it was boring. Professor Manny Estrada spent his afternoons either in class, teaching, or in his office seeing students. He attended department meetings and committee meetings, and I used those times as opportunities to case the surrounding areas, figuring the G-men wouldn't try to take him out in front of a roomful of anthropologists. There wasn't much out of the ordinary to discover, though. Once I thought I spotted the two of them, lurking in their suits by the Kline Biology Tower, but when I got closer, they had vanished.

Then, one day, when I was outside Professor Estrada's office helping Dorothy with the mimeograph machine, I heard his phone ring. He picked up and spoke, hurried and low, and I couldn't make out what he was saying. I heard him hang up, then a few minutes later he emerged from his office, locking his door behind him. Mumbling some excuse, I left Dorothy holding a sheaf of fragrant, wet stencils and ran after him.

When I got to the sidewalk, Professor Estrada had already turned left toward Science Hill. He crossed Sachem and climbed the slope, cutting through Kline Biology, where I thought I'd seen the two G-men lurking. From there he proceeded toward the Wright Nuclear Lab. He didn't see me following. He never looked behind him, neither left nor right. He just kept moving straight ahead, head down, body angled forward as though he were walking into a stiff wind.

I trailed him to the parking lot behind the electron accelerator, where he stopped. I ducked behind an old Studebaker that was parked nearby and pressed my forehead to the cool, chrome fender. My heart was pounding. My tongue throbbed and tasted of metal. I waited for a moment, then rose slowly and peered around the tail fin.

Across the lot, I could see Professor Estrada, leaning down and talking to someone through the window of an idling car. I was pretty sure it was the G-men—I could tell from the car, a sleek black Ford with a profile that meant business—but I was still too far away. Like a crab, I scuttled closer, moving down the row of parked vehicles, keeping low to the ground. As I approached, I could hear the smooth purr of the Ford's engine and the murmur of voices. I stopped again, gathered my courage, and lifted my head over the hood of a VW. Professor Estrada was partly blocking my view, but I thought I could see two men sitting in the car. The tinted glass of the driver's window was rolled partway down, and it looked like they were wearing matching mirrored sunglasses. A moment later, Professor Estrada straightened. He shook hands with the driver, and then he took a step back and watched as the black Ford glided away. He looked hot in his tweed jacket, which was unusually rumpled, and for a moment he seemed genuinely anthropological. When the car pulled out onto Whitney Avenue and merged into traffic, I thought I saw his shoulders slump. He ran his fingers through his hair, only he held them there a little too long, as if clutching his head on either side might keep it from rolling off his shoulders.

That night at dinner, I waited until my mom had served us and sat down, and my father had taken his first bite—I think it was beef in black bean sauce, one of his favorites—and then I broached the subject.

"I saw the G-men down by the atom smasher," I announced.

Dad sighed, put his chopsticks down, and wiped his mouth. "They're not G-men, Georgie."

"But Mom said . . ."

"Your mother has her reasons to distrust the government, and she's perfectly within her rights to do so, but that was then, and this is now. You mustn't go around imagining things."

"I'm not imagining!" I cried. "I saw them in the parking lot. They were in a black car." I hesitated for a moment. "They were talking to Fatima's dad."

Dad picked up his chopsticks again. "Are you sure?"

I nodded. "They were talking, and then he shook hands with them, and then they drove away." I waited for my dad to take in this information, then I added, "Does this mean that they're not going to assassinate him?"

Dad looked confused. "Where on earth did you get that idea?"

"You said things were heating up in his part of the world. You said they wanted to talk to him."

"So I did." His face looked pained.

"What were you doing in the parking lot?" my mother demanded. "You were supposed to be at your father's office doing your homework."

"I thought Professor Estrada was in trouble. I was trying to save his life."

"Oh, for goodness' sake," my mother said. The two of them fell silent, and for a while there was just the sound of chewing. Then my mother looked at my father. "Do you think . . . ?"

Dad shrugged. "I don't know," he said. "I hope not."

"Poor Samira," Mom said.

• • •

Professor Estrada didn't get tenure. Dad told us at dinner, several weeks later. I don't remember what we were eating that night. Leftovers, probably. My mother was a great fan of leftovers. When Dad broke the news, she pursed her lips, and I could see her shoulders tighten.

"He's going back to the Philippines," Dad said. "He's taking the family."

My heart sank at this news, and then something terrible occurred to me. Was this my fault? I didn't want to ask, but I had to know. "Dad?"

"Yes, Georgie, what is it?"

"Is this because of the G-men?"

Dad looked at me, puzzled. "The G-men?"

"I saw Professor Estrada talking to them, remember? And I told you. You said you were opposed to this kind of thing. Is that why you didn't give him tenure?"

"Oh, that!" Dad said. He seemed amused, but then he saw my stricken face. "No, Georgie, of course not. These tenure decisions are very complicated. This had nothing to do with any G-men."

"Poor Samira," Mom said to herself, and then she turned to my dad, and her voice was angry. "It's hardest on the wives, you know. Uprooting the family, moving the children, going here and there and starting all over. You men don't understand that."

Dad bowed his head slightly, acknowledging her point, and then he shrugged. "Well, at least Manny's found the funding he needs for his fieldwork," he said. "His research depends on it."

"*Research?*" my mother said. "Is that what you people call it?"

"Michi, it's his choice."

Mom stared at her plate.

"They'll be okay," Dad said. "Manny's a survivor."

"Don't you talk to me about survivors," my mother said.

• • •

As it turned out, Dad was right. Manny survived. So did his family. Fatima went to university, until she dropped out and joined the Moro Islamic Liberation Front during the uprising in 1987. I heard the news from Dorothy, who had retired by then but still kept up with former department members. She used to stop by 51 Hillhouse from time to time to check on things, and she happened to be there when I was home from college for a visit and had stopped by to pick up my dad. Dorothy had always had a soft spot for Manny Estrada.

"I never understood why the department didn't give him tenure," she said to me. "He was such a charming man, so outgoing, and his little girl was a darling."

She looked up, and seeing my expression, she reached out and patted my hand. "You two were good friends, weren't you, dear?"

The Estradas had moved away as soon as the semester ended, and that final month had been a bad one. Fatima continued to avoid me, refusing even to meet my eye in the corridor between classes, and traveling en masse with her classmates like a quick, shiny fish in the middle of a migrating school. I was desperate to talk to her, but she never gave me the chance. In the afternoons, her mother would be waiting for her on the sidewalk in front of the main entrance where the other mothers pulled up in their station wagons. Samira always wore a longish coat and a headscarf, and she and Fatima would walk to the corner and wait there for the public bus, never raising their eyes from the ground.

Right around that time, some of the kids in school started bullying me. They would encircle me and chant:

*Georgie Porgie, puddin' and pie*
*Kissed the girls and made them cry . . .*

It certainly wasn't the first time I'd heard this rhyme—with a name like Joji, you come to expect it—but this was different. The first time they chanted it, I felt my blood surge, certain that Fatima had told them what had happened at the Peabody. Now, thinking back, I realize it was probably my newly acquired lisp that made me the butt of my classmates' teasing. The lisp gave my speech a fey quality, a signifier they seized on. But at the time I was overwhelmed with fury, and I blamed Fatima both for my shame and for the vileness of her betrayal. After that, I avoided her too. I stopped trying to talk to her. I stopped talking to anyone.

*When the boys came out to play,*
*Georgie Porgie ran away . . .*

On the last day of school, I hid in a classroom and watched Fatima go, and I didn't even say goodbye.

• • •

We did communicate one last time. Although we never spoke again, I wrote her a letter. I was in graduate school, doing a doctorate in postcolonial studies. I was thinking a lot about my childhood and what it was like growing up in the Anthropology Department at Yale, and of course I thought of Fatima. Professor Estrada had gone on to get tenure at one of the larger universities in Manila, and I addressed my letter to Fatima care of him. I figured that, as an anthropologist married to an Oriental wife, Professor Estrada had probably been sheltered from most of what had transpired so many years ago, and the chances were good that he would forward my letter to his daughter. When I didn't hear from her, I thought the letter had gone astray or that she had simply decided not to answer. But then, almost a year later, I received a letter back.

"Dear Joji," Fatima wrote. "Thank you for your letter and your apology. I don't remember dancing with you in the Peabody Museum, and I certainly don't remember anything about a kiss. If you say it happened, maybe it did. What I do recall is the decadence of American children—how spoiled they were, how greedy and how cruel. I remember that you, in particular, were obsessed with treasure and material gain. I was interested to hear about your paper, 'Manichaean Allegory and the Polarization of Gender and Identity.' Now I have a question for you: Why are you Americans so obsessed with your identities? Why don't you know who you are? We know who you are. The rest of the world knows exactly who you are."

Harsh, but somewhat accurate. I wanted to explain that it wasn't always like that. There was a time when I knew, or at least I thought I did.

"Dear Fatima," I wrote. "Here, in America, we are what we own." I quickly realized that this was an overly simplistic analysis, so I tried again. "Here, in America, we think we can be anyone, and so we are no one at all."

I never finished or sent the letter.

She was entirely right about one thing: I was obsessed with treasure. I still have three little plastic treasure chests, the size of sugar cubes, which I remember getting from the dentist to hold my baby teeth as they fell out. The chests were cheap things, made in Hong Kong, in garish colors, and I was surprised to come across them many years later when I was cleaning out the New Haven house after my parents died. They were in the back of an old junk drawer, under a tangle of string and wire twist ties, covered in dust. I fished them out and lined them up in front of me on the counter. Seeing them there, blue, yellow, and red, all in a row, I remembered how precious they had once seemed. Their little covers were attached by flimsy plastic hinges. I picked up the blue one and pried it open with my fingernail. Inside was a pearly molar with a brittle, brownish root, which I don't remember losing but which must have been mine. The next chest, the yellow one, held a trembling ball of mercury, which I do recall. Those were the days of better living through chemistry, and words like "toxicity" hadn't yet entered our lexicon. My mother let me keep the mercury after I apologized for breaking the thermometer, and I used to play with it like a quick, silvery pet.

The third chest, the red one, contained a bedraggled, dried-out thing that I could not identify at first. I tipped it into my palm and studied it. It was the size and shape of an olive pit, but light and covered with what looked like silver fur. Turning it over, I saw that it was pussy willow, and suddenly I remembered how I'd gotten it.

It was the very first time I met Fatima. I was with a bunch of kids, playing on the slope behind the Divinity School. I don't remember why I was there, but the other kids were mostly white, so it couldn't have been an anthropological gathering. Fatima was there, and she stood out, as I did. She was just a little thing, recently arrived from the Philippines, and I had never seen her before, but I recognized that her face, like mine, bore the telltale traces of hybridity. She was being looked after by one of the older girls, and she had to go to the bathroom. She was begging the girl to take her inside, but the girl was busy talking to her friends, and she told Fatima to go behind a bush.

"I can't," Fatima whimpered, pressing her knees together.

"Sure you can," the girl said, smirking at her friends. "Just pull down your underpants and squat. Isn't that how you do it in your country?"

"No," Fatima said, "we sit down. I have to sit down."

"Oh, honestly!" the girl exclaimed. She rolled her eyes and shook her head. Her friends snickered, and the girl grinned. "Listen, Fatima. You see those pussy willows over there?" She pointed to a bush growing by the wrought-iron gate. "All you have to do is find a nice fat one of those and stick it up your nose. You'll never have to go to the bathroom again."

"Really?"

"I promise," the girl said, solemnly.

The others nodded in wide-eyed agreement. Fatima hesitated, then hobbled toward the bush.

I was watching the whole thing from the swings, not far from the pussy willows. Being a boy, it had never occurred to me what it must be like to be a little girl, playing outside, and suddenly having to pee. It meant interrupting everything and running inside with the other kids knowing why, so instead you held it and held it until you were about to burst. Seen that way, I could imagine how the older girl's alternative might seem attractive, and I was curious to see if it would work. At first it was funny, watching little Fatima go cross-eyed with concentration as she plucked a soft, gray pussy willow and fitted it into her nostril. The big girls all started to laugh—*Oh my god, she's really doing it!*—and Fatima looked up, and I could see the elation flood her face. She had succeeded, finally, in joining in the fun, and the pleasure in this small accomplishment distracted her briefly from the pain and pressure in her bladder.

"It's working!" she said proudly, then she inhaled.

Up shot the catkin like a sleek silver bullet, lodging high in her nasal passage, and it wouldn't come out however hard she exhaled. The shafts of fur lay in the wrong direction. So the first time I ever spoke to Fatima, she had peed her pants and was running around in little circles, snorting like a spooked pony. The big girls hadn't yet realized what had happened. They were sitting on the picnic table, still cracking up. So I walked over and took Fatima's hand and led her away from the Divinity School, down St. Ronan Street, across the parking lot by the atom smasher, up and over Science Hill, past the Peabody Museum to 51 Hillhouse Avenue. There, I brought her, sobbing, up the broad stairs of the Anthropology Department to my father's office.

My dad was sitting at his desk, grading papers. "Oh my," he said softly, dropping his pencil and coming around to kneel in front of us. "What have we here?" It was a reasonable question. Even for a trained anthropologist, it would have been hard to tell by observation alone that the damp little girl weeping before him had a pussy willow stuck up her nose, let alone deduce how it had gotten there.

"Aren't you Manny Estrada's daughter?" he asked, pulling out his handkerchief and gently wiping her tear-streaked face.

She gulped and nodded, and then I explained what had happened. My father frowned. Without saying another word, he pocketed his keys, scooped Fatima up in his arms, and drove us to the emergency room. He carried her straight up to the admitting desk and spoke to the nurse, and Fatima was quickly whisked away. My dad went with her. By the time they came back out again, both Manny and Samira had arrived. They were newcomers to Yale, baffled and helpless. Manny clasped my dad's hand and thanked him over and over for his kindness. Samira scolded Fatima, then hugged her, then scolded her again. Fatima gazed at me with eyes as dark and wet as a fawn's.

"I'm proud of you," my dad said later on, patting me on the shoulder as we drove home that evening. We sat side by side on the broad bench seat of the Pontiac. "You should always help other people. That's what we do."

I nodded, listening to his words. I remember feeling unsure, wondering who he meant by "we." Did he mean we, anthropologists? We, our family, in our Pontiac sedan? We, Americans? I didn't quite understand, but it didn't matter. Sitting up tall, next to my dad, I clutched my new treasure in my hand and knew that he was right.

Earlier, when we were leaving the hospital, Fatima had sidled over to me, still smelling faintly of pee.

"Here," she said in a small voice, holding out her hand.

I looked down and noticed for the first time the darkness of her skin and how white the underside of her arm looked in comparison. Her palm was pink and damp, and centered in the middle lay the bedraggled silver catkin.

"You can have it," she whispered, and I took it. I heard the tremor in her voice, saw tears in her eyes that I took to be tears of gratitude, and I experienced an intoxicating surge of power. I felt immensely proud. The order of the world made sudden sense to me, and for that brief moment, I knew exactly who I was.

# LEAFBLOWER

L*eafblower.* It's a lovely word, really. "Leaf" from the Old Norse *lauf* and the Old English *lēaf.* "Blower" from the Old English *blāwan* (to blow, take a breath, make a sound). The sort of word you might find in a poem, something old and epic:

> Lo! The Leafblowers' glory through splendid achievements
> And the Lawn Kings' prowess we have heard . . .

• • •

She has heard their prowess. How could she not? They are displaying it all over the neighborhood. Scourge of the block, wreckers of the morning's quiet. Lawn tractors, branch-shredders, edge-trimmers, Weedwackers, ride-'em mowers, cutting swaths across the broad, green lap of the world.

Their truck, emblazoned with the Lawn Kings logo, is parked in the driveway of the neighbor's house across the street. Mel, balanced on a spindly chair by the bookshelf, watches them through the rippled glass of the old woman's bedroom window. An ancient rhododendron partially blocks her view, but through the upper reaches of its sprawling branches she can see the men readying for the assault, lowering their tailgate and priming their diabolical tools of Nature's subjugation. Of these tools, the leafblowers are by far the worst—the insect-whine of their two-stroke engines, insistent, throbbing. Like being fucked in the ears by a giant mosquito.

Fuck. From the Old English *fuke* or *fucken*.

The old woman is still sleeping in the small bed below. Mel listens for the sound of her breathing, afraid that the racket outside will wake her and cause her to open her eyes and see Mel on the rickety chair, looming above her with the heavy tome in her hands. The book is a dusty translation into modern English of the Nowell Codex, which Mel has taken from the top shelf. She was flipping through the first few pages of *Beowulf* when the commotion distracted her, but the old woman's breathing is steady and loud. She is mostly deaf without her hearing aids, a sound sleeper, even without the pill that Mel had given her the night before.

The old man is a different story. The Professor is a fitful sleeper, and through the thin walls Mel hears him yawn, and yawn, and yawn again—great, aching, cavernous sounds that follow one after another for what seems like an eternity—until they stop, and then there is silence. Mel wonders if he has fallen back to sleep or if he is dead. She hopes he's not dead. She has grown fond of the Professor and his wife, and she doesn't want either of them to die, not on her watch, although she knows it's a possibility. She doesn't want to be the one to find their bodies. She can't afford to lose the sweet deal she has on the rent.

The bedroom where the old woman sleeps used to be the daughter's room. The daughter, Rosamund, lives in California now, and she has a kid, and a husband, and a PhD from an Ivy League university, and a high-powered tech job, and she rarely comes home. It must have been a bright, sunny room when Roz was growing up here, but now it's as dark as a cave. It's late summer, and the monstrous rhododendron outside the window has dropped its flowers, but the leathery green leaves still block the light. It was just a small shrub once, the Professor told her, when Rosamund was a child, but over the years, it has grown and grown until it has swallowed the entire corner of the house and part of the roof as well.

When Mel suggested that the Professor hire someone to prune it back, he shook his head. Those landscaper fellows are all crooks, he said. They think they can get away with overcharging old folks, but not him, and besides, he doesn't want them bringing their infernal chainsaws and power equipment onto his property. The racket they make! The Professor has a perfectly good handsaw. He will prune the thicket himself one of these days. He just hasn't gotten around to it, and until he does, they will have to be content to live inside the dark and tangled bowels.

It was an evocative image, Mel thought, and she told him so. She was not trying to flatter him. At the time of the conversation, they had already signed the rental agreement, and he was just showing her around. They were standing in front of his wife's bedroom window, looking out into the understory of the giant shrub, crisscrossed with contorted branches, pricked with light.

"Wow," she said. "You're right. It's like being inside the plant's intestines or something."

"Intestines?" he repeated, looking puzzled.

"Bowels," she said. "Isn't that what you said?"

"Boughs," he said. "I said boughs, but bowels is better." He smiled and gave a courtly little bow in her direction. He was wearing an old tweed jacket and a collared shirt with a tie. If he'd been wearing a hat, he would have tipped it. "But then again, I'm not the poet."

She suspected he was being ironic. During their first meeting, the Professor had commented on her name. "Is Mel short for Melody or Melanie?" he asked.

"Neither," Mel said. "It's actually Malory, but I've never liked it, and Mal is even worse, so I just go by Mel."

"Ill-fated," he said. "Not the most auspicious of names. Is that Malory as in Thomas?" And when she looked confused, he added, "Thomas Malory? *Le Morte d'Arthur*?" And when she still didn't catch on, he sighed. "One *l* or two?"

Later, in her car, she googled it.

Mel does not have a PhD, or a high-powered job, or a kid, or a partner, or even someone to hook up with from time to time. What she does have is an MFA in poetry (she should have known who Thomas Malory was) from a second-tier state university (which is why she didn't). She also has a crappy job doing technical writing and editing, and an unmanageable student loan debt. After she got her MFA, she wanted to move to New York, but she couldn't afford to live in the city. She can't afford to live in this crappy college town, either, but neither can she afford to leave, so for now, she is stuck in a one-room studio above the Professor's garage, where she gets a deal on the rent in exchange for looking in on the old man and his wife and helping them out when they need it. Daughter Roz, who is a few years older than Mel, texts her with frequent requests to check on her parents, or run errands, or do odd jobs around the house. The texts are framed as requests, with hearts and exclamation points and namaste emojis, but it's clear to Mel that they are commands. She and Roz have never met, but the woman sends her kissy faces.

Outside, the pulsing treble whine of the leafblower is joined by the basso roar of the tractor mower, but the old lady sleeps on, emitting soft puffy little snorts that create a countertempo to the rhythms of the engines outside. A tiny woman, batty with dementia, she was once a preeminent oncologist, but now, lying in bed on her back with her hands crossed over her heart, she is more like Sleeping Beauty. Even her name is right out of a fairy tale: Rose Fae O'Reilly. Mel calls her Dr. Fae. She calls the professor the Professor. She likes Dr. Fae more than the Professor and feels sorry for her, dozing through her last days on earth.

It's only a matter of time before the Professor emerges, and Mel needs to pack up and get out of there. The walls of the little bedroom are lined with shelves, and the shelves are filled with the Professor's many books. He taught medieval studies, Old and Middle English, and Old Norse, at the local college, and there are a great many books on a great many shelves throughout the house. The shelves in his daughter's bedroom hold the overflow, books he seldom looks at. He says he needs to downsize, and one of Mel's jobs is to help him cull his library, but when she asks which titles he wants to get rid of, he keeps changing his mind, and so she spends a lot of time moving books from the shelves into boxes and then back onto the shelves again. Dr. Fae has a habit of hiding cash inside her husband's books and then forgetting, so the Professor has instructed Mel to check the pages. He has also told her she should feel free to borrow any books she likes, but what he means is that she should read them and return them, not take them to the used bookstore and sell them and keep the money for herself. Still, she is just trying to help, she tells herself, and since the books she takes are from the overflow, he won't miss them. She finds forty dollars tucked between the pages of *Beowulf*, and as she pockets the bills, a passage catches her eye.

> So blessed with abundance, brimming with joyance,
> The warriors abided, till a certain one began to
> Dog them with deeds of direfullest malice . . .

Outside, the engine of a power edger starts up, followed by the whine of a brush cutter. She closes the codex, climbs down from the chair, and slips the volume into her backpack, which is now full. It's the end of the month, and her loan payments are due. She returns the chair to the corner of the room next to the bed. The old woman looks peaceful lying there, her skin crumpled and soft, her fine white hair fanned across the pillow like an aura. Mel takes a few tabs of Ativan from the pill bottle in the drawer, pockets them, and leaves the room, closing the door quietly behind her.

Back at the garage, she unpacks the books and puts them into the box in the trunk of her Kia, along with the others she's culled. She brings the codex upstairs and sets it on the makeshift desk she's rigged from a hollow-core door and two sawhorses. The studio above the garage is adequately renovated but underfurnished, and when she moved in, she brought little with her. The Professor told her she could help herself to whatever she needed from the garage downstairs, and now she has enough to get by. There's a sagging armchair in one corner. A wobbly office chair on wheels. A metal-topped table in the kitchen area where she eats. A fold-out sofa bed where she sleeps. On the desk sits an ancient manual typewriter, a Remington Rand, that once belonged to Dr. Fae, whose initials, RFO, MD, are embossed on the front of the carrying case. Mel found it under a pile of old luggage and brought it upstairs. The ribbon was dried up, so she ordered a new one online. The blank paper she borrowed from the Professor's printer tray, and now she slips a sheet into the roller and centers it. She had never used a manual typewriter before, but she watched a video on YouTube explaining what the various mechanisms did, and she's been practicing.

Outside, the Lawn Kings are still loudly showcasing their prowess, so she puts on her noise-canceling headphones to dampen the sound. The headphones were a present from her ex, the expensive kind that she could never have afforded herself. When she moved out, she meant to leave them behind as a statement, along with everything else Allie had gifted her, but she's become addicted to the way they hug her head and cup her ears. The firm, steady pressure soothes her and helps her focus, and when she puts them on, her body melts into a velvety quiet, and the clacking of the typewriter keys seems very far away.

`Word-hoard`, she types, followed by the date, and then she opens the codex and starts to read, pausing from time to time to add to her list. She never studied Old English in grad school, and this list is an ongoing project. She's not hoarding words for any purpose. She just likes the way they sound, and she needs something to type.

```
Earth-cave: an underground dwelling

Life-house: the body, physical form, where life
resides

Gold-friend: a noble person who gives gifts of gold

Shield-wall: a defensive formation

Sky-candle: the sun or the moon

Death-spell: a curse or fatal enchantment
```

The problem with a manual typewriter, she is learning, is that when you make a mistake, you can't undo it. You can't erase, and you can't back up; your only choice is to type on.

• • •

At nine o'clock, she moves to her laptop. The company she works for is based on the West Coast, but her team leader lives in Philadelphia and lets Mel set her own hours, more or less, as long as she attends the staff meetings and Zoom socials that are supposed to boost their morale, which is particularly low right now on account of the new AI platform they are helping to bring online and which will eventually replace them. Management insists that human editors will always be needed for quality control, to ensure accuracy and maintain ethical standards. Human expertise, deep domain knowledge, and creativity are essential, they assert; only human people can edit for tone, style, nuance, and cultural sensitivity. But Mel and her human colleagues know perfectly well that the prose they are producing requires little in the way of expertise or creativity, never mind tone, style, or nuance, and as for ethical standards, well, that ship sailed long ago. Still, because they are human people, HR maintains that staff socials are essential to help them relax, bond, and build rapport, and it's the responsibility of the team leader to make these socials fun and engaging. Mel's team leader outsources this task to Mel, directing her to come up with icebreaker games and activities, and Mel outsources the task to the AI, instructing it to generate a catalog of games—Online Trivia, Virtual Bingo, Escape Room, and Desert Island—that can also be executed by the large language model while she and her human colleagues shop or nap or check their socials. Mel uses game time to play Sudoku or check on the old woman if she's having a bad spell.

Just before noon, she removes the headphones and listens, and this time there is quiet outside. The Lawn Kings must be taking a lunch break. She goes to the main house, heats up some tomato soup in the microwave, and melts some cheddar on slices of toast. The toaster oven dings, the microwave pings, and the tinny sounds make the hairs on the back of her neck prickle. Appliances and their infernal nagging, she thinks, and she notices, too, that the inside of her mind is starting to sound a lot like the Professor. She wonders if she's channeling him.

Tomato soup is the Professor's favorite, and before long she hears his study door open. He shuffles into the kitchen, sits down at the table, and digs his spoon into the thick red soup.

"That damn cardinal is back."

"Did he wake her?" Mel asks.

"No," he says. "Nothing wakes her. Not even those infernal Lawn Kings."

"Did they wake you?"

"Of course they did."

His face is inches from the red surface of the soup. He has a bad tremor in his right hand, so he tries to minimize the distance the spoon needs to travel. Mel watches, holding her breath, and when he swallows safely, she exhales.

She checks her phone. It's hard to juggle the job she does for a paycheck and the job she does for rent. She has a production meeting this afternoon for the paycheck job, but she also has to take the old woman to Senior Joints at three, and she's not sure how she's going to manage both.

"I'll look in on her," she says. "She should eat something before class."

Dr. Fae is sitting up in bed, looking out the window. When she sees Mel, her face lights up. "Look!" she cries, pointing.

There's a flash of red in the dappled darkness of the rhododendron, and the cardinal comes to rest on the windowsill. He is a beautiful, bright red male. He cocks his head, puffs out his chest, and stares at them with his beady black eye.

"Such a handsome bird!" the old woman says. "Such bright red feathers!"

And a rakish, slicked-back crest, and a plump beak, pink and waxy. The bird is insolent. He makes sharp, strident noises as he hops back and forth. He wears a fine black mask across his face.

"Like a bandito," Dr. Fae whispers. She looks up at Mel, and there's something in her tone that is a little coy, a little challenging. "He steals things, you know."

Mel knows better than to contradict her. "He does?" she says, trying to sound intrigued instead of paranoid. "What does he steal?"

The old woman's eyes slip slyly sideways. "He comes in the night."

• • •

Back in the garage, Mel types:

```
Once upon a time in a dark shrub
Once upon a time in a dark, cave-like shrub
Once upon a time in the dark and crooked bowels of
a monstrous shrub
Once upon a time a cardinal
```

This is as far as she gets before the leafblower starts up again. She hears the gas engine fire and the throbbing *vroom vroom vroom* as the operator fingers the throttle. He's enjoying that, she thinks. Fucker. She thinks about hurling rocks at him, or stealing his lawn tractor and mowing him down, or cutting him off at the knees with his Weedwacker, but her lunch break is over, and the message board from work is blowing up. She pushes the typewriter away, puts her headphones back on, and responds to the most urgent messages, but when she settles down to copyedit the draft of the natural language processing application programming interfaces (NLP API) documentation for the AI system that her team is currently working on, she finds the adaptive algorithms of her high-end headphones are not up to the task of canceling the leafblower. The thin whine of the engine coils like a hot, insidious wire through the foam-padded earcups and into her ear, and from there snakes its way into the language processing centers of her brain. Even her favorite '60s K-pop playlist can't buffer the sonic interference. She goes to the window.

From the second floor of the garage, she has a clear view of the driveway across the street. The leafblower guy is young and pale and slouching, the kind of kid she used to date in high school. Her first boyfriend had a summer lawn care job, and she remembers the way his hands smelled, like gasoline and grass clippings. This guy is wearing a red ball cap under a pair of cheap plastic ear protectors which, from a distance, look a lot like her expensive headphones. The two-stroke engine, strapped to his back like a rocket pack, is emitting puffs of smoke, but he doesn't seem to notice. He's swinging the long blower tube lazily back and forth, aiming vaguely at the lawn clippings that litter the black asphalt. A few clumps of grass scatter reluctantly in front of him, but the leafblower isn't paying attention. He stares up at the clouds and smokes a cigarette, lost in a dream. *Puff puff* goes the pale smoke rising from his cigarette. *Puff puff* goes the pale smoke rising from his rocket pack. He takes a final drag, plucks the butt from his lips, and flicks it to the asphalt, and then he aims his nozzle at it. A small shower of errant sparks flies up into the air. They arc over the leafblower's head! They ignite the volatile oil-and-gasoline mixture that fuels the engine strapped to his back! They blow him sky-high into the heavens!

> The heavens wept, and the welkin grieved for hastening death . . .

None of this actually happens, and yet she watches, ever hopeful, pondering the odds. But the leafblower remains earthbound. He pulls out his phone and starts scrolling with his thumb, all the while swinging the heavy, phallus-like tube in long, slow arcs before him.

• • •

At three o'clock, the Lawn Kings' truck is still parked in the street. The leaf-blowing equipment has been retired and replaced by a Weedwacker, now squealing from the backyard. She packs up her laptop, collects the old woman, and drives her to Senior Joints. She sits on the sidelines in a molded plastic chair and logs on to the Zoom meeting. She's late. She mutes herself and blurs her background, praying that the treadmills and Stairmasters behind her won't be visible on screen. She tries to focus on what her supervisor is saying, but she is distracted by all the vigilantly masked old ladies marching in circles and waving their crooked limbs like ancient sea creatures in the ventilated, HEPA-filtered air. Their handsome and able-bodied trainer, whose name is Axel, tries to motivate them by playing disco hits from the '70s and '80s through a tinny portable speaker. *Don't rock the boat, baby. What's love got to do with it? We are family!* The old ladies like Axel, and they try to please him. They try to move to the disco beat. Their concentration is impeccable.

Mel's concentration is less so. As her production meeting drones on, she uses the AI, whose NLP API documentation she is supposed to be copyediting, to research the amount of air pollution caused by the volatile organic compounds emitted in the exhaust of gasoline-powered grounds-keeping equipment. The AI informs her that operating a leafblower with a two-stroke engine for thirty minutes is comparable to driving a Ford F-150 pickup truck from Texas to Alaska. The AI cites the study, and the data seems legit, and knowing this gives Mel a grim sense of satisfaction. Her production meeting ends just as the class is over, and she logs off in time to see Axel, unmasked, give Dr. Fae a big hug. She frowns at him and then realizes that she is again channeling the Professor. It occurs to her that she would like a big, unmasked hug from Axel too.

She and the old woman have a weekly routine: Senior Joints, then a drive-thru fast-food fried-fish sandwich and a chocolate shake, and finally a shopping spree at the Cancer Connection Thrift Shop. The ladies at Cancer Connection all know Dr. Fae and treat her like an oncological goddess. The Professor says this is good for his wife's morale, even though the old woman often has no recollection of her medical career and can't remember the ladies from week to week. She just likes shopping.

"Look!" she cries, pulling a shimmery off-the-shoulder cocktail sheath from the rack and handing it to Mel. "This is very elegant. You should try it on."

The Cancer Connection gets a lot of pricey brand-name donations, since wealthy people die of cancer too. The cocktail dress, a Halston, is not something Mel would ever think of wearing, but to make Dr. Fae happy, she obliges. She stares at her reflection in the dressing room mirror. The dress is too small, and she looks like a flabby mermaid with seaweed for hair, but she steels herself and parts the curtains with a flourish. Ta-da.

The old woman's face lights up with genuine delight. "Brava!" she cries and claps her hands. "Bellissima!"

The shopping is good for Mel's morale too.

The old woman vetoes a pale-pink Fair Isle sweater and the

pull-on paisley harem pants that Mel has chosen for her and disappears into the maze of racks. When she emerges, she's wearing a black *Ghost in the Shell* hoodie with a manga illustration of a naked girl with tubes and wires going in and out of her body. The girl is on her knees, holding a submachine gun, but Dr. Fae has cataracts, and Mel doubts she has noticed these details. The black hoodie looks good with the old lady's white hair. Mel finds her a leather jacket to wear on top, and the old woman is delighted. She makes Mel try on a gorgeous Helmut Lang suit that fits her perfectly and would be great for job interviews, should she ever have one.

She and the doctor can entertain each other for hours this way.

As Mel waits in line at the cashier, Dr. Fae wanders off again, and when she returns she has on a red-checked hunting cap with ear flaps and a long-peaked visor. She holds up a bright red cardigan sweater and drops it into their basket.

"Who's that for?" Mel asks.

The old woman looks confused. She doesn't remember. This happens. She digs in her purse and hands Mel her credit card. The cocktail dress is expensive, and so is the suit. Mel doesn't press her for an answer.

The Professor hears the car pull in and comes out to meet them. He opens the passenger-side door and unfastens his wife's seat belt. She's still wearing the hoodie and the hunting cap, the flaps pulled down low over her ears. The Professor looks at Mel, and she shrugs.

• • •

The cardinal is back the next morning at dawn. When Mel pokes her head in, Dr. Fae is sitting up in bed and staring out the window. She's still wearing the red cap, and when she sees Mel, she points.

"Look!" she cries. Outside, in the rhododendron, the bright bird sits on a crooked branch. As if in response to the old woman's voice, he flies toward her and lands on the windowsill. He flicks his tail and hops back and forth, peering at them and pecking at the glass. Flirting.

"Such a handsome bird!" the old woman says. "Such bright red feathers!"

The cardinal preens and pecks some more. Dr. Fae climbs out of bed and moves to the window. "Is he someone's pet?" she asks. "Is he trying to come inside?" She leans until she's level with the windowsill and the bird's beady black eye. She places her finger on the glass next to the bird's head. "Hey you," she says. "Hey bird." She taps the glass with her fingernail, and he taps back with his beak. He doesn't seem at all afraid, doesn't fly away.

"Maybe it's your red hat," Mel says. "Maybe he likes it."

The old woman raises her hand to her head. She has forgotten about the hat. She takes it off and looks at it, wondering where it came from. "Do you like my red hat?" she asks the bird. Her nose is almost touching the glass now. They are beak to beak. The cardinal pecks her nose gently.

“Such a handsome bird,” the old woman says to Mel. “He likes my hat, you know.”

Mel hears slippers in the hall, and the bedroom door opens. The bird flits, turns, and flies back to a branch, where he perches, glaring at them.

“Damn cardinal,” the Professor says.

He stands in the doorway, holding the jamb for support. He’s wearing the red cardigan over a pair of threadbare flannel pajamas with pale blue stripes. The Professor always dresses in jackets and button-down shirts. He wears dull, muted colors, the subdued browns and grays of a nuthatch or a thrush. Mel has never seen him in red before. It feels wrong, and she wishes he would go put on some normal clothes, but instead he crosses the room to stand next to his wife. He scowls at the cardinal.

“I detest that creature.”

As if he has heard, the bird flies at the window and hits the glass hard. The impact is shocking.

“Oh!” the old woman cries.

In a flurry of feather and claw, the bird scrabbles against the slick surface of the glass, then he catches the air with a scarlet wing and retreats. Frenzied and battle-keen, he attacks again and again, battering himself against the pane, until the glass is streaked with faint pink scratch marks.

Dr. Fae clutches her husband’s red sleeve. “Why is he doing this?”

“I’m going to catch that damn bird,” the Professor says.

“Such bright red feathers,” his wife says.

“I’m going to buy a net.”

The image lodges itself in Mel’s mind: the tall, spindly Professor in his bright red cardigan, chasing the bright red cardinal with a net.

```
Spear-wielder
Peace-breaker
Battle-hunger
Blood-revenge
Death-spell
```

• • •

Back in the garage, the AI informs her that the bird in the old lady’s rhododendron is *Cardinalis cardinalis*, a territorial and adaptable species now expanding its range. As the New England forests are clear-cut to build strip malls and suburban housing developments, the climate of the eastern seaboard warms, and the cardinal, who prefers warm clearings to cool forests, moves north.

Mel grew up on a street called Deforest Drive. Their house was a split-level ranch in a suburban development of identical tract houses in Columbus, Ohio. The developers bought up the land, cut down all the trees, and then came in with the bulldozers. They scraped up all the humus-rich topsoil and hauled it away to sell and then built the houses on the sandy subsoil. The hopeful new homeowners scattered lawn seed that washed away whenever they watered; they stuck cuttings in the ground and watched them die. The irony of the street name did not escape them, as they cursed the developers and bought the precious topsoil back again, bag by bag. When Mel was a child, it was a barren, lunar place. Her parents dreamed of fruit trees and flowering dogwoods, but only the crabgrass and thorny locusts survived.

She was twelve when her parents lost the house on Deforest Drive in the subprime mortgage collapse. They moved Mel and her younger brother into a two-bedroom rental, and soon after, they got divorced—unlike *Cardinalis cardinalis*, who, the AI tells her, is monogamous and typically mates for life. Cardinal parents often stay together year-round, Mel learns, and unlike her parents, they share responsibilities for nesting and feeding their young. They are known to be fiercely territorial. A male cardinal may exhibit aggression when he sees his own reflection in a car mirror or a window and mistakes it for a rival.

For lunch, she makes egg-salad sandwiches for Dr. Fae and the Professor and tells them what she's learned.

"So, he's attacking himself?" the Professor asks.

"Yes," she says. "It's a thing."

"A thing, is it?"

"A guy thing, mostly," Mel says. "It's called mirror aggression."

Dr. Fae is eating her sandwich with a fork. "Such a beautiful red bird," she says.

The Professor wipes his mouth. "Good to know I don't have to take it personally," he says, "but that rhododendron is my territory, and that bird needs to go."

"He wears a mask," Dr. Fae says. "He's a real bandito."

Back in the garage, Mel types:

```
He was a beautiful red bird, a real bandito. Ever
cocky, he claimed the tangled depths of the old
wife's understory.
"That bush is my territory," her husband said.
"That bird needs to go."
```

• • •

The AI notes that under the Migratory Bird Treaty Act of 1918, it is illegal to kill, capture, or harm cardinals or any other native migratory birds. Penalties for violating the MBTA can include fines, imprisonment, or both. Good to know, Mel thinks.

• • •

The Professor wears the red cardigan every day. He says it's to make his wife happy, but Mel wonders if this is true. Dr. Fae is enchanted by the cardinal. She has pulled the spindly chair from the corner to the window. Dappled sunlight pricks the gloom of the rhododendron, and the leathery leaves are spotted with white droppings. She sits there with her hunting cap pulled down low over her eyes and watches the bird as he flits back and forth. His red plumage is as shocking as a wound. He seems to be in a perpetual state of agitation, which gets worse when the Professor comes into the room, so maybe it is personal after all, Mel thinks, and she wonders about the provocative red sweater. She doesn't say anything, only watches as the cardinal's battle frenzy escalates. He hurls himself against the glass, until the window is cloudy with his pale blood.

"Oh!" Dr. Fae cries. "Why won't he stop?"

"Come away, my dear," the Professor says, putting his hands on her shoulders and pulling her from the window. "Let's leave him be."

• • •

`"Come away!" the red bird cries. "Come away! Leave him be!"`

Interesting, Mel thinks, as she pushes aside the Remington, boots her computer, and logs on to work.

• • •

Later that afternoon, when Mel comes back with the groceries, she finds the Professor sitting at the kitchen table, surrounded by art supplies: a pad of colored construction paper, scissors,

Scotch tape, a glue stick, and a box of crayons. There's an *Audubon Field Guide to North American Birds* lying open to a page of owls, and he's bending over a fierce-looking bird that he's copying onto a sheet of paper. His concentration is deep, like a young child's. He's not a bad drawer, and she compliments him.

"It's a great horned owl," he says. He's working on the owl's scowl.

"His horns are great," she says. "They're very savage."

"They're not horns," he tells her. "They're plumicorns."

"Good to know," she says, putting away the oat milk.

He looks up from the page. "Do you know what plumicorns are?"

"Feather-horns?"

The Professor smiles and goes back to work. He puts the finishing touches on the intricately variegated plumage, his face inches from the paper. The owl is life-size, with a barrel-shaped body, talons, and a gunmetal beak. Its hooded, saucer-shaped eyes are made of shiny gold foil, which the Professor cut out and glued to the owl's face. They reflect the light and glare menacingly up at him as he works.

"Where did you get all the art supplies?"

"The basement. They're my daughter's. My wife can't bear to give away any of Rosamund's things, but sometimes her hoarding comes in handy."

He puts down the crayon and picks up the scissors and, with painstaking concentration, cuts along the outline of the owl, freeing it from the page. He holds it up by its plumicorns to show her. "There," he says. "That ought to put a fright into him."

"Who?" she asks, though she knows perfectly well.

"That damned cardinal." He gets to his feet, takes his owl and the roll of tape, and marches off to his wife's bedroom. Mel follows. Dr. Fae is napping, but she wakes when they come in, and he shows her his handiwork.

"Oh!" she says. "What a fierce-looking bird!"

The Professor is pleased. He positions the owl on the window, taping it so that its menacing yellow eyes face out into the rhododendron. He steps back and admires his work.

"There," he says grimly. "That should scare the living daylights out of him."

It doesn't.

• • •

The texts from Roz are increasing in frequency.

> Whassup with this damn cardinal business?
>
> Mom's sounding loony. Dad's sounding obsessed. Sigh.
>
> Are they ok?
>
> Mel? Can you deal with this please? Call an exterminator or something?
>
> Send me the bill!

The text was followed by three winking smiley faces. Why were they winking, Mel wondered?

• • •

When Mel first moved into the garage apartment, she didn't have to do much more than help the Professor with his books once in a while and drive Dr. Fae to her appointments. But lately her duties have increased. Roz signed her parents up for a high-end gourmet meal delivery service that delivers premium ready-to-heat meals to their door. At first the Professor handled the heating, but little by little the task migrated to Mel. She isn't quite sure how that happened. Probably Roz suggested it. Now she does the supplementary grocery shopping, makes their lunches, heats their dinners, takes out the garbage and recycling, manages Dr. Fae's meds, and drives her around. Roz is good at making suggestions, but not so good at taking them. When Mel suggested that Roz talk to her father about a further reduction in rent to reflect all the additional labor she's providing, Roz agreed, but nothing came of it, so Mel has figured out other ways of compensating herself. Roz is a busy woman. Mel doesn't want to bother her.

There are several local used bookstores nearby, but the Professor is well known in the small college town, so Mel prefers to drive to a large bookstore in the city, which specializes in academic texts and where she can get a better price. Joe, the guy who buys books on weekdays, is a poet she met in her MFA program. He's been working at the store for less than a year, and while there's a cap on how much he's allowed to pay out in cash without getting approval from his boss, he always gives her the max. When he sees what she's brought this time, his eyes light up: a translation of *The Saga of the Volsungs: The Norse Epic of Sigurd the Dragon Slayer*, a collection titled *The Poetic Edda: Essays on Old Norse Mythology*, and Snorri Sturluson's *Heimskringla: History of the Kings of Norway*.

"The boss will be happy," Joe says, as he looks over the stack. "This Viking shit really sells."

He tallies the total, and she signs the receipt with a fake name while he pretends not to notice. When she first started coming here to sell the Professor's books, she and Joe used to talk about writing. They talked about local poetry readings, classmates who'd had chapbooks published, and projects they were working on. Now these subjects are awkward territory.

"You doing okay?" he asks as he hands her the cash.

"Yeah," she replies. "Fine. You know."

"Yeah," he says.

"You?"

"Same," he says. "You know."

He starts putting the books back into the box, and she turns to go.

"Oh, hey," he says, holding up Snorri Sturluson's *Heimskringla*. "This reminds me. Some guy was in here the other day asking the boss about one of the books you brought in by this Snorri dude."

Mel stops. "Who?"

"I don't know. Old guy. Professorial type. Said the book was signed by the author, and he recognized it."

"Not possible, Joe. Snorri Sturluson died a thousand years ago in Iceland."

"Oh. Okay, well, there was somebody's name in the book, and this guy was asking about it. My boss wanted to know if I'd bought it, and I said I couldn't remember."

"Right," Mel says. "Okay. Thanks."

"No biggie," Joe says. "Just thought you should know."

"Totally."

• • •

That evening, when she goes to rouse Dr. Fae for dinner, she finds the Professor sitting on the edge of the bed. His owl is still in the window, and his wife is napping. The cardinal is flapping and pecking loudly at the glass, but the Professor doesn't seem to notice. He's looking up at the top shelf of the bookcase, head cocked to one side, reading the titles. He's frowning. There are gaps on the dusty shelves where books used to be.

In the doorway, Mel hesitates. "Is everything all right?"

"Oh, Malory," he says, looking startled and almost guilty. "I didn't hear you. Is it time for supper already?"

After dinner, the Professor retreats to his study to make a few phone calls, he says. He's still on the phone when she knocks quietly on his door.

"Recycling?" she mouths, so as not to disturb him. She holds up the bin.

He frowns. "Just a moment," he says into the phone, and then he places his hand over the mouthpiece and watches Mel as she collects his discarded paper. She closes the door behind her, then lingers, listening as he goes back to his call.

"Yes, of course, I understand. I hope there's some other explanation, too, because if not, it's extremely concerning. Yes, I'll keep an eye out. I'm sorry to bother you. I appreciate your taking the time to check . . ."

• • •

Meanwhile, the cardinal attacks are increasing in both fury and duration and can be heard all over the house: the relentless beak against the glass, the frantic scraping of the needle-sharp claws like fingernails on a chalkboard. The bird pursues the Professor from room to room, following him into the kitchen, his study, even the bathroom. Cardinals are generally known for their confident, cocky attitude, the AI tells her, which can be quite entertaining to observe. Their striking, iconic appearance, bold behavior, and beautiful songs make them a favorite among bird enthusiasts. Trying to be helpful, she passes this information along to the Professor.

"I hate that bird," he says. From the window of her garage, she sees him outside in his red cardigan, beating the rhododendron with a broom handle. "Shoo! Shoo!"

The Lawn Kings, too, are launching a fresh assault. They have shifted the base of their operations and are attacking from the opposite side of the house, farther from Mel's garage but closer to the Professor's bedroom. This neighboring property was recently sold, and in addition to the usual yard maintenance, the new owners are having some large nuisance trees removed, so the Lawn Kings have added several high-powered pieces of machinery to their arsenal: a wood chipper, a shredder, and a heavy-duty Stihl Magnum chainsaw. They like to get an early start.

"Aren't there laws about this sort of thing?" the Professor cries in despair, and the AI informs her that yes, towns and cities do have noise ordinances designed to regulate the amount, duration, and source of noise in a community; that excessive noise is a form of pollution linked to stress, hearing loss, sleep disturbances, and other physical and mental health problems; that ordinances try to balance competing interests while allowing businesses to operate in order to ensure a peaceful and harmonious environment; and that in their town, landscaping equipment may not be operated in residential areas before 7:00 a.m.

Mel relays this information to the Professor. At 6:45 the next morning, she watches him stride forth in his slippers and striped pajamas, cordless phone in hand, as the Lawn King drives his mower in ever-tightening circles around the neighbor's broad, grassy lawn. "Hello! Hello!" he shouts into the phone. "Yes! That's right, a noise complaint! Listen—" He holds the receiver up toward the roar of the engine.

In the garage, Mel types:

```
Spear-armed
Battle-weaver
Dragon-fury
Blood-revenge
Death-song
```

Mel? Can we do something about this, please???? Rox texts, followed by a long string of exploding-head emojis.

• • •

At meals, the Professor is quiet, wincing whenever the bird's wings beat against the window or when an engine fires up. Battle-weary, he is tired and pale, neglecting to shave. He's curt with Mel, and she worries about the missing books. If he asks, what will she say? She would have to tell the truth, which would mean losing her affordable housing, but she could lose that regardless.

I'm counting on you!!! Roz texts. If it's too much for them to live on their own [weepy face] you have to tell me so I can make other plans!!!

He hasn't been sleeping well in his own bedroom, and Mel knows this because early one morning, when she goes into Dr. Fae's bedroom to return the Nowell Codex, she finds him there, lying next to his wife in their daughter's small bed. Dr. Fae is cradling his head as he sleeps and stroking his snowy white hair. When she sees Mel in the doorway, she puts her finger to her lips.

"*Shhhh*," she whispers.

They're doing fine! Mel texts, cheerfully, adding a smiley face with teeth for emphasis.

• • •

Mel has an idea. When it's time to drive Dr. Fae to her gerontology appointment, she brings her noise-canceling headphones to the house. The Professor is in his study with the door closed. She knocks, and when he doesn't answer, she tries again. Finally, she opens the door and pokes her head in. He's sitting at his desk with a wool ski cap pulled down over his ears. The cardinal is pecking at the window behind him, and the leafblower is revving in the yard next door. She waves her arms to get his attention. He takes off the ski cap and removes the wads of toilet paper he has stuffed into his ears.

"Yes?"

"Is that helping?" she asks, pointing to the roll of toilet paper on his desk.

"Not in the least." He swivels and throws a pencil at the cardinal in the window.

She shows him the headphones and explains how they work. He looks at them skeptically, but he puts them on.

"May I?" she says. She comes around the desk to stand behind him and adjusts the foam cups to better cradle his ears. His thin, wispy hair has grown long and brushes his frayed collar. She activates the noise-canceling function on the earpiece and sees his face soften as he exhales. Shield-warrior, she thinks. War-torn and hoary with winters. He could really use a haircut.

"Better?" she asks, resting her fingertips lightly on the bony ridges of his shoulders.

"What?"

• • •

Dr. Fae walks into the hospital like—well, like a doctor, except for the hoodie she insisted on wearing. She asks the desk nurse about her plans for the holidays and greets the gerontologist like an old colleague, which he is. He compliments her on the hoodie. It's the one with the naked girl with tubes going in and out of her body—the Professor tried to get her to change before she left, but she refused, and now she seems pleased that the doctor has noticed. Mel doesn't sit in on the appointment. She hasn't yet reached that level of clearance. But afterward, when Dr. Fae is in the restroom, the gerontologist calls her into his office. He knows who she is and the arrangement she has with the family.

"So, what's this about a bandit?"

Mel tells him about the cardinal, and the doctor laughs. "Well, that explains it. She was talking about a handsome red bandit who's stealing her money and attacking her husband and absconding with his books. I assume the Professor is okay?"

"Oh, yes," Mel says. "He's just fine."

"She says the bird wants to steal her away too. She's not wandering, is she?"

"No, mostly she sleeps and watches TV. She likes to watch the sports channels. And wildlife shows."

"Good. Well, keep an eye on her, and please tell the Professor to call me. Nothing urgent, but we need to think ahead."

"Right," Mel says.

The doctor nods, thoughtfully, and then he smiles. "That's quite the sweatshirt she's got on. She said it reminds her of a young patient she once had." He hesitates. "She was a remarkable physician, you know. Treated my wife's cancer. She had an intuitive sense for the disease, almost as if she could see the malignancy inside a body." He shakes his head. "Not your concern, of course. Sorry. I forget sometimes you're not their daughter."

Back in the garage, Mel types:

```
She could see the malignancy inside the life-house
of the body.
```

• • •

Mel's ex has been phoning her every few days for several weeks now, and one afternoon, during an online icebreaker social, Mel has nothing better to do, so she picks up. "What do you want?"

"Where have you been?" Allie cries. "I've been calling and calling. I thought something happened to you!"

Mel thinks about reminding Allie that they're no longer together, that they broke up over a year ago, and that she is under no obligation to talk to her or take her calls. Instead, she asks, "How's Humbert?"

The man Allie left her for is not named Humbert. His name is Bernard. He's a professor in their MFA program and twenty-three years older than Allie. He's a novelist, and Allie wants to be a novelist too. Mel no longer trusts fiction writers of any kind. She thinks they are unrealistic, lack integrity, and have a slippery hold on the truth. Unlike poets, who are unrealistic but honest because they have less to lose.

Allie is distraught. Bernard, it seems, has gone back to his wife, even though he swore they were separating, papers had been filed, divorce proceedings were underway, and soon he and Allie would move to his cabin in Vermont and live off the grid and focus on their writing and on each other—all of which confirms Mel's beliefs about fiction writers.

She doesn't gloat. She doesn't say I told you so. Instead, she listens—patiently, kindly—and when Allie asks if maybe they could meet up for a drink, she even hesitates. Once upon a time, not so very long ago, Mel loved Allie very much, and the truth is that part of her still loves Allie and would really like to see her, and the truth is, too, that Mel is lonely, desperately so, and she would like nothing better than to turn back time and be magicked out of the garage into the spacious condo she and Allie once shared, uncorking a bottle of excellent wine with Allie's fancy French corkscrew, curling up together on Allie's comfy Norwegian sectional that felt like a big leathery hug, which was how all of life with Allie felt until Humbert appeared and the hug turned into a sucker punch. Allie did not throw Mel out—Allie is not unkind—but neither did she seem sorry. As soon as Mel figured out what was happening (which took longer than it should have because Allie is a good ~~fiction writer~~ liar), she packed her bags and left. Not that she had much to pack. It was all Allie's.

So now Mel hesitates as the ache of the loss of their love trembles in the silence between them. There's a hint of yearning, and even tenderness, in the pain she feels. She waits, still hoping for something . . . for what? An apology would be nice. Some small sign of remorse. She wonders how she will answer, what words will come out of her mouth, and so when she hears herself say, "Fuck you, Allie. I trusted you. Now you know how it feels," she's genuinely surprised. She didn't know she still felt that way too.

She disconnects, and the world is silent and frozen. Then she realizes it isn't the world; it's her Zoom screen, which is not actually frozen—it's still operational and the session is still live—but although the icebreaker game has ended, no one in the gallery of participants is moving, no one is talking, and then she sees the frame of green light around her little square, which indicates that she is unmuted and that her team leader and all her coworkers have been listening to her phone call and watching her cry.

Awkward.

• • •

The noise-canceling headphones are not a solution to the noise problems, but they provide some relief. Mel helps the Professor order them online and figures out how to pair them with his ancient stereo receiver so he can listen to music too. Grimly triumphant, he summons her to his study one day when the Lawn Kings are hard at work to announce his discovery: that the consort music of the sixteenth century provides an effective buffer against the din of the twenty-first.

"Does a much better job than Wagner or even the Russians," he says, handing her the headphones. "It's that distinctive buzzy sound of the double-reed Renaissance instruments that masks the frequency of those infernal engines."

He plays her a gavotte for three crumhorns by Michael Praetorius, and as soon as she puts the headphones on, she sees what he means: the noise of the hedge trimmer dissolves into the old music and is absorbed by it.

• • •

Nice job with the headphones!!! Roz texts. Just FT'd with Dad but omg he needs a haircut!

The smiley face she chooses is the hollow-eyed screaming Munch emoji, which seems to Mel like an overstatement.

• • •

The email from human resources regarding the termination of her employment does not come as a shock. She knows her conduct has not aligned with the company's team-oriented values and behavioral standards. She acknowledges a persistent pattern of behavior that affects team dynamics, but she takes exception to their choice of the adverb "adversely." To the contrary, she would assert that her creative input has had a positive impact on team dynamics and productivity, though she realizes there's no point in quibbling about diction with the bot that wrote the email.

In their offboarding meeting, her supervisor is also interested in word choice. "Mel, what you did is called cheating. And you encouraged others to do it too."

Mel points out that she used the very same large language

model that the team was working on to perform the unnecessary and unpleasant task of socializing online—wasn't that the point? How could this possibly be cheating? Isn't it more like proof of concept?

"The point, Mel, is *trust*. How can I possibly trust you?"

Mel doesn't have an answer for that.

• • •

"It's criminal," the Professor tells her. "My old barbershop is now a Salon and Day Spa. They use the word 'spa' so they can gouge you. Do you know how much they want to charge for a haircut?"

He plugs a pair of clippers into the kitchen outlet and turns them on and off. "Still works," he says. "Could do with a little oil."

Mel sees where this is going. She wonders how much the Salon and Day Spa charges.

"My wife used to cut it," the Professor is saying. "She trained as a surgeon, said she knew enough to cut our hair without cutting off an ear." He chuckles and squirts a drop of oil onto the blades from the little tube. The motor clicks and hums.

"I guess you want me to cut your hair?" Mel says. She has no choice but to offer. She's late with the rent.

"Oh?" the Professor says. "Would you? Do you know how to use these things?"

"Enough not to cut off your ear."

She used to cut her little brother's hair after they moved from Deforest Drive and her parents got divorced and her dad moved out. Before that, her dad used to buzz Paulie's head because he didn't think a little kid's haircut was worth paying good money for, and also because Paulie was autistic and the sound of the buzzer in his ears made him crazy. Mel's job was to hold him down in the chair, which they both hated, and so she learned how to distract him with stories instead. He liked stories about knights and dragon slayers and trolls who lived under bridges that rattled when the knights rode over on their clattering steeds. When her dad moved out and she took over cutting her brother's hair, she would time the telling so the buzzer was rounding his ears just as the trolls and the dragons attacked. Paulie didn't mind so much. He knew that Mel would make it so the knight would win in the end.

She remembers all this as she runs the clippers up the back of the Professor's head.

"You certainly seem to know what you're doing."

"Yeah," she says. "I used to work at a salon and day spa." It is a lie, but maybe if he thinks this, he will pay her.

"So you cut ladies' hair as well?" he says. "How fortuitous. Perhaps my wife would like a trim too . . ."

When their mother died, Paulie moved in with their dad to the small one-bedroom apartment he rented behind a 7-Eleven.

Before the 2008 financial crisis, their dad had been an inventory control manager at the regional headquarters of a national office-supply chain. After he was downsized, he found another job working as a stock clerk in a local supermarket. It was a comedown, status-wise, but only temporary, he told them, a stopgap measure. Six years later, he'd been fired from the supermarket and was working the night shift at the 7-Eleven.

There wasn't enough room for Mel to move into the apartment, but that was okay because she was going off to college. That was always the plan. Her mom had been an administrative assistant in the principal's office of the local junior high school, and she understood the value of a good education. Mel was bright, and the plan was for her to go to state college and study something practical like accounting or nursing, find a stable job in the financial or health-service sector, and help out with Paulie's special ed and care. The plan was never for her to get an MFA in poetry.

Luckily, Paulie didn't need her help. In high school, he discovered he had a talent for coding, and he landed a lucrative IT job right out of college. Now he supports their father, who lives with him in the house Paulie bought, and he sometimes has to bail his sister out when she gets behind on her student-loan payments or can't make her rent. This was not part of the plan either.

"Why did your parents give you an unfortunate name like Malory?" the Professor asks as she works on his sideburns.

"My mom just liked it. It was the name of a character on her favorite TV show. She didn't know French, so she didn't know what it meant."

"Where's your mother now?"

"She died."

"I'm sorry."

"Yeah, well, it was a while ago." She changes the clipper attachment to do the top.

"The Malory you're named after," the Professor says. "Was she ill-fated?"

"I don't know," she says. "Maybe? I think she was a total airhead, but supposedly she had a high IQ."

"What was the name of the program?"

"*Family Ties*. It was a stupid show."

When she finally called Paulie to ask for a loan, he didn't say anything at first, but his silence was not that of a concerned brother contemplating his sister's plight and considering how he might help her.

"Arrrgh," he said, finally. "Shit."

He was playing a video game—the pirate one, *Sea of Thieves*.

"Paulie, did you hear what I said?"

Another silence, and then, "I dunno, Mel. You have to ask Dad."

"Why? It's your money, bro."

"Yeah, but Dad's my financial manager . . . *Yes!*"

"Paulie, what are you talking about? Dad couldn't manage his way out of—"

"Avast, ye scurvy rat . . . !"

"Are you in treacherous waters?"

"Yes," he said. "We're being boarded, but I'm listening to you too. I'm doing two things at once, which is bad, so I have to call you back."

When her phone rang, she heard the mournful strains of the hurdy-gurdy in the background and knew that his sloop was becalmed and the pirates were singing. This was her chance, but he cut her off.

"Listen, Mel," he said. "I know Dad's a loser—he knows it too—and his self-esteem is in the toilet, so I gave him a job title, all right?"

"A job title?"

"Yeah. Financial manager. Life coach. People like job titles. Job titles give you self-esteem."

She listened to the wistful lyrics. *Our ship, she dreams of wind in her sails* . . . Becalmed was a lovely word to describe such a frustrating impasse.

"I like job titles too," she said, although she'd never had one, so she couldn't honestly say if this was true.

The wind picked up. The music swelled.

"Please, Paulie?" she pleaded. "I'm a loser too. I need help. Just to tide me over . . ."

"Sorry, sis," he said, as his sloop sailed away. "Dad says it's not a good idea to lend you money. He says you need to be more entrepreneurial."

• • •

Her father was right. Since that call, Mel has been thinking about her failed attempts at entrepreneurship. More specifically, she's been thinking about the Professor's books. She uses a dish towel to brush the little silvery hairs off the back of his neck and then unties the garbage bag that she has draped around his shoulders like a cape. Maybe her business model was too small. Maybe she should have expanded while she had the chance. It's too late for that now. Maybe she needs a life coach.

She hands the Professor a small mirror. "What do you think?"

He puts on his glasses and holds up the mirror. "Very nice," he says, turning his head from side to side. "As good as a barber. Better, even." As he stares at his reflection, she sees that the mirror is trembling.

"You okay, Professor?"

He closes his eyes as his shoulders slump. Heart attack, she thinks. Ministroke.

"My daughter," he says.

"Roz?" Mel says helpfully.

He bats his hand at her. "I only have one, and I know what her name is."

"Right," she says. "Sorry."

He shakes his head. "No, no. It's just that . . . well, she's worried about us. When I spoke to her on the FaceTime, she said it won't be long before I'm no longer capable of taking care of Fae. She wants to move her to a *facility*."

He spits out the word, its taste repulsive in his mouth.

"A *memory care unit*, she called it. I told her I can care for her mother's memories perfectly well, thank you. I meant it to be funny, a lighthearted quip, but she didn't take it that way. She's never had much of a sense of humor. In any case, my wife's doctor agrees we need to plan ahead, so I've been doing some reading."

He looks up at Mel. Behind the lenses of his glasses, his eyes are watery and blue.

"The *Post* just did an investigation of these facilities," he says. "Cases where residents wander off and die of exposure. Nobody notices. 'Fatal elopements' they call them. Who comes up with language like that?"

His tone is imploring, as if somehow she might know the origin of the offending phrase. As if her knowing would correct it, make it go away. But she has no answer. He sighs and shuts his eyes again.

"I know about the books, Malory."

Finally—the moment she's been dreading.

He continues. "I'm not dead yet, you know, and even if I were, my library is not yours to plunder. Do you have an explanation? What were you thinking?"

Again, she has no answer. She waits for him to say more. His eyes are still shut, and his overgrown eyebrows are drawn together in a bushy frown. She should have trimmed them, too, she thinks. Outside, everything is silent: the engines, the cardinal, the cars on the street. She wonders if she might slip away now before he opens his eyes. Pack up her stuff and drive away while he sits here in the kitchen. Where will she go? Where will she sleep? She has no job, no apartment. She could live in her car—

Suddenly, he starts to laugh. It's a high-pitched, wheezy sound, and at first she's not sure if it's a laugh or if he's having a seizure. She's never heard him laugh before.

"Are you okay, Professor?"

He nods, pressing one hand to his chest. "It's just so ironic," he says, when he catches his breath. "My daughter wants to put my wife in a facility, and she wants Medicaid to pay. 'We need to bankrupt you, Daddy,' she tells me. 'We need to spend down your assets, get your savings below the eligibility threshold.'"

He takes off his glasses and wipes his eyes. "I told her you would help," he says.

Mel feels her face flush. "I'll pay you back."

He holds up a hand, as if signaling traffic to stop. "I haven't finished. I told her you would help look after Fae. I told her that with your help, we could manage."

He's watching her now.

"What about your books?" she asks.

"Consider it back pay."

"I didn't have to steal them."

"True. But we've been asking too much of you."

• • •

They come to an agreement. Mel will serve as a caretaker to Dr. Fae in exchange for free rent and a wage that she considers fair. The work itself isn't much more than what she's already been doing—preparing their meals, cleaning up afterward, taking Dr. Fae to her appointments and seeing to her needs, and generally keeping her entertained and active. They start going to Senior Joints three times a week. Axel is especially solicitous with Dr. Fae during class, and she seems to enjoy the attention, so when Axel asks Mel if she wants to get a drink sometime, Mel wonders if she should accept. Dating a trainer seems like a lot of work. "He's such a nice young man," Dr. Fae says in the car, as they eat their fried-fish-fillet sandwiches. "He's very handsome."

They still go to the Cancer Connection, but Mel has discovered some funkier thrift shops in town, and little by little, their wardrobes grow bolder. When she finds a youth-sized tuxedo that fits the doctor perfectly, they decide to dress for dinner that night. Mel wears her shimmery cocktail dress for the first time and helps the doctor buckle her cummerbund. The Professor wears a polka-dot bow tie that goes nicely with his red cardigan. When they're not shopping, they take walks in the neighborhood or go for drives in the country. Fall is coming, and already the days are getting colder, and when there's a chill in the air, they sit on the couch together in front of the television while Dr. Fae dozes and Mel reads books from the Professor's library. Tennis or golf tournaments stream quietly on the screen, and the hushed patter of the sportscasters provides an ambience that they both find soothing. The Professor gives Mel a biography of Sir Thomas Malory and suggests she read it; she learns that the person she's named after was a criminal and a thief. He wrote *Le Morte d'Arthur* while in prison, a fact she finds oddly comforting.

Sometimes Mel dozes off, too, and awakens to find Dr. Fae watching her. Once, a gentle tapping on her chest woke her, and when she opened her eyes, she saw Dr. Fae leaning over her, fingertips resting lightly on her sternum, just below her heart. The old woman's touch was firm and sure, a physician's hands, and her expression was serious. She cocked her head, as though she were listening, and then she took her hand away and patted Mel's shoulder.

"Well, Doctor?" Mel asked. "What's the prognosis?"

"You'll live," the doctor said.

• • •

The Lawn Kings move through the neighborhood in cycles, like the moon, like the seasons, like a band of marauders or a viral contagion. As the lawns lose their summer vigor and wither into dormancy, the mowers and Weedwackers are retired. Soon the autumn leaves will start to fall, and the leafblowers will come into their full glory, and when the last leaf is gone, it will be time to plow the snow. Throughout the summer, the cardinal has kept vigil in his rhododendron, defending his shrub against his archrival, the man in the red cardigan sweater, and the constant *tap-tap-tapping* of his beak against the glass marks the tempo of their days. Cocooned in sixteenth-century harmonies and buffered by crumhorns and shawms and curtals and racketts, the Professor no longer frets about the noise outside, but the cardinal is not doing so well. He is a shadow of his former self. His wings droop, and his sleek, glossy feathers are ruffled and dull. Dr. Fae, with her keen diagnostic eye, has noticed the bird is ailing. Mel often finds her in her bedroom, sitting on the spindly chair, leaning in toward the window, so close that the brim of her red cap touches the glass.

"He's sick," she tells Mel. "My bandito."

• • •

When the last of the nuisance trees, a towering Norway maple, starts to drop its abundant yellow leaves, the new neighbors decide to have it removed. The Lawn Kings set up an encampment for the felling. They bring in a bucket truck with outriggers and a long, articulating hydraulic boom arm. They bring in a flatbed truck, a container truck, a generator, a chipper, and a stump grinder. Mel and the Professor watch from the kitchen window as the forces mobilize.

"It's going to be a long day," Mel says.

"It's going to be a noisy one."

The workers position the bucket truck next to the maple and deploy the outriggers. They put on hard hats and harnesses, step into the bucket, and ascend into the brilliant golden canopy to lop off the tree's limbs with chainsaws. It's a beautiful tree, especially in autumn.

"How tall is it, do you think?" Mel asks.

"Fifty feet? Sixty? It must be over a hundred years old."

One by one, the great branches creak and fall to the ground, where they are fed into a chipper. It doesn't take long to strip the tree—a few hours, maybe. Shorn of its limbs, the tall trunk stands naked against the clear autumn sky; then they start to dismantle it. Working from the top, they wrap chains around its girth and slice off one section at a time, lowering each to the ground and loading it onto the flatbed. Throughout the day, the tree grows shorter and shorter, until it is reduced to a stump.

Mel and the Professor come out to watch the final phase of the operation and stand side by side in their matching noise-canceling headphones.

"Unbelievable!" Mel shouts, but the Professor can't hear her over the stump grinder. He pulls off one earcup.

"What?"

She points at what is left of the tree trunk, just a few inches now. "A hundred years, gone!" she shouts. "It's crazy. Like turning back time."

The Professor nods and puts the earcup back into place. Behind them the screen door opens, and Dr. Fae comes out to join them. She stares at the splintered branches, the raw slices of trunk, the wood chips flying up into the air. The stump grinder is deafening. She's wearing her red cap with the earflaps pulled down, and she has her hands pressed tightly over them. Her mouth is open; she looks like the hollow-eyed Munch emoji. Maybe she's screaming—with the noise of the stump grinder, who would know?

By the end of the day, the tree is gone. The fellers have packed up their trucks and driven off, and the Lawn Kings have decamped. Only the slouching leafblower is left to clean up. A late-afternoon rain shower settles the sawdust, and the air feels chilly and damp. He trains his nozzle on a single yellow maple leaf plastered to the wet asphalt of the driveway. The leafblower is blasting 900 cubic feet of air per minute through the hose at 250 miles an hour. The leaf trembles, refuses to budge.

"I don't understand," the Professor says, fretful. "Why can't he just bend down and pick it up?"

"It's a standoff," Mel says.

"Against a leaf?" They watch for a while longer. "Astonishing," the Professor says. "That gives me an idea."

The next morning, after breakfast, he asks her to accompany

him outside. On the neighbor's side of the fence, only a patch of dark raw earth and yellow sawdust marks the place where the old maple stood. Brandishing a tennis racket, he leads her around to the side of the house. He stops in front of the giant rhododendron.

"I was thinking about what you said yesterday about a standoff," he says. "And I've come to the conclusion that you're right. I've been meaning to cut this bush back myself, but why bother? These people have all the powerful machines. They can get it done in a matter of hours and haul away the debris too."

"Sure," Mel says. "I guess."

"It will be good for the house," he says. "Turn back time, you said, right? Freshen things up. There's been some damage to the gutters and the roof from the buildup of mold and mildew, not to mention the vermin."

"Your wife likes the vermin," Mel says, but he's not listening. He's bushwhacking, using the tennis racket to part the branches of the rhododendron, fighting his way through the heart of the shrub toward his wife's bedroom window.

"Let some sunlight into her room," he says. "She'll like that, don't you think? Maybe she'll wake up a little."

Taped to the window, the fierce paper owl stands guard over Dr. Fae, who is napping on the little bed inside. The Professor peers through the glass. "All she does is sleep."

He takes out his handkerchief, spits on it, and wipes away the pale scratch marks the cardinal has left.

"Damn cardinal." He studies the paper owl, who glowers back

with golden-foil eyes. "You know, I'm surprised this fellow didn't work."

• • •

Daddy says he's going to chop down my Dark Lord!!!! Roz texts, followed by a string of livid, red-faced emojis.

? Mel texts back, and as she waits for the reply, her phone rings.

"He says it's *your* idea!"

"Hi Roz," Mel says.

There's a pause, during which she hears Roz take a deep, calming breath.

"You don't understand," she says. "I *chose* it, see? When I was *seven*!"

"I'm sorry, but what are we talking about?"

"The *rhodo*! Mom and Dad let me choose it from a catalog, and we planted it outside my window. It's a Dark Lord—the variety, I mean—and I loved the name. It's so totally goth."

"You were into goth when you were seven?" Mel can't quite picture it.

"Inside was like a little cave, and I used to hide there. Inside my Dark Lord. It was my secret place."

"It's not so little now, you know."

"Listen, it was your idea, so you have to make him stop."

"Actually, it wasn't my idea. Your dad thinks it would be better for the house. And better for your mom, if she had more light—"

"I'm okay if they prune it a little, but they absolutely can't cut it down. It'll hurt the resale value to have a big old ugly hole in the landscaping. Don't tell him I said that. I'm sending you some info. Just make sure he reads it, please?"

She texts a bunch of AI chat transcripts with pruning tips: Count the bud scars to determine the branch's age (each scar marks a year); never cut back more than three years' growth or more than one-third of the plant at a time—this "rule of thirds" preserves spring bloom; severe pruning can stress or kill the shrub.

"Roz asked me to show you this," Mel says, holding out her phone.

"Yes, she sent it to me too," the Professor says. "I've made an appointment with the Lawn Kings for Tuesday afternoon. It's during Fae's exercise class. Best to do it when she's out of the house, I think. They said it wouldn't take more than a couple of hours, so we'll have plenty of time before you get back."

"Roz seemed pretty concerned . . ."

"Yes, well, Roz isn't here," he says. "You are."

Rhododendrons bloom in spring, and Mel has only seen this one bloom once. The trumpet-shaped blossoms were a dark crimson, with white tips on their stamens, like stars.

• • •

When she pulls into the driveway, she sees the rhododendron is gone. The Professor is waiting for them in the yard, triumphant in his red sweater.

“Mission accomplished,” he says, as he helps his wife out of the car and retrieves her shopping bags.

From the driveway, the garage blocks the view of the garden where the rhododendron once stood, so Dr. Fae doesn’t notice its absence. They take her into the house and follow her to her bedroom. The late-autumn sun pours through the window, which now has an unobstructed view of the garden and the garage and the street beyond. Dr. Fae glances around the room and then turns to leave.

“What is it, Fae?” the Professor asks. “Don’t you like it?”

His wife glances up at him and smiles. “Oh, yes,” she says. “It’s a very nice room.” She takes the shopping bags from him and continues down the hallway, pausing to look into each room before moving on. When she gets to the living room, she sits down on the couch, as if in a waiting room, to wait.

“Problem,” Mel says.

“What is it?” the Professor says.

“I don’t think she recognizes her room.”

In the sunlight, the bedroom looks dingy, with cracks on the ceiling and mildew stains on the walls. There are cobwebs in the corners, and the bookshelves are dusty too. Roz has arranged for a woman to come once a week to clean, and Mel makes a note to speak to her.

They close the curtains, fetch Dr. Fae, and lead her back, and this time she walks into the darkened room with no hesitation. She goes straight to the window and pulls back the curtains, and the sunlight pours in. Slowly she surveys the room, as if seeing it for the first time, then turns back to the window and taps the glass. She peers down at the cluster of lopped-off rhododendron stalks outside and then looks up at Mel.

"Where did he go?"

• • •

"'Rejuvenation pruning,'" the Professor insists. "That's what the young fellow called it. He said the plant was old and diseased, riddled with galls and stem cankers. There was too much dieback from all the mildew and fungi, and the only solution was hard pruning. He assured me it would come back in the spring."

The Professor sounds fretful again. Mel suspects this information may not be quite accurate, that late October may not be an optimal time for hard pruning, that there may have been other solutions. She changes the subject. "Roz keeps texting me. She wants photos. I haven't answered her."

"I know, I know," he says. "She's texting me too. She's worried about the resale value."

"Did she tell you that?"

"No. But I know my daughter." He falls silent, but when she puts the bowl of soup in front of him, he looks up. "Was I wrong? They're professionals. I thought I was paying for their expertise. I thought they would know best."

"Rhododendrons are tough," Mel says, although she actually has no idea. She suspects the Lawn Kings are full of shit.

Dr. Fae no longer sits on the living room couch. She has stopped watching TV and napping. Instead, she perches on the spindly chair by the bedroom window, waiting for the cardinal to return. She's restless, agitated. She gets up, sits down, gets up again, wanders around the house, and peers out the windows before returning to the bedroom. The Professor hears her padding from room to room, bumping into things, opening and closing doors, curtains, blinds. Once she tripped and fell, and he didn't hear her right away. She was okay—just a bruised hip, a twisted ankle—but now he's afraid to wear his headphones in case she falls again.

"At least she's not sleeping as much," Mel says. "That's good, right?"

"It's a miracle she didn't break anything." He shakes his head. "I thought she would like it. All that light."

To distract her, Mel takes her on long drives. There's a dairy farm in the country with an ice-cream stand that is always crowded with families in the summer; now, at the end of the season, the place is empty. They get vanilla cones with multicolored sprinkles and sit in the car with the heat on and watch the cows. When ice cream dribbles down the front of Dr. Fae's parka, Mel wipes it with a napkin. She wipes sprinkles off the doctor's chin, and the doctor smiles. Mel remembers wiping her mother's chin when her mother was in hospice. She remembers wetting her mother's mouth with a small sponge on a stick. When Dr. Fae has finished her cone, she likes to get out of the car and go right up to the fence where the cows are. She likes to watch the cows eat. If their big heads are close, she reaches out to touch their wet noses, and they let her. They seem to trust her touch.

Her memory is getting worse, and Mel hopes she will forget the cardinal, but she doesn't. Instead, driving home at dusk, it's Mel's name she forgets.

"Rosie?" she says, worried, looking at her from the passenger seat. "No . . ." Her voice trails off.

"I'm Mel," Mel tells her. "Rosie's your daughter."

"Yes," she says. "That's right. I have a daughter. Her name is Rosamund. She lives in the garage. She takes care of me, you know."

She looks out the window. The tired brown fields are waiting for winter. They pass a pumpkin patch with a few bright orange pumpkins. Mel switches on the headlights. It's getting dark earlier, and the nights are getting colder.

"You see," Dr. Fae says, "I have a medical condition. It starts with an *a*. It's called adrena . . . no. Adeno . . . No—that's not right. I can't remember what it's called, but it causes me to forget things."

"It's good that your daughter takes care of you then."

"Yes." Dr. Fae closes her eyes and rests her head on the back of the seat, then she opens them again and looks at Mel. "I'm very sorry, my dear, but I seem to have forgotten your name."

After dinner, when Mel goes in to check on her meds before leaving for the night, she finds the doctor sitting by the window in the darkened bedroom. Plugged into an outlet in the corner is the blue, moon-shaped nightlight that Mel bought at the Dollar Store after the doctor lost her way back from the bathroom one night. The bluish glow from the moon is dim, so Mel turns on the bedside lamp. "That's better," she says, tapping a pill into the doctor's palm. "Don't you want to watch a little TV before bed?"

The doctor swallows her pill and looks up at Mel. "This is your room."

"It's your room now," Mel tells her.

"It is?" She glances around the room at the lamp, the nightstand, the bed. "Where will you sleep?"

"I have a very nice bedroom above the garage. Look, it's right over there." Mel bends down and points over the old woman's shoulder, out the window, then turns off the bedside lamp again so they can see past their own reflections. The garage, once blocked by the rhododendron, is visible on the far side of the garden. Mel points to the small, bright window under the eaves. "That's my window, see? You can wave to me." She waves at the window. "Hi Mel," she says.

The doctor waves too. "Hi Mel," she says. And then, "Who is Mel?"

"I'm Mel," Mel says.

Dr. Fae turns in the chair to face her and waves. "Hi Mel," she says, and Mel waves back, and the doctor looks happy because she's made a joke and it's funny. The night sky is clear, the moon is bright, and the temperature is still dropping. Mel reaches past her to close the curtains, but the doctor stops her. "No, please leave them open."

• • •

Back in the garage, Mel types:

`Who is Mel?`

Then she types:

`I am Mel.`

Then she types:

`Where will you sleep?`

She has finally reached the bottom of the page. She rolls it out of the typewriter and adds it to the pile, which is not much of a pile, really—just a few sheets of paper with words from her word-hoard and random sentences that got stuck in her mind at the end of the day. Scraps of archaic language that mean nothing now. Sentences that don't add up.

Which is fine, because it's not like she's actually trying to write anything. She's just typing. Or, rather, practicing typing. Typing is a useful skill. A practical skill that will look great on her résumé: thirty wpm, 60 percent accuracy on a 1942 Deluxe Model 5 Remington Rand. Awesome.

*The world will never not need nurses, Malory.* Her mother's voice was shredded by cancer by then, which had spread from her lymph nodes to her throat and her lungs. Mel was seventeen. She was about to start college, but she came every day. She was the only one. The hospice freaked Paulie out too much, and her mother always found her ex-husband exhausting. When the doctor said Mel had a good bedside manner, her mother patted her hand. *She's going to college*, she wheezed, proudly. *She's going into the medical field.*

At the beginning of the semester, Mel registered for Anatomy & Physiology, Nutrition, Chemistry for Health Sciences, and a required English Composition course. Two weeks later, when her mother died, she dropped all except English Composition and added Contemporary American Poetry, Introduction to Literary Studies, and an astronomy class for nonscience majors called Exploring the Universe. Since then, a decade has passed, and now she's working as a home health aide with no credentials and no job prospects in her field of choice.

There were never any job prospects in her field of choice.

On the far side of the garden, the old woman's window is a small blue rectangle floating in the darkness. When the doctor sits in her chair, Mel can see her silhouette. Her face is in shadow, but her snow-white hair catches the blue light and makes a silvery halo around her head. She is sitting there now, motionless, and as Mel watches, she lifts her hand and waves. Mel waves back, and it's like a scene in an old movie: one person on the dock, and the other on an ocean liner, waving as the great ship pulls slowly away.

• • •

The next morning, Mel wakes to the Professor calling from the bottom of the garage stairs. His voice is thin, hoarse, desperate.

"Mel!" he cries. "Mel!"

She looks at her phone. It's 5:30 a.m. Her phone vibrates—it's Roz, so Mel doesn't answer. Outside, the sky is still dark. The Professor is standing at the foot of the stairs in his bathrobe, leaning on the railing with his hand pressed to his chest.

"Oh, thank goodness," he says, breathless, when he sees her. "Fae's gone. I can't find her."

She gets dressed quickly, and together they search the house, but there is no trace of the doctor. The morning is cold, and there's frost on the ground.

"Her puffer's gone," Mel says. "And her red cap too." The red hunting cap will make her easy to identify. They are thinking about fatal elopements: the seventy-five-year-old Alzheimer's patient who froze to death on the patio; the seventy-eight-year-old man whose body was found covered in fire ants; the woman who drowned in a puddle. The Professor is frantic now. He wants to get in the car and search for her, but Mel makes him sit down at the kitchen table and puts water on for coffee. She's trying to stay calm. "We'll go, but first tell me what happened."

It was just after five. He had gotten up to go to the bathroom, and on his way back he heard a noise coming from his wife's bedroom, so he went in to check. It was that damn cardinal, back again, scrabbling around on the windowsill. When the bird saw him, it flew off. That's when he noticed the bed was empty. He looked everywhere—all the rooms, the basement—but he couldn't find her. He phoned Mel, and when she didn't pick up, he tried his daughter, but it was the middle of the night in LA.

"So I went to the garage to wake you."

Mel's phone vibrates. "It's Roz."

She holds it out to him, but the Professor shakes his head, and so she lets it go to voicemail and calls the police precinct instead. She puts the phone on speaker and lays it on the table, and when the dispatcher answers, she pushes it toward him.

"I'm calling to report a missing person," he says, leaning over the phone, speaking too loudly. "Her name is Rose Fae O'Reilly—Dr. Rose Fae O'Reilly. O'Reilly is her maiden name, but it's the name she used professionally. She's a doctor. She is eighty-seven years old and has been diagnosed . . ." His voice cracks; he swallows, tries to take a deep breath. The dispatcher's distant voice cuts in.

"Sir, I need your name and relation to the missing—"

The Professor pushes the phone to Mel. "I can't. You talk to him."

Mel picks it up. "Hello, Officer? His name is—"

"Hang on," the dispatcher says. "Who are you?"

Mel hesitates and looks at the Professor. "I'm the daughter."

• • •

"It wasn't a lie," the Professor says. "You didn't say you were *our* daughter."

"Still," Mel says. She scrolls through the photos on her phone, looking for a picture of the red hunting cap to send to the police. She finds one, but the doctor is wearing her *Ghost in the Shell* hoodie, and the Professor is worried that the naked girl with tubes will give the police the wrong impression. She finds another one of the doctor in the red cap and her tuxedo.

"That's better," he says. "That's a nice one."

She attaches the photo to the email and sends it off, along with another of the doctor in her puffer coat, standing next to a cow.

"We can't just sit here and do nothing," the Professor says, pushing back his chair. "We have to go look for her."

"I'll go," Mel says. "Someone needs to be here in case she

comes home." She takes their cups to the sink, and her phone vibrates again. It's Roz, calling for the third time. "I should answer. What should I say?"

The Professor takes the phone from her. "Hello, sweetheart," he says, smoothly. "You're up early."

He's watching Mel as he speaks. "Yes, I know it's Mel's phone. We were just having coffee . . . No, nothing's wrong—your mother's fine. She's just . . . No, no, no. She woke up early and went for a walk, and I couldn't find . . . I know she shouldn't. I forgot to lock . . . Yes, I'll tell her. Everything's fine. I'm sorry to scare you, honey; I shouldn't have . . . Yes, love you too."

He hands the phone back.

"She'll be upset if she finds out you lied to her," Mel says.

"Let's hope we don't have to tell her."

It's six thirty, and the sky is getting light. She goes to the garage, grabs her coat and wallet, and when she comes back out, he's standing in the driveway, still in his pajamas and slippers, his red cardigan wrapped tightly around him.

"Go back inside," she says, getting into the car. "You'll catch pneumonia."

He's got something in his hand, so she rolls down the window. It's a paper map, old and creased from being folded and refolded. He leans in and jabs at the map with his forefinger.

"I've marked the routes she used to take when she still drove—here's Rosamund's elementary school, and here's the playground, the community center pool. Also the neighborhoods where our friends used to live." His hands are shaking, so the map is shaking too. He has circled all the places with a red pen. "I should go with you."

"No," she says, taking the map from him. "Stay by the phone. I'll be back."

She rolls up the window and puts the car in reverse. He stands there, looking frail and cold, then he raises his hand and waves.

"Go inside!" she yells, backing down the steep driveway, but now he's lurching toward her, waving his arms over his head.

"Stop!" he cries. "Stop!"

She brakes—just in time—barely missing the Lawn Kings' pickup as it swings into the driveway and parks, blocking her exit. She twists around in the seat.

"Hey!" she yells, but the driver doesn't hear. He jumps down from the truck and jogs around to the passenger door, and she sees then that it's the leafblower. He opens the door and reaches inside.

"Hey," she yells again, getting out of the car. "What the fuck!"

The leafblower hears her this time and looks up, and now she can see Dr. Fae sitting in the front seat, holding onto his arm. Her feet are dangling out the door. The leafblower lifts her from the seat, sets her down on the ground, and then, still holding her hand, starts walking her carefully up the driveway.

• • •

His name is Caleb, he tells them. He remembers the Professor from the shrub-removal job. He and his dad were working on a property about a mile away when they saw the lady walking down the middle of the street. They thought it was weird because it was still kinda dark—they like to get an early start, you know? A little later they saw her again, this time standing next to the truck. She seemed dazed and out of it, so his dad went over and talked to her. She didn't know where she was, but she'd recognized their truck and thought she lived nearby. One of the guys remembered seeing an old lady in a red hunting cap near where they took down the big Norway maple, and his dad told Caleb to take her in the truck and bring her back. He did, and when she saw the house, she remembered.

The Professor holds tightly onto Dr. Fae's arms. He keeps thanking Caleb, inviting him in, offering him coffee, but Caleb's on a job and he's gotta run.

"Such a nice young man," Dr. Fae says, as Mel helps her take off her coat. "He likes my hat. He has a red hat too."

She seems a bit tired and chilled, but otherwise fine. She doesn't remember why she left the house or where she went, but she says she enjoyed the ride back in the pickup truck. "It's very high up off the ground, you know. It has excellent visibility. You can see the whole world."

She wants to lie down, so Mel takes her to her bedroom, and

when she comes back, the Professor is standing at the stove, heating tomato soup in a saucepan.

"I thought some soup might warm her up."

"She's sleeping now."

"Well, you have it, then. I can make some more for her later. Sit down. Relax." He takes a wooden spoon from the drawer and stirs the soup.

"We should call the police," she says. "Let them know she's back."

"Yes, of course."

"And we should talk about what we're going to do." She hesitates. "We were lucky this time, but—"

"Yes," he says. "Thank God she's fine."

"Thank the Lawn Kings, you mean." Did she really just say that? She watches him, a rickety old man with a wandering wife, stirring tomato soup with single-minded concentration. It was pure chance that Dr. Fae was returned to them safely. Anything could have happened. She could have tripped and fallen, or been hit by a car, or died of exposure. Soon it will be winter, and there will be snow and ice on the ground. "I don't know how much longer—"

"We can manage for a while," he says, still stirring. "Thanks to you. You handled it well."

Is it relief she feels, or apprehension? She's not sure—a bit of both. She feels her shoulders loosen and her stomach unclench.

"You know," the Professor says. "Caleb is one of the fellows who pruned the rhododendron."

"I know," she says. "He's the leafblower."

"Leafblower?"

"The guy who operates that infernal contraption you hate. The one who wouldn't bend down to pick up the leaf."

"Oh, yes. The leafblower. Of course."

He stirs the soup, watching it go round and round. "*Leafblower*," he repeats. "You know, it's a lovely word, really. Like something you might find in a poem . . ."

# IMMORTAL

People say I have a disorder. The medical name for it is *pica*, which is Latin for "magpie," because magpies eat anything. But I don't. I only eat plastic. So no, I don't have pica. Plastic is just who I am. I do not eat sand. I do not eat metal. I would not eat a magpie, unless it was plastic.

The first time? When I was a baby, of course. I was teething and crying, and Mother put a plastic nipple into my mouth. Ever since that moment, plastic has pacified me when I am upset.

Toothbrushes came next. I didn't eat them. I chewed on them while savoring their fresh minty flavor.

. . .

I remember the first time I swallowed. It was a Bic pen—the ballpoint kind with the conical cap. The proper name for that model is the Bic Cristal, but nobody remembers the Cristal part anymore. Everyone just calls them Bics. Mostly they were blue, red, or black, sometimes green. The first one I ate was blue, and ever since, I've found blue to be the most delicious.

Blue—with that irresistible prong that keeps the pen upright in your pocket. I used to chew that prong, which is also called the clip, until it was mangled and flat and as thin as paper. It became a challenge to see how papery-thin I could make it, tapping with my big front teeth. Sometimes little slivers broke off. At first I spat them out, but I got in trouble for spitting, so I started swallowing instead. The swallow became part of the challenge, bringing a small satisfaction and making me hungry for more. Soon I was eating the whole prong and then the whole cap too.

There's a little plug at the end of a Bic with a sharp flat top and a short hollow stem. If you suck the air from the hollow, you can make the plug stick to the tip of your tongue. That is the power of suction. If you still live at home, you can wiggle your tongue with the plug on it at your baby sister and make her laugh. The plug smells like ink, which is nice, but the ink tube is even better—delicate, pliable, and chewy. It can turn the inside of your mouth blue if you're not careful, which will get you in trouble with your home health aide.

The chewy parts of a Bic are the cap, the plug, and the ink tube. They are polypropylene, which is a semicrystalline plastic. The hard parts are the long hexagonal barrel and the point with the ball in it, which is also called the nib. (The nib isn't plastic. It's a vitrified metal called tungsten carbide, which I would never eat. I spit out the point with the ball.) The hexagonal barrel is made of polystyrene, which is amorphous.

I love these words: *semicrystalline* and *amorphous*. They taste delicious in my mouth. Some words are like that. They taste the way they sound.

The first time I ate the barrel of a Bic, I was surprised at how brittle the amorphous polystyrene was. It's hard to describe. You have to use your back molars to crunch it, and when you do, it splinters into small shards that keep changing texture as you chew. This is very satisfying.

. . .

CD cases are made from polystyrene too. So are plastic knives and forks, disposable cups like the ones on airplanes, and some plastic food containers. I like to eat all of these. I also like the following: buttons, beads, soda bottles, water bottles, bottle caps; combs, earbuds, ice cube trays, sunglasses; the round dome lids from a Starbucks iced latte (as long as there's no milk foam stuck to them); clean clamshell packaging, plastic soldiers, TV remote controls (with nice rubbery buttons), cocktail swords (the kind for olives—but I never eat the olives), credit cards, computer keyboards, my brother's Hot Wheels. Plastic flowers too. Sometimes I'm allowed to go into a dollar store and buy a bouquet of plastic daisies for a dollar, and later I eat them in the park. Daisies are sweet and good, but I have to be careful to eat only one or two or they'll notice and I'll get in trouble.

Once I ate the keys off an old Smith-Corona typewriter. They were the perfect size to pop into your mouth. All the letters were clean and delicious, but the vowels tasted best.

Flyswatters would be delicious, too, except for the fly guts, which are gross. Lawn furniture is too big to eat, but yes. Sometimes in the waiting room at my therapy clinic, the molded plastic chairs look delicious, and when nobody is looking, I lick them. Once, Mandy caught me licking, but she said she would turn a blind eye. Mandy used to be my registered behavior technician. She is very pretty, but she isn't blind. I know this because I asked her, and she said no, so I told her if that was the case, I didn't understand what she meant. She said "turning a blind eye" was an idiom, and then she explained it. I like Mandy, but I didn't like her explanation. I said it was stupid, because if her eye was really blind, she wouldn't need to turn it. You only need to turn your eye if your eye can see. She said I was absolutely right, and so I made a joke. I said I thought it should be called an *idiot*, not an *idiom*, and it must have been a good joke, because Mandy laughed. That was a very good day.

Not all days are good days. I tried to eat a balloon once, but it was too chewy, and I was afraid of asphyxiating myself, so I spit it out. You could say I had a panic attack. That was a bad day. The same with plastic bags—too shapeless and baggy, too imprecise.

Once I ate a kitchen timer. It was shaped like an egg. That was super-precise.

. . .

There's precision in eating plastic. It's clean and tidy. Mandy told me that you are what you eat, but I said she was wrong about that. I told her I am a human being, but I don't eat other human beings, right? She said that was a good thing. Then I said maybe if I did eat other human beings, it would make me more human. I didn't mean to scare her or make her mad. I shouldn't have pretended to bite her. I was only trying to make her laugh with my joke, but she didn't understand. That was a very bad day. She didn't have to go away. I would never have eaten Mandy.

Sometimes I wonder if I am a human being. Maybe I am not even alive. I do not like to eat living things. Living things are gross because they rot. Vegetables, like stinky broccoli, are living things, even when they are as small as squishy peas. Meat is not a living thing, but it is only recently dead. Not dead enough. I only like things that are small and hard and have been dead long enough to be purified by heat, time, and pressure. Plastic falls into that category. Plastic comes from tiny, precise organisms—zooplankton and algae—that have been dead for so long they cannot die. That's perfectly dead, in my book. Pure. Safe. Super-clean. Immortal.

. . .

Mandy once told me that words are immortal too. She likes words, and so do I. We used to look them up in the dictionary to find out where they came from and what they meant. For example, "immortal" comes from the Latin *immortalis* (*in-* "not" + *mortalis* "mortal"). "Plastic" comes from the Greek word *plastikos*, meaning something that can be changed.

After Mandy left, I wrote her a letter with some immortal words that I typed on the old Smith-Corona (before I ate the keys). I was very careful. I wanted her to come back and be my registered behavior technician again, but I didn't want to scare her by asking straight out, so I started by telling her about some very cool scientific studies of environmental pollution that I read on the internet. Mandy cares a lot about the environment, so I knew she would be interested. The studies reported that plastic is everywhere in the food chain. The researchers estimated that human brains contain enough microplastic to make a plastic spoon, and that an average person consumes about a credit card's worth of plastic each week in their normal diet. I wanted Mandy to see that it's not so weird to eat plastic anymore. "See?" I wrote. "I'm not so different from a normal person. I'm not so different from you!"

. . .

It was a very persuasive letter. I ended it by telling her about "neuroplasticity," how our brains are always changing, and this is an example of how plasticity is actually a good thing. "Because someday, when your mind changes, you can come back!"

I haven't heard from her yet, but it's okay, because if there's one thing I've learned from plastic, it's how to be patient. That's the best thing about plastic—even when it's broken down, it persists.

# THE DEATH OF THE LAST WHITE MALE

The death of the last white male occurred on the first day of the Chinese New Year—and, to make matters worse, it was the Year of the Cock. When Grace found the body, she was filled with foreboding. He was a Silkie, a magnificent bird with showy, snow-white plumage, sapphire-blue cheeks, and a powder puff crest on the top of his head. His name was Gorgeous, although mostly they called him the Wimp, on account of the limp he'd picked up in a fight with his predecessor, Bootsie, a white alpha male who had ruled the roost until he died of a mysterious flu-like illness. They put the Wimp in charge of running the hens after that, but he never quite rose to the occasion, probably because of the damaged leg. He could never quite get on *top* of things, Grace complained, and after he took over, the number of fertilized eggs dropped precipitously, as did the count of new white chicks. In fact, the survival of the entire white line had been looking iffy for some time now.

Death came from the sky in the form of *Buteo lagopus*, a rough-legged hawk, pausing on its spring migration to Alaska for a quick bite of lunch. Like a Chinese roadside buffet, Grace thought. All you can eat. She had known something was amiss when she passed the chicken run on her way to the grocery store and there was nary a bird in sight—not a cluck to be heard nor a feather to be seen. She thought they had flown the coop until she looked beneath it and found them tightly huddled, a quivering ball of feathery terror. She straightened, scanned the sky, and spotted the hawk perched in a snag, staring down at her with its nictitating yellow eye.

Of course, Grace couldn't actually see the nictitating membrane slide across the eye. The hawk was too far away, and lately her vision had worsened. Bob blamed the long hours she spent in front of LED screens—computer-vision syndrome, he said. Blue light was hard on the eyes; it was only natural. But Grace didn't buy it. She had always taken pride in the acuity of her vision. Like a hawk's.

She considered doing something to protect the flock, but they were safely hidden for now, and the store was closing. She needed to buy nine perfect oranges for New Year's luck. They had cause to celebrate. She had entered her fifth month—more than halfway there—and the baby was due in May. The chickens would be fine, she told herself, as she hurried along.

Bob was out in the forest cutting firewood when *Buteo lagopus* made its kill. Later, when he came in and Grace told him about the death of the last white male, he raised his eyebrows at her choice of words but didn't take it personally. Grace did have a habit of fetishizing whiteness, at least when it came to fowl.

"And husbands," her husband added.

"Foul white husbands," Grace replied.

"Don't say things you'll regret," Bob said. "Death could strike me down in the blink of a nictitating eye."

His words unsettled her. She pictured the yellow eye, and the way hawks hover, riding an updraft, their wingtips hardly moving; she thought about the trembling ball of earthbound chickens, and the Wimp, strutting bravely out to confront the deadly raptor. A fool's errand, apparently.

"He tried to protect them," she said. "He sacrificed his life to save them. Now all our chickens will be brown."

"I like the brown ones," Bob said. "They have a beautiful, henna-colored variegation."

"The white ones are more exotic."

"There's a reason the brown ones survive, you know. They're better adapted. If you were a hawk half a mile up in the air and you saw a brilliant white bird and a dun-colored one, which would you go for? Which is the better target?"

"White males do make good targets."

"Glad to oblige."

• • •

Grace didn't actually see Gorgeous make his suicidal run. When she passed the henhouse on her way back from the store with her oranges, the deed was done, and only the aftermath remained: a small, flocculent white pile she took for a drift of melting snow—until it moved. Drawing closer, she made out the victorious raptor, straddling the now lifeless Gorgeous, flipping him over and searching for his heart.

Her own heart sank. It's my fault, she thought. I should never have gone to the store. I should have stayed and guarded the coop. She took a step forward.

Sensing her approach, the hawk paused and glanced at her, but only briefly, then went back to ripping the brilliant white feathers from the rooster's breast.

Should I scare it away? Yes, of course I should. We can't have hawks killing our chickens. Can't have them thinking that our hens are easy. And yet there was something in the hawk's utter indifference to her that she was loath to disrupt.

Perhaps it's endangered, she thought. Perhaps I should let it finish. A rooster is a small price to pay for the survival of a species—even if he was our last white male. Besides, he's already dead.

She stepped closer and stopped. Why isn't it scared of me?

Curious now, she picked up a small stick and advanced. The

hawk looked up again. She raised her arms and waved the stick. "*Shoo!*"

The hawk blinked, unimpressed, then dipped its head and sank its beak into the rooster's breast, extracting the bright red heart. It looked back at Grace. Now that she was closer, she could see the clear membrane slide sideways over the fierce, yellow eye. The hawk flipped back its head, opened its beak, and transferred the heart to its crop. Then, leisurely, it spread its great wings, flapped them once, twice, thrice, and flew away.

Grace carried her stick into the run and approached the pile of feathers that had once been Gorgeous. There was a neat incision where his heart had been; the breast feathers were stained bright red. She couldn't see his head.

Maybe it's not him, she thought. Maybe it's one of the hens.

She bent and poked the corpse with her stick until the head flopped over. It was definitely the Wimp. The plum-colored walnut that he sported on his forehead in place of a comb marked him as a Silkie male. Beneath the fluffy white feathers his skin was blue-black; his sapphire cheek patch had already dimmed, and his eyes with it. Faced with the dullness of death, she didn't want to touch him.

She straightened and ran her hands over her belly. Stupid, she thought. He's just dead, not contagious. But even so, she went to the barn for the rubber gloves Bob used when cleaning chicken shit from the coop and brought back a bucket as well. With a gloved hand, she lifted Gorgeous by a foot and lowered him headfirst into the bucket. But that felt wrong, so she turned him so his head was up and his feet were down. That was better. His body felt frail through the thick rubber. She retrieved the plastic bag of oranges she had left by the gate and carried the bag and the bucket to the house. She didn't want to leave the rooster in the run in case the hawk returned to finish him off, and besides, the sight of him might demoralize the hens.

• • •

She left him in the bucket on the porch, next to the front door where Bob would see him, then arranged the oranges in a blue bowl on the kitchen counter by the window. The nine perfect orbs of California sunshine looked waxy and unreal in the surly Pacific Northwest twilight. It was February, and the days were short.

"Crepuscular," she whispered, glancing up from the oranges and out at the mist that weighed heavy on the boughs of the cedars.

She had spent the previous week thoroughly cleaning the kitchen—a Chinese New Year ritual she had learned from a feng shui expert on a home-and-garden show. Grace's parents had immigrated before she was born, and in the States she had never felt the need to get in touch with her heritage. Here in Canada, however, where people wore their multiculturalism more openly, she felt she should make an effort. In the lead-up to the lunar holiday, she set to work clearing out the stagnant energy of the old year to make room for abundance and luck in the new—something that felt especially important now that they were bringing a new life into the world. She emptied the pantry and refrigerator of stale food. She filled or discarded jars that were less than half full. She tidied the magnets and mementos on the refrigerator. She replaced worn sponges and dish towels with new ones. Then, broom in hand, she swept the old year's dirt from the kitchen, straight down the hallway and out the door.

Bob helped. His job was to locate and remove all the dead shrews he had stashed in Ziploc bags and tucked into the deep recesses of the freezer—offerings that the cat, intent on winning Grace's love, had killed and dragged in along with deer mice, rats, squirrels, and small birds. Sometimes he would leave a single organ on the floor by her side of the bed—a gleaming liver, a tiny kidney—for her to step on with her bare feet when she went to the toilet in the middle of the night. Bob wasn't interested in those leavings; he saved only the tiny intact shrews to take to the island shrew expert, who was studying the mandibular morphology of the Vancouver Island water shrew, *Sorex palustris brooksi*, which was an endangered species.

"Everything around here is endangered," Grace complained.

Bob sighed. "Yes," he said. "It is." Patiently, he tried to answer her question about why their freezer needed to be filled with dead rodents.

"It's our duty to count," he said. "To keep track of the losses. And anyway, shrews aren't rodents."

"I thought they were." She had always lived in large cities. Shrews looked like kitchen mice, the kind her mother trapped with glue boards. She would set the traps behind the stove at night and in the morning collect the stuck mice and beat them to death with a rolled-up newspaper as they struggled to free themselves from the adhesive.

"Different order," Bob said. "Shrews are Eulipotyphla. They have five toes, like Silkies, not four. See?" He held up a foot.

Her mother tried to check the traps before Grace woke up, hoping to spare her the sight. But often Grace saw anyway. Once, a small mouse had gotten his foot caught in the glue—just one hind foot. By the time they found it behind the stove, it was already dead. It died trying to chew off its leg. No one thought to count the toes.

"The deer mice, on the other hand, are rodents," Bob was saying. "And we have plenty of those."

Grace thought of all the deer mice the cat had dragged in. Deer mice carried hantavirus, which could cause miscarriages and be fatal to babies. Cats carried *Toxoplasma gondii*, a parasite a pregnant woman could pass to her fetus, causing birth defects in the child. She knew all this because Bob had told her—not to scare her (these illnesses were rare and, with good hygiene, largely avoidable)—but because it was always better to know. Bob was a pragmatist, a fount of information.

"Right," Grace said, turning away from the dead little shrew. "Just please get rid of them by New Year's."

• • •

The nine oranges were for the final part of the ritual. Once the kitchen was clean, she and Bob would stand on the threshold and roll the oranges, one by one, through the front door. This was meant to symbolize the luck entering their household. She knew it had worked last year because she'd gotten pregnant. Now, with the baby on the way, they needed more luck. But as she waited for Bob to come in from chopping firewood, she kept thinking about Gorgeous, dead in the bucket on the porch, and her enthusiasm—for the New Year in general and orange rolling in particular—faded, replaced by that old foreboding. She knew it was silly. They could get another white male; Silkie cockerels weren't a dime a dozen, but neither were they rare. Still, the knowledge did nothing to dispel her dread, which felt like a toxic fog, heavy and pestilent, settling in a hollow. The feeling was not new. It predated 9/11 and the war. Maybe it had started with Y2K.

They both felt it back then, and they had hoped moving to Canada would help. They'd come to the island every summer since before they were married; after 9/11, they decided to try living here year-round. Canada seemed like a better place to raise children. There was public health care. Bob could continue his research away from the distractions of the city, and Grace, who worked as a freelance copy editor, would take fewer jobs while she concentrated on getting pregnant. For a while her spirits did lift, but as time passed, the political goings-on down south felt even more disturbing, and from this northern vantage there was even less she could do. She felt helpless. Bob didn't mind if the islanders thought of them as "the Americans," but Grace preferred to be regarded as Chinese. A week after she turned forty, she learned she was pregnant. Bob was ecstatic, and at first so was she. They had wanted a child for so long. Then, slowly, the dread returned.

The bright oranges in the blue bowl looked cheerful, she decided. She sat at the kitchen counter to wait for Bob and turned on the radio—a decision she regretted almost immediately. Was it really always better to know? A host in Toronto was interviewing an expert from the Centers for Disease Control about the H5N1 influenza virus. The clock was ticking, the expert said. Transpacific migration of the Asian avian flu was occurring at an alarming rate. A pandemic was no longer a question of *if* but *when*. Hundreds of thousands of chickens in Southeast Asia were shivering and dropping dead. Migratory birds were being infected. The flu was spreading to house cats and pigs. Forty-five black-striped Bengal tigers in a Bangkok zoo had died and more than a hundred others had to be destroyed. And people were starting to die too—babies, mostly. Children who'd come into contact with chickens. Women were miscarrying. If the virus continued to mutate—if it learned to swap its avian genes with human genes—the flu could infect 25 to 30 percent of the world's population. Hundreds of millions could die.

In December 1997, when the same flu had hit, Grace had watched reports on television as every last chicken in Hong Kong was killed and buried in landfills. She still had family there, aunties and uncles and cousins. She watched the trucks drive up to the farms and the men in moon suits and biohazard gear jump down like aliens landing. They stuffed the living chickens in white bags and gassed them. Earthmovers and cranes shoveled the bags into enormous holes in the ground. A million and a half birds.

She looked at the bowl of oranges. How could they protect her family against all the plagues and political pestilence that beset the world? It was a lot to ask, but maybe it was better than nothing. Maybe they should get rid of all the chickens. She would talk to Bob. The cat, seeing her sitting in the kitchen doing nothing, decided he might as well get off the chair and solicit food. He circled her ankles, then jumped up onto the counter. She butted foreheads with him and gave him a treat. She would not get rid of the cat. She loved the cat, even if he wasn't supposed to be on the counter.

She heard Bob's boots scrape across the porch. She picked up the bowl of oranges and carried it out. He was squatting by the bucket with Gorgeous in his hands, turning him over to examine the clean incision. He looked up when he heard her on the threshold.

"Hawk?"

She nodded. "He's our last white male," she said.

He raised his pale eyebrows.

• • •

They would bury Gorgeous under a tree in the orchard, and Bob asked her to choose which one. She chose a flowering Santa Rosa plum—her favorite—whose beautiful white blossoms in spring reminded her of snow and feathers. As she watched her husband dig, she thought about how wasteful it was to bury a perfectly good chicken, especially a Silkie, whose black flesh and bones were prized in China for their health-giving properties; yet she didn't want to cook and eat him either. It felt wrong to eat an animal that had died of natural causes, as if the act of killing were what transformed a living creature into food. She knew that was silly.

"Not to worry," Bob said, tamping the earth. "Nothing is wasted. He'll make good fertilizer. When you eat a sweet plum in August, you can think of Gorgeous."

"Great," she said. In August their baby would be three months old. In August she would be eating sweet plums and nursing her child. She would not want to be thinking of Gorgeous. She shook her head to dislodge the image, then ran her hands over her belly as if to keep it from passing to the baby. They had learned a few weeks ago that they were having a boy. There was so much to protect him from. She remembered the oranges, but after what had happened, she wasn't sure.

"Maybe it's too late," she said. "Maybe they're unlucky now. Maybe we shouldn't roll them in."

"Don't be silly," Bob said, taking her hand and pulling her up the hill to the house. "Come on."

She let him lead her, but she wasn't convinced. He was so American. What did he know about luck? Americans thought that they could manufacture their own good fortune. Chinese people knew better. The blue bowl of oranges was still sitting on the porch where she had left it. When he offered her one, she shook her head. He shrugged, took aim, and bowled, cheering as the orange caromed down the long hallway. The cat, seeing this, leaped off his chair and gave chase. Bob handed her another orange, which she accepted, and then they took turns. One by one, the oranges bounced off cedar walls, bumped down the basement steps, and careened into the bedroom, the kitchen, even the bathroom. The cat went wild, skittering and spinning as he chased the sunny orbs, and Grace felt her heart lift. Bob laughed, and she laughed too. What her husband didn't know about luck, he made up for in enthusiasm.

"There," Bob said, bowling the last one. "Done!" He grinned, hugged Grace, and picked her up in his arms. Following the route of the oranges, he carried her over the threshold, setting her carefully in the middle of the kitchen. He fished an orange from under the stove, dug a blunt thumb into its thick rind, peeled it, and broke it into sections. He offered her one, slipping it between her lips.

"Pure California sunshine," he said.

She tasted citrus oil on the rough edge of his thumb. She bit into the pulp, expecting a burst of sweetness, but the flesh was dry, the flavor both sour and insipid. She wrinkled her nose but swallowed anyway.

"Ew," she said. It had looked so perfect from the outside.

He smiled, shrugged, and held up the rest of the orange. "Compost?"

"Compost," she said.

He tossed the fruit into the bucket and came back to the counter. Her lips were still puckered, so he leaned in and kissed her. Despite herself, she smiled.

He wrapped his arms around her, holding her tight. "Don't you worry," he said. "Just you wait for them plums."

# SHIPS IN THE NIGHT

Baby slept in the eaves, under the rafters. Her room was shaped like a wedge of cake on its side, so when she lay in bed and looked up at the steeply pitched ceiling, she felt as though a lid were being slowly lowered on top of her. She had grown so tall in the months since they moved to Vancouver that now, if she pointed her toes, the tops of her toenails scraped the slope. When she mentioned this at breakfast, Guy's answer was, "*C'est facile, Bébé.* We will chop off ze legs."

"You're horrible!" Cayenne exclaimed, swatting his arm. Then, to Baby, "He's just kidding, hon. I won't let him cut your legs off, I promise."

Guy whinnied through his nose. He was smoking a joint, which was all he ever had for breakfast. Baby ate dry Froot Loops from a bowl because Cayenne had forgotten the milk.

"Oh, lady! *Comme tu es bête,*" Guy said, taking a toke so the words came out strangled. "Not ze legs of *Bébé*! Ze legs of ze *bed*!"

They didn't get it, so Guy rolled his eyes and exhaled. "I will cut a few inches from ze legs of the bed," he explained through the smoke. "That way we will gain in length what we lose in height."

Guy had been in engineering school until he did too many psychedelics and dropped out. He was older than Cayenne. He was not Baby's father, but Baby liked him. She liked the way he pronounced her name. *Bébé.* His own name was pronounced *Ghee* because he was Quebecois.

Baby's bed was a mattress on a sheet of plywood, supported by two-by-fours that Guy nailed together after she saw the rat on the floor. He drilled holes into the plywood "so it can *breeeeathe*," he said. They were living off his unemployment checks and the money he made selling weed, while Cayenne worked on her romance novel. She said she was going to sell it for a lot of money, and Baby believed her, because Cayenne didn't know shit about engineering, but she knew plenty about romance. She'd named herself for a hot pepper, after all. It was going to look great on the jacket of her book, she said. No last name, just *Cayenne*, in big, raised, golden, swirly letters. They'd been living with a guitar player in a trailer park in El Paso back then, and everything was very romantic—*muy caliente*—until it wasn't anymore, so they moved on.

• • •

They were always moving on.

"You don't have to take that shit," Cayenne said, gripping Baby's arm as she dragged her from the trailer. "Remember, you don't have to take it lying down." She pushed Baby into the Chevette and slammed the door, then went back for the rest of their stuff. It was hot in the car. Baby rolled down the window and watched as Cayenne crossed the small yard, tugging the broken suitcase with one hand and clutching her typewriter case with the other. The typewriter was her prized possession, a portable pink Olivetti. Her long India-print skirt dragged in the dust. One of the suitcase latches came undone, spilling some of the contents—a torn shawl, a platform sandal. For a moment Cayenne looked like she was going to cry. Instead she picked up the sandal and hurled it at the car.

Baby's arm ached where her mother had gripped her. There were red marks like a rope burn and a smear of blood from the cut on Cayenne's knuckle. Baby licked her thumb and rubbed off the blood, then she spread the road atlas across her bare knees. The cover was sticky with spilled Coca-Cola. She fingered the tattered pages. She was glad to be leaving Texas.

The car slumped as Cayenne got in. Baby opened to the big map of the United States and waited, but Cayenne just sat there, frozen, clutching the steering wheel and staring straight ahead.

Her hand was still bleeding a little from when she hit the guitarist. There was a darkening bruise below her eye from when he hit her.

Baby traced the nation's blue veins and red arteries with a dirty finger. "Where are we going, anyway?"

Cayenne sighed, let her forehead drop to the wheel. "I'm sick of the whole damn country," she muttered. They sat there for a moment longer. Suddenly she straightened. "Hey!" she said. "Canada! What do you think?" She turned the key and gunned the engine. "Buckle up, Baby. We're going straight to the top!"

• • •

They reached Vancouver and slept in the car until Cayenne hooked up with Guy. He had an extra room, which he said they could use until they found a place of their own, but Baby knew it wouldn't take long for things to get romantic.

"Oh, Baby," Cayenne whispered, setting down the suitcase and her typewriter in the living room and looking around. "What do you think? Screw America, right? Canada is awesome!"

She took Baby by the hand and pulled her through the house and up the narrow stairs, opening every door. The floor creaked, and the lintels were crooked. It had been a carriage house, built behind the main house where the Chinese landlord lived. Baby's window faced the back, looking down into the wide alley that the carriages once used, only now it was delivery trucks and garbage trucks and dumpsters.

Cayenne gazed out past the dirty rooftops, splattered with seagull shit, to the ragged, snow-capped ridge just visible beyond. "The vast north," she sighed. "Can't you feel it? Look at those mountains. We've got room to *breathe* here, Baby."

Her eyes were like hot stars on Baby's horizon.

• • •

Baby remembered the stars.

"It's all about experience," Cayenne said, as she drove the battered Chevette through the star-filled desert night. "Real-life experience. A writer needs that, you know?"

Baby nodded. She didn't go to school much, but she had plenty of real-life experience.

"I've got it all figured out, see? The heroine is from Texas. From El Paso. Maybe she's the daughter of a rich oilman who falls in love with a musician. What do you think?"

Baby turned to face her mother, leaning back against the car door and stretching her legs so her feet rested on Cayenne's lap. The window knob dug into her backbone. "Is she beautiful?"

"Of course she's beautiful," Cayenne said. "Is your door locked? I don't want to have to circle back and scrape you off the tarmac."

Baby twisted and punched down the button. "How beautiful?"

"Extremely beautiful. The most beautiful girl in all of Texas.

She's got flaming red curls and a temper to match. Like you, Baby. She gets her looks from her mother."

Cayenne's profile was the only thing that stayed the same—her face encircled by the moon and stars, framed against the landscape, blurred by speed.

"The musician guy . . . is he a guitar player?"

"Hmm." Cayenne tilted her head. "That's a good idea. Should he be?"

"Yeah," Baby said. "A guitar-player creep."

Cayenne glanced over. "You glad we left El Paso, hon?"

Baby nodded.

"Well, I think you're right," Cayenne said. "We needed some distance. You can't write about a place until you leave it behind."

• • •

The old glass pane in Baby's attic window looked like it was melting. When she knelt on her mattress and stared down into the alley, everything outside wavered—an underwater world with steel dumpsters like rusting shipwrecks, and girls like gaudy fish flitting up and down.

It was called the Stroll, Guy told her. At one end was Hung Lung Enterprises, a chicken-processing plant that filled the alley with the sweet stink of death when the wind came warmly off the Burrard Inlet. The seagulls rode the pockets of air, perching on splintering utility poles that rose and tilted like a forest of crosses.

The poles' trussed limbs, dotted with ceramic insulators, carried looping strands of high-voltage wire, heavy and rubber-coated, that tied the grid to the house just below Baby's window. The sash was swollen, leaving the window stuck slightly ajar, so when the wind blew through the alley, Baby could lie on her bed and watch the curtain lift and settle above her.

Cayenne had made the curtain from a worn housedress she'd found at the Union Gospel Mission Thrift Store.

"Look, Baby! It's vintage. You can't buy fabric like this anymore." She held the dress up to herself. "I don't know—do you think it's too domesticated?"

The thin, yellowed fabric was printed with blue cornflowers and smelled of the thrift store, of vinegar and mold. When puffs of wind billowed the curtain above Baby's face, it was like looking up a mother's dress—except mothers didn't wear housedresses anymore. They wore polyester sweatpants in pastel colors. Cayenne had pointed out the moms as they crossed America. They had names like Madge and Dot and Gert, Cayenne whispered. Terrible names. Not romantic.

• • •

Standing in line at a convenience store late one night, waiting to pay for gas, Baby found a little booklet called *What to Name Your Baby*.

"What's the Texas girl's name?" she asked.

Cayenne was looking at *People* magazine, but she put it down. "Let me see that." She flipped through the booklet, then pretended to return it to the rack. Instead, she slipped it into Baby's pocket and gave her a quick smack on the head.

"Ow!" Baby said.

"I told you to stop touching everything," she said loudly, so the cashier would hear. "Get back out to the car and wait for me."

As Baby left, she heard her mother talking to the cashier. "Kids," she said.

She came back with a supersize bag of popcorn and tossed it into Baby's lap. "What a team!" She held up her hand for a high five, but Baby ignored her.

"That hurt," Baby said, but Cayenne just laughed. She pulled out of the lot and flicked on the dome light. "Go on," she said. "Start with the *L*s."

Baby flipped through the booklet. "Liz?"

"Boring."

"Laverne?"

"Cheap." Cayenne frowned. "*L*s should be sensual. Like *love*." She curled her tongue, touched the tip to her teeth, and Baby could hear it vibrate. "Can't you hear the difference, Baby?"

• • •

In the alley, Baby watched the girls as they scratched through the gravel. "Like chickens," Guy said. "Looking for their stash."

Cooch grass cracked the asphalt in patches, shot up tall, then went to seed. The girls traveled to Vancouver from the prairie provinces, Guy told her. They were not much older than Baby—from places like Moose Jaw or Cut Knife or Qu'Appelle.

"*C'est la ville terminale*," Guy croaked through the smoke he held in his lungs. "It iz Terminal City, Bébé! End of ze line."

Across the alley, rickety wooden steps led up to the Golden Happiness Printing Company, and underneath the steps, to the clatter of the presses, the girls did things with men. Rhythmic. Fast. Sometimes they did it behind the Union Gospel Mission, against the dumpster wall or on broken sofas leaking stuffing in tufts.

When a storm came in from the Pacific and rattled the glass, Baby lay in bed and listened to the poles creak. The wires swung like heavy rigging on a pitching ship. Now and then she would hear the rat in the wall, and when it rained, the girls in the alley would start to swear, their heels clicking faster as they ran to the eaves for shelter. Baby was about to turn fourteen. She felt the restless breath of the alley play across her face as she watched the curtain swell.

Sometimes, when Guy was doing a deal downstairs, Cayenne would come and lie on Baby's bed, and they would gaze out the window together. "It's like we're princesses," Cayenne whispered. "Kidnapped by pirates, or imprisoned in a tower, biding our time and plotting our escape."

Down below, homeless men pushed shopping carts across the

gravel. They climbed over the dumpster's tall steel walls and dropped down inside. When too many went in at once, a fight would break out. Like a tangle of rats, they would rise to the surface, wrestling for a prize—a torn sweater, a broken toaster.

"Look at that," Cayenne said, cupping her chin in her hands and leaning into Baby. "What do you suppose he wants with that toaster?"

Under the streetlight, a hooker in a Spandex tube dress was doing jumping jacks in stiletto heels. Her ankles wobbled; she kept slipping off the edges.

"She's doing aerobics," Baby said. "She's got a needle in her mouth."

"That's enough," Cayenne said, trying to close the curtain, but Baby opened it again. The girl hiked her dress to her waist and folded over like she was hinged.

"No," Cayenne said, pulling Baby back from the window. "Don't look."

But Baby shook her off. The girl was bent, swaying, then her knees buckled and she plopped, bare-assed, into the gravel. Legs splayed, she did something between them. She sat up and fell back, and when her hand dropped away, Baby could see the patch of pubic hair and next to it a needle, sticking out from where the girl had forgotten it.

Cayenne sat on the edge of the bed, shoulders slumped, rubbing her temples. "I'm going back to work," she muttered.

"What about your novel?" Baby asked.

Cayenne frowned. "That's what I meant. What did you think I meant, Baby?"

"Nothing," Baby said. "You said *work*. I just thought—"

Cayenne held up her hand. "I don't want to know." They listened to the whore moaning, "*Come on. Come to Mama . . .* "

"*That's* not work," Cayenne said, her voice low and charged. "In case that's what you were thinking. I have *never* done that." She got to her feet and walked down the hall to the bedroom she shared with Guy. After a while, Baby heard the clack of the typewriter keys. Slow. One letter, then another. A pause. Barely a word, even. Certainly not a long word, one worth any money at all.

• • •

A narrow patch of kitchen garden separated the carriage house from the landlord's place in front. On one side lived the Wongs, and on the other the Fongs, and the landlord was a lady named Lily. They were always screaming at one another in Cantonese across the chain-link fence that separated their gardens. Lily lived with her mother and a man who, Guy insisted, was a former politburo cadre from the Guangdong Province and had once shared a bottle of *mijiu* with Li Ping.

"He iz Triad now," Guy said. "A real gangsta."

"*Ce n'est pas vrai*," Cayenne said. She was trying to learn a little French from Guy so she could use it in her novel. She had typed the first chapter and was reading it at the kitchen table. Beside her lay a clipped advertisement for a company that published novels. Cayenne was planning to send them the chapter.

"It iz the truth," Guy protested. "Mrs. Wong told me so."

"Mrs. Wong doesn't speak English," Cayenne said. "And you don't speak Cantonese."

"*Kam tin tin hei hou . . .* " Guy said, and it sounded like singing.

"What's that?" asked Baby, giggling.

"'It iz a fine day today!'" He reached across the table and tickled her. "What do you say, Bébé? *Hoi sam ma?*"

"I don't understand!" she said, giggling harder now. Guy was so funny.

"'Are you happy?'" Guy said. "Say it. *Hoi sam ma?*"

"*Hoi sam ma?*"

"*Bien,*" he said. "Now, listen: *Hoi* means 'open' and *sam* means 'heart.' *Ma* makes it a question. So, 'Do you open your heart?'" He waited for an answer. "Well, do you?"

"*Oui!*" Baby laughed. "*Oui! Oui!*"

Cayenne shook her pages and rolled her eyes. "Hello? I'm trying to concentrate?"

• • •

Lily worked at Hung Lung Enterprises, boning chickens. Mrs. Wong rose early and gutted fish. Her garden was overgrown with vegetables—bok choy, yu choy, snap peas, and chard. She dug her kitchen scraps straight into the earth. Whenever Baby left the little house to buy cigarettes for Guy, she had to pass Mrs. Wong, squatting outside with her sleeves rolled up, doing something wet and violent to food. She scrubbed black soil from white radishes as fat as thighs, cracked ribs of pork, scaled red snapper for luck, decapitated turtles for longevity. Often, when Mrs. Wong spotted her, she would wipe her forehead with a bloodstained knuckle and call "*You! You!*," hoisting herself up and parting the pea tendrils that climbed the chain-link. Her gap-toothed smile squeezed her eyes into crescents as she thrust gifts into Baby's hands: a dusty bunch of mustard greens, a cabbage head. Guy told Baby she must always accept and always say thank you. She could say *do jeh*, which meant, "I appreciate you many times."

One day Mrs. Wong hauled a garbage bag from the house.

"*You! You!*"

Baby went to the fence. Mrs. Wong heaved the bag over the top and pushed it toward her. It smelled raw and was leaking blood, and Baby recoiled into the hydrangeas. But Mrs. Wong just stood there holding the bag, so Baby had no choice but to take it. She held it at arm's length.

"*Do jeh*," she remembered to whisper.

Mrs. Wong nodded and grinned. She peered up at Baby's face. "*Hoi sam ma?*" she asked, but Baby had already forgotten what the words meant and didn't know what to answer.

• • •

"What the fuck—?" Cayenne said, as the blood dripped onto the linoleum.

"Fish heads!" Guy cried. He shoved back his chair. "It's Chinatown, Bébé!" He and Cayenne had been weighing out weed—Guy had an excellent supply chain up and down the BC coast and was famous for God Bud and Sweet Island Skunk—but now he cleared the table, flung open cabinets, and started pulling out spices—star anise, dried dates, bone-white shark cartilage. The heads slithered from the bag, sticky and wet. An hour later he lifted the lid from a heavy clay pot, ladled the steaming contents into three big bowls, and set them down on the table. Baby stared at her fish head, resting on a nest of glassine noodles. It stared balefully back.

"Eat!" Guy cried, poking his chopsticks into the cheek.

Baby pushed the bowl away. "It's gross."

Guy reached over and skewered the large, milky eyeball. He waved it in front of her.

"Stop tormenting her," Cayenne said.

Guy shrugged. "I am not tormenting. I am *teaching*. It iz better she learns to eat foods from other cultures, no?" He popped the eyeball into his mouth, closing his own eyes and grunting with pleasure. His lips worked as he sucked, his forehead slick with sweat and steam. He opened his eyes, spat out a hard white kernel, the size of a small pearl, and held it out for Baby to see.

Baby shoved back her chair and ran upstairs to her room. From her bed she heard Cayenne complaining, and then Guy declare, "*Bien*. If she must eat ze hamburger, then take her back to America."

Their voices dropped, and after a while it was quiet, save for the wind in the alley and the dry, sporadic cough of an asthmatic hooker. The sound made Baby feel lonely, like she might cry. The coughing went on. She lifted the curtain and peered into the gathering dusk. A girl stood alone in a cone of light from the streetlamp, weaving and dancing—two steps left—cough—two steps right. She was wearing bike shorts that hugged her rear end in a way Baby admired. Her head looked like a balloon on a string, bobbing and partly deflated.

The stairs creaked, then footsteps. Guy's voice low, Cayenne giggling. "*Shhh*." Their bedroom door clicked shut.

Outside, the girl started wheezing and gasping for air. She dropped to her knees and spat. Baby wanted to call Cayenne to come see, but she didn't. The girl clutched her stomach and lifted her face to the moon—catching sight of Baby instead.

"Hey!" she called.

It was the hooker from before, the one with the needle in her crotch. Now Baby could see she was a kid, maybe fifteen or sixteen years old. Her black hair was razored into a bad shag. It might have been the streetlight or the wavering glass, but the girl's eyes, staring up, seemed to cross and uncross as she swayed.

"Yo, Princess!" the girl called. "Yeah, I'm talking to you! You got any money?"

A princess, Baby thought. In a tower. Just like Cayenne said. Sounds were coming from the bedroom. The house seemed to tremble when Cayenne and Guy made love. Baby could hear her mother moaning, "*Oh, Guy, je t'aime . . .*" but she was faking. Baby could tell. Guy wasn't romantic anymore. Baby wondered where they'd wind up next.

The street was silent. When she looked out again the girl was still there, windmilling her arms in wide arcs.

"What's your name?" the girl yelled. Her voice sounded thin coming through the warped glass.

Baby didn't answer.

"My name's Lulu," the girl said. "You got any money? I gotta get to the hospital . . ."

She began wheezing again and covered her mouth with her hand. Her shoulders shook. Baby watched.

"Come on, Princess. Help Lulu out, please. I'm fuckin' dying down here . . ."

Just then Mrs. Wong peered over the back gate, brandishing a large pair of pruning shears. "*You! You!*" she yelled.

Lulu spat and stared at the old lady. Baby held her breath. Mrs. Wong had a small brown paper bag that she waved at the girl like a flag. When Lulu came closer, she reached over the gate and thrust the bag into her hands. Lulu opened it and pulled out a round white bun—the steamed kind filled with barbecue pork that Guy sometimes bought at the Chinese bakery. She peeled off the paper from the bottom and took a bite, then another. Mrs. Wong grunted, nodded, and disappeared back into her garden.

"Hey—thanks, lady!" Lulu called.

Then, like an afterthought: "And fuck you, Princess!"

Baby let the curtain fall. "*Hoi sam ma*," she whispered to the sloped ceiling in the dark.

• • •

"But Bébé is fourteen!" Guy said. "She is a big bébé now. She is in need of a name!"

"Baby will choose her own name when she's ready," Cayenne said. "That's the deal, right, Baby?"

"What's in a name?" asked Julien. He was Guy's customer, a poet from Seattle who had come north to score. "Would a rose by any other name smell as sweet?"

"Rose is nice," Baby said. "I like Rose."

Baby liked Julien. Cayenne did too. She thought he was TDH—tall, dark, and handsome—plus he'd brought lots of money. He was funny and mimicked Guy's accent. "I wan' ze *wheeeeelchair*, man," he said, pointing at a plastic freezer bag of BC bud and counting out bills.

"Rose is a terrible name," giggled Cayenne. She was in a mood. There weren't enough chairs, so she shared Baby's, then pulled

Baby's head into her lap and noogied her scalp. She was playing cool mom. She did that when she wanted to impress a guy.

"Cut it out," Baby said. She stood and moved behind Julien. Her hair was tousled. "I like Rose. *Je m'appelle Rose.*"

Cayenne sniffed. "Flower names are so bourgeois."

Guy lit a joint and passed it to Julien, who took a long toke. "Oh yeah, man," he said. "Iss ze fuckin' *wheeeeeelchair*!"

"How come you need a wheelchair?" Baby asked, bumping her hip against the back of his chair. "You a cripple or something?"

She knew she wasn't supposed to say that word, but Julien only snorted, rocking forward as he exhaled, and Cayenne laughed, too, high and tinkly.

"Oh, Baby, that's priceless," she said. "He's talking about the weed, silly. Messes you up so bad you need a wheelchair, that's all."

Baby kept nudging Julien's chair. "I knew that. I just think it's stupid."

Julien caught his breath and looked at her, tears from the smoke sparkling in his dark eyes. "She's pouting," he said admiringly.

"I am not. I just think it's fucking dumb, is all."

"Oooh," Julien said. "Such a potty mouth."

"Yeah," Cayenne said. "Watch it."

"Look at that lip," Julien said. He flicked a red curl from Baby's cheek and fingered her mouth. He pinched her bottom lip and tugged. His fingertips were hard and smelled like burned tar. Baby decided she didn't like him anymore.

"Cut it out, fuckface," she said. Talking hurt with him pinching her lip, and the words came out funny. He held on.

"Hey, mama," he said to Cayenne. "You got yourself one bitchy little baby—"

"Julien," Cayenne said. "Watch out for her, she—"

"*Ow!*" Julien cried as Baby bit down on his finger.

"—bites," Cayenne finished, as Baby thundered upstairs.

• • •

Baby lay on her bed, toes still scraping the ceiling. Guy hadn't gotten around to cutting off the legs. He'd meant to, but he kept forgetting. The voices from the kitchen dipped and swelled.

"More wine!" Cayenne cried. "We have to celebrate. Look!"

The alley was empty, but the wind was up. The utility poles creaked, and a seagull cawed overhead.

"It's from that publishing place," Cayenne said. "The one I sent my chapter to. They liked it!" Her words bubbled up through her laughter.

Baby's heart began to pound.

"Listen." There was a pause, then Baby heard her mother reading: "'Thank you for sending us your riveting first chapter. Our editorial team is unanimous in thinking that *Ships in the Night* is a real, steamy bodice ripper, and upon receipt of the finished manuscript, we will be thrilled to help you publish this promising romance and launch you, Cayenne, as a hot new debut author . . .'"

The excitement in her mother's breathless voice bruised Baby's heart. *Don't tell them*, she thought. *Tell me!*

Downstairs they were pouring wine and toasting. Julien congratulated Cayenne—"This is just the beginning!"—and she thanked him for all his positive energy. Guy wanted to see the letter. Baby rolled onto her stomach and buried her face in the pillow. After a while she took off her jeans and crawled under the covers. They were talking about money and contracts, which didn't interest her. She tried listening only to the wind, but she could still hear their voices rising and falling.

Then she heard Julien say, "Where's the bathroom?"

"Upstairs," Cayenne said. "Come on, I'll show you."

Chair legs scraped. Guy said, "He don't need you to hold his dick."

"Don't be silly," Cayenne said. "I'm going to check on Baby."

Baby listened to their feet on the stairs. She shut her eyes and slowed her breathing. Outside her door their voices softened and slurred.

"In here," Julien whispered.

"No! That's Baby's room . . ."

"Where, then?"

"Oh, Julien. Not now. I can't . . ."

"Hey, come on. Ships in the night, right?"

The floorboards creaked under their shifting weight. Baby barely breathed. She heard rubbing sounds against the wall, other sounds too—puffs of air, a low humming in the throat.

"We're alike, you and me," Julien murmured. "Writers. Kindred souls . . ."

"Oh, Julien . . ."

"*Cayenne!*" Guy hollered from the kitchen, and Baby's heart leaped.

"The bathroom's right there," Cayenne said loudly, then her footsteps clattered down the stairs.

Baby breathed again. She heard the bathroom door shut and the *shushing* sound of Julien peeing. In the kitchen, Guy and Cayenne were already fighting. Then, a crash. She got out of bed and crept to the landing. If she sat on the top step and leaned down, she could just see into the kitchen. A chair lay on its side. She hugged her bare knees.

"We were just *talking*," Cayenne said. She stood with her back to the kitchen counter. "You don't understand, Guy. He's a writer, like me. We're kindred souls."

Guy snorted. "*Bien.*" He brandished Cayenne's letter. "These people want cash to publish your book. You won't get it from me, so you think maybe you will go and suck his kindred dick, eh?"

"Give me that!" Cayenne said, grabbing for his arm, but he held the letter high, out of reach. Her breasts were heaving. "Don't be so mean, *mon amour*," she pleaded. "I'll pay you back, you know I will! It's going to be a bestseller! They said so . . . !"

From the stair, Baby peered through the balustrade at her mother's upturned, teary face. The tears were real. Maybe she still cared about Guy, Baby thought. Maybe it's still romantic. A noise behind her—the toilet flushing—sent her quickly back to her room. Downstairs, the back door slammed. She knelt at the window, lifted the faded cloth, and watched Guy stomp down the rickety steps into the alley. A moment later Cayenne ran after him, catching up with him at the dumpster. Baby chewed her thumbnail and watched.

Just then, her bedroom door eased open, sucking in wind from the alley through the gap. The flimsy curtains billowed, catching the light from the streetlamp in such a way that, from the doorway, what Julien saw was a half-naked Baby, kneeling on the bed in her underpants, thumb in her mouth, enveloped in a lucent field of yellow cornflowers. She was perfectly still, except for her tousled hair which lifted in the draft, red tendrils playing about her face. Riveted by the tableau, he stood there, and then she moved, raised a hand, as if in invitation or to fend him off—it hardly mattered which.

"Hey there," he said softly, stepping into the room and pulling the door closed behind him. "Don't be scared."

"I'm not scared," Baby said, though she was.

He moved to the bed and sat on the edge, reaching for her face, toying with a strand of her hair. "So pretty," he said. "Such a beautiful Baby."

She batted his hand away. "Cut it out."

He smiled. "Oh, that's right—you're dangerous. I'll have to watch my fingers." He fished his wallet and keys from his jeans pocket and tossed them on the chair beside the bed—like he lived here, Baby thought—then he lay back and tried to stretch out. The bed was too short, so he rolled on his side, knees bent. "I'm beat," he said. "I'm just going to close my eyes for a bit."

"You're not supposed to be here."

He patted the mattress. "Don't be selfish. There's room for both of us."

"My mom's gonna kill you if she finds out. Guy will too."

He glanced at the door, hesitated, then put his finger to his lips. "*Shhh*," he whispered. "We won't tell them, okay? Our secret."

He closed his eyes again, pretending. She knew he wouldn't pretend for long. *You don't have to take that shit*, Cayenne had told her in El Paso. *You don't have to take it lying down.* Baby backed away toward the window and looked out. Below, her mother and Guy were still by the dumpster; she couldn't tell if they were fighting or not.

"Hey, Baby," Julien said. "Come back. I'm getting lonely."

It looked like they were just talking. Maybe they were making up. She made a fist and rapped her knuckles on the windowpane.

"Hey!" Julien said. He sat up and banged his head. "Ow—what are you doing?"

She rapped again and waved. They still didn't hear, didn't look up.

"Who's out there?" Julien said. "Who are you waving to?"

"No one."

She turned to face him, and he held out his hand. She crawled to him and climbed on top. Straddling him, she reached for his wallet.

"Ah," he said, smiling and raising up on his elbows. "So that's how it is."

There was still a lot of money inside. Big bills. American.

"Don't get greedy now." He made a feeble grab for it, but she held it behind her back.

"I won't," she said. "Take off your pants."

"Sure thing, Baby," he said, and when he obeyed, she emptied the wallet and threw it across the room.

"Oh no you don't," he said, lunging at her—but she was already back at the window, banging hard on the glass with a fistful of bills.

"*Mom!*" she yelled, yanking open the window. "*Guy!*"

They looked up, and she waved. Julien froze. "What the *fuck*?" He scrambled from the bed.

She turned to watch as he struggled into his jeans. "You wanted to rape me," she told him. "That's bad."

He zipped up his fly, fumbled for his keys, his empty wallet. At the door he paused, started to speak, but she cut him off. "I won't tell," she said. "Our secret."

• • •

Cayenne lay on Baby's bed, staring at the ceiling. "Canada is a backwater," she said. "We're getting stale here, don't you think?

It's time we went back. I was thinking Seattle. That's a *real* city. We'll live in a cute Victorian and I'll finish my novel. Julien said it's a great place for writers. Won't that be fun?"

Outside, the streetlamps blinked on. Baby pressed her lips to the cold glass. "I hate Seattle."

"How do you know?" Cayenne said. "You've never been there." She was wearing a white embroidered peasant blouse with red laces that she wrapped around her fingers until the tips turned white. "Why are you being so negative?" Her voice tightened, rising into a whine. "Why are you ruining everything just when things are going my way?"

Baby didn't answer. Cayenne sighed, sat up, and went to kneel beside her. "Hey," she said, bumping shoulders. "Forget I said that, okay?"

Baby nodded. Down below, a chicken truck from Hung Lung Enterprises rattled past the streetlamp, sending a hooker stumbling into the spill of light. Stacked high with empty cages, the truck shed a wake of feathers drifting in the air.

"Is that the same girl?" Cayenne said.

It looked like Lulu. She was staring up into the light, milky-eyed and confused. She caught a feather. Then another, falling like snow. "Hoooo hoooo," she laughed like a loon, then doubled over coughing. It was definitely Lulu. The cough was worse. Baby wanted to rap on the pane, to call down to her, to help. Maybe they could be friends. Baby had never stayed anywhere long enough to make a friend—but that was okay, Cayenne said, because they had each other. Dazed, Lulu spun, a demented ballerina in a snow globe, reaching for the feathers as they drifted down. *Hoooo hoooo.* It looked like fun. Her mother would hate it if Lulu were her friend. In a way, that was perfect. Beside her, Cayenne was talking about Seattle again, about the bookstores, the cafés. Baby let the curtain fall.

"You just want Julien to fuck you," she said.

She heard Cayenne gasp, saw her turn, then felt the slap. It wasn't a hard slap, but Cayenne had never hit her before—not in the face. Her hand flew to her cheek, and Cayenne went white.

"Oh, Baby, no!" she cried. "I didn't mean it!" She threw her arms around Baby's neck and pulled her close. "Sweetheart, I'm so sorry . . ."

She held Baby's head and rocked her, crooning apologies into Baby's curls. Cradled at her mother's breast, Baby felt small again—small, but potent. When a sob welled up, she let herself cry a little. She hadn't cried in front of her mother in ages.

"Oh, no, Baby. Please don't cry! I didn't mean to do that. You have to believe me. I've just been so stressed . . ." But the more Cayenne pleaded, the harder Baby cried, until she was sobbing and gulping for air. Her face—crushed against the laces on her mother's blouse—was hot and wet with tears and snot. She tried to breathe, to push away, but Cayenne held on, still trying to explain.

"It's not what you think, Baby. Really. It's different with Julien. We have a special connection. We're alike. We're writers. We're—"

"No!" Baby shouted, shoving her back. "No! You're *not*!"

Cayenne blinked. "Not what, sweetheart?"

"You're *not* like him! You're *better* than him. You're better than all of them."

Cayenne's shoulders slumped, and her head dropped to her hands. "Oh, Baby," she said. Her voice was muffled. She stayed like that, and when she straightened, her face looked naked, old. She reached out her arms, but Baby turned toward the window. Cayenne sighed.

"You liked Guy, didn't you? And you'll like Julien too—you'll see. You're just upset about having to move, but trust me. You'll change your mind when we get to Seattle, I promise."

*When we get to Seattle.* Baby rested her forehead against the cold glass. Lulu was still down below, spinning and coughing. Next door Mrs. Wong shouted something in Cantonese. *Hoi sam ma?* Do you open your heart? If they stayed in Vancouver, Mrs. Wong could teach her more words. Mrs. Wong was kind. She gave everyone gifts. Guy was kind—mostly—and he taught her things too. He was going to look for a school she could go to.

"If we go to Seattle, I'm changing my name to Lulu."

"Lulu?" Cayenne said. "God, that's awful!"

"*L*s are sensual—you said so."

"Okay," Cayenne said, shrugging. "It's your choice." She stretched and smiled, and her eyes went dreamy. "That reminds me—did I tell you? I'm thinking of changing the story. It'll take place in Canada, see? The heroine's this poor girl from the prairies who's been forced into prostitution, and the villain is a French fur trapper. Then there's this Chinese drug dealer, and . . ."

Lulu looked up at the window. Baby waved, and Lulu waved back. Baby thought about the money hidden in her underwear drawer. It was supposed to be for Cayenne, for her novel. Maybe if she gave it to her now, the novel would get published and they wouldn't have to go to Seattle. But then she'd have to explain where she got it, and Cayenne would get mad, or jealous.

Maybe she should give it to Lulu instead. Take her to the hospital. Or not. She went to her dresser and opened the drawer. Cayenne was lying on her back, staring at the lowering ceiling. Baby slipped the bills into her pocket.

"I can still call it *Ships in the Night*," Cayenne was saying. She pulled the letter from her bosom and unfolded it. "Did I show you this? Look! It's a real steamy bodice ripper, Baby!"

Baby closed the drawer. "That means they like it, right?"

"It means they *love* it."

"So how come you want to change it then? It's good the way it is."

"Really?" Cayenne's face lit up like a child's.

"Totally," Baby said. "You just need to finish it." Her mother would never finish her novel. Baby knew this now. "And we should just stay here until it's done. So you can focus."

Cayenne nodded slowly. Baby watched her mother think. Maybe she should give her the money—maybe tell her how she got it—or maybe it was better to hang on to it until they really needed it. She fingered the bills in her pocket. It was her choice, and she would decide later.

# FEELINGS

Once upon a time, a long time ago, there were two little girls who lived in a small university town in New England. Their names were Meghan and Kai, and they were best friends—and if anyone had asked, they would have sworn they'd be best friends forever. This was back when even fairly young children could still walk home from school by themselves, so every afternoon they walked to Meghan's house, where they played until Kai's father picked her up after work. Kai's father was an underpaid, part-time psychology professor who taught introductory classes on neuroses and psychoses. Meghan's father was a famous neurosurgeon in the city who cut people's heads open and actually fixed what was wrong inside. He made a lot more money than Kai's father, so Meghan's family lived in a big Edwardian near the university, close to the private school they both attended. Kai's family lived in a small prefab ranch house in a working-class suburb. Sending her to the private school was a stretch, but when it came to education, her parents wanted the best for their only child.

Meghan was the middle of three sisters. Her older sister, Cecily, was pretty and mean. She had boobs, wore a bra, and wanted nothing to do with Meghan and Kai—which mostly meant pretending they didn't exist—and that suited them fine. Meghan's younger sister, Izzy, was annoying and still sucked her thumb, which was pathetic. Her skinny pink thumb was raw and wet as an earthworm, so Meghan and Kai refused to hold her hand, even when they were crossing the street, even though they were supposed to.

Meghan was thin and plain, but she said she didn't mind because she was the smart one in the family. "I'd so much rather be interesting and intelligent, wouldn't you?" she'd say, in a low, confiding voice that made Kai feel interesting and intelligent, too, although she suspected she wasn't. According to her dad, Kai had lots of emotional intelligence, but when she repeated this to Meghan, Meghan shook her head. "That doesn't count," she said. "That's just *feelings*."

Something in her intonation struck them both as very funny. Afterward, whenever either of them said the word, they'd draw it out long, and when someone else said it, they would glance at each other with wide, mocking eyes: *Feeeeeelings*. It cracked them up.

Their English teacher was a hippie and big into feelings. When they studied Gratitude for Thanksgiving, she made them keep diaries and share what they were thankful for, which was incredibly embarrassing. Now, for Christmas, they were doing Compassion, and the teacher said they would need to acquire some before school let out for the holidays.

Meghan raised her hand. "Is compassion like a *feeeeeling*?" she asked, which made Kai snort so hard she had to pretend she was having an asthma attack and use her inhaler.

It was a good question, their teacher said. Compassion was a feeling, but it was more than that. The prerequisite for compassion, she explained, was empathy—the ability to put yourself in someone else's shoes. Compassion was empathy in action. For their project, they were to do one compassionate act and then write about it. The class groaned and bombarded her with questions: *You mean a report? An essay? What about a poem? A story? A play? How many pages?* She held up her hand. They had studied the different genres of writing all semester, she reminded them, and this was their chance to choose the one they liked best. On the walk home, Meghan said she thought it was an interesting assignment.

• • •

That weekend, when Meghan was in the city with her mother, she spotted an old bum panhandling on the corner and saw her opportunity. While her mother stepped into a phone booth to make a call, Meghan dug in her pocket for change and darted forward. The man held out his hand, and she dropped a nickel into his palm. His skin was covered with dirt and thick yellow calluses. When she looked up, he was watching her.

"Seriously?" he said.

"I beg your pardon?"

"That's all you got?"

In fact, it wasn't. Meghan had a twenty in her backpack and her dad's credit card, but she couldn't exactly ask the bum to break the twenty, and she doubted he took Visa. That's what she told Kai later. "It's not like he took Visa, right? So what was I supposed to do?"

"Totally," Kai said. "Twenty's way too much. You gave him what you could. It was very compassionate."

"Thank you," Meghan said.

What she didn't tell Kai was that, besides the twenty, she had a few crumpled singles in her pocket—the change from the hot-pretzel man. She'd just decided a nickel's worth of compassion would satisfy the assignment.

"I know you got more," the man said with X-ray eyes. "I can't get nothing to eat with a nickel."

He was right on both counts, but just then her mother looked up and saw her daughter talking to a bum on the corner.

"I take my eyes off you for one second," she said, grabbing Meghan's arm and pulling her away. She spat on a Kleenex and wiped Meghan's hands. "What were you thinking?"

"I was feeling sorry for him," Meghan said, sulking. "I was putting myself in his shoes."

"Well, don't," her mother said.

• • •

"But did you?" Kai asked later.

"Did I what?"

"Put yourself in his shoes?"

Meghan made a face. "Ew. No way. His shoes were disgusting."

"Did you feel sorry for him?"

"No. The guy was pathetic. He was gross. And he smelled."

"Doesn't count," Kai said. "It's not compassion unless you feel the *feeeeeling*." She was trying to be funny, but Meghan ignored her.

"My mom told my dad, and he said he was proud of me and gave me another twenty—but I know he did it just to piss her off."

When Kai told her parents the story at dinner, they raised their eyebrows at each other across the table.

"Twenty, huh?" her father said. "Not a bad return."

Her mother shot him a look. "Don't." Then, to Kai: "You girls think you're so clever. Do you know where the word *compassion* comes from?" Kai's mother taught English at the public high school and turned everything into a teaching moment, but Kai liked repeating what she learned to Meghan, so she listened. "It comes from the Greek word *pathos*, meaning 'suffering,' and *com*, meaning 'with.' Compassion means 'suffering with.' That poor man was suffering, but your little friend certainly wasn't. She gives him a nickel, and *she* gets twenty dollars? That's not compassion. That's exploitation."

"That's what I told her!" Kai said—though she hadn't.

"You tell her to go find that poor man and give him every last cent."

"Sure, Mom," Kai said. *Fat chance*, she thought. When she told Meghan, they both laughed.

• • •

There was an older girl in Cecily's grade at school named Patty Potts. Patty Potts wasn't poor, and she wasn't a bum, but she was totally pathetic, or so Cecily said. Cecily called everyone pathetic, but in Patty Potts's case, it seemed true. Patty Potts had no friends. She looked like a sack in her school uniform. She had terrible posture. She was perfect.

"She always seems so sad," Meghan whispered.

"So sad," Kai said. "She's suffering because nobody likes her."

"*We* like her," Meghan declared, as if saying it could make it so.

And with that it was decided: Patty Potts would be the object of their compassion—their pity project—and they would ask the teacher if they could do the assignment together. Kai suggested they write a short story (she wanted to be a writer, preferably a novelist), but Meghan, who intended to become either a journalist or a detective, insisted on a report. The teacher was reluctant, but Meghan talked her into it.

"*Com* means 'with,' right? And *passion* means 'suffering.' Kai and I want to suffer together to do the assignment."

Strictly speaking, that line belonged to Kai—her mother had given her the etymology—but Meghan stole it. This was typical, but Kai didn't mind. In fact, she felt a little proud. They both made tragic, suffering faces; the teacher laughed and told Meghan she was too clever for her own good.

They began by observing Patty Potts at school—between classes, at recess, in the lunchroom—as she hovered at the edges, ignored and unseen, while all around her kids were laughing and talking and messing around. After school she walked home alone, and they followed, discreetly, at a distance, careful not to look directly at her. Keeping their spines stiff and their eyes fixed straight ahead, they leaned into each other until their shoulders touched and spoke from the corners of their mouths.

"It's like she doesn't even exist," Meghan said from the left side of her mouth.

"Nobody ever talks to her," Kai said from the right.

Left. Right. Left. Right. The rule was that they couldn't turn their heads to look at each other.

"Nobody ever walks with her," Meghan said.

"Nobody sits with her at lunch," Kai said.

"That's because her lunch is so sad," Meghan said. "She has a sad lunch. She has to make it herself, you know. Every morning."

"Yeah," Kai said. "And she doesn't know how to make anything except egg sandwiches."

They fell silent, enchanted by the pathos of Patty's lunch.

"Egg sandwiches smell like farts," Meghan said.

"That's why nobody will sit with her in the lunchroom," Kai said.

"Who smells like farts?" Izzy cried, breathless, breaking the spell. They had forgotten Izzy at school again, but she had seen them leaving and ran to catch up. Her enormous backpack kept slipping off her skinny shoulders.

"You," Meghan said. "You smell like farts. Go away. We're having a private conversation. You know the rule."

The rule was that during private conversations Izzy had to walk ten steps behind them. Meghan counted as Izzy walked backward. "Bigger steps," Meghan said.

On the next block, Patty Potts stopped at the intersection to wait for the light. Meghan knelt and pretended to tie her shoe. Her hair fell forward, curtaining her face.

"Her mother's an alcoholic, you know," she said from behind the curtain. "She doesn't get out of bed in the morning."

"She stays in bed all day," Kai said. "She's clinically depressed." Kai knew a lot of psychological vocabulary from her father.

Meghan pulled up her knee sock. "That's because Mr. Potts is having an affair."

"He left her for a *younger* woman," Kai said. She had overheard her parents say this—not about Mr. Potts, but about some other father. Kai didn't know who, and she didn't care. She just liked the hush of it, the way they breathed into the secret, stretching it out long. When they caught her eavesdropping, they told her not to sneak around listening to grown-up conversations that were none of her business.

Meghan didn't seem impressed, so Kai tried again. "The younger woman was his *secretary*," she said, with more emphasis this time. No reaction. Meghan was looking right past Kai at Izzy, who was inching closer. Meghan glared; Izzy stopped.

Ahead, Patty Potts stood at the crosswalk like a zombie, staring into the traffic. It was a busy intersection. Would she step off the curb into the path of the oncoming bus? They were half a block away, but if Kai ran, maybe she could save Patty Potts's life. That would totally count.

The light changed. Cars stopped. Patty Potts crossed safely, and they hurried after her.

The Potts house was a gloomy Tudor revival set back from the curb, its dark facade and steep gables shrouded by overhanging cedars. It was perfect. The perfect house for Patty Potts. They ducked behind a privet hedge as she turned up the path. From the sidewalk they watched her let herself in with a key.

"After Mr. Potts left," Meghan whispered, "Mrs. Potts tried to kill herself."

Kai thought about this. "With sleeping pills," she decided. She knew more than most kids about the ways people kill themselves. "Patty Potts found her passed out on her bed, and she called 911."

Meghan nodded. "They took her in an ambulance. They had to pump her stomach."

"Patty Potts saved her mother's life!" Kai said, triumphant.

Meghan shrugged, still watching Izzy over Kai's shoulder. "I guess. But Patty Potts never recovered from the trauma."

"She has PTSD," Kai agreed.

"And Mrs. Potts has pretty much been a vegetable ever since."

Meghan usually got the last word. There was a small window in the peak of the gable. "That's Patty's bedroom," Kai said. "She lives in the attic, under the eaves."

"No," said Meghan, whose bedroom was in the attic, under the eaves. "Patty Potts lives in the basement. The attic is her crazy mother's."

"She takes care of Crazy Mother," Kai said.

"Feeds her egg sandwiches on a tray."

"Up and down. Up and down."

"Crazy Mother is very demanding for a vegetable," Meghan said. "That's why Patty never has time to shower or do her homework."

"That's why her hair is dirty and she has BO."

"That's why her skin is so bad."

"That's why she gets D's in math."

"Poor Patty Potts!"

"Poor Patty Potts!"

• • •

"We have to *do* something for her," Meghan said. "Otherwise it doesn't count." They were sitting on the floor of Meghan's bedroom under the eaves, brushing her plush ponies. Kai coveted the ponies; Meghan owned the entire herd. Spurs and crops, bits and bridles, and an assortment of oxers lay scattered around them. Meghan had real jodhpurs, shiny leather boots, and a black velvet helmet. She took real riding lessons, and Kai coveted those, too, but her parents said don't be silly.

They were too old to play with ponies, but the slow brushing of the plush coats while basking in pity for Patty Potts put them in a delicious trance—tragic and pleasurable at once. Then Meghan got impatient. "We have to *act*," she said, tugging a tangle from her pony's tail. "If it's just a *feeeeeling*, it doesn't count."

"Maybe we could write her a letter," Kai said. She was grooming Popcorn, her favorite, a posh palomino with a plaitable mane. Meghan's was a dapple-gray show jumper named Silver Whisper, draped with ribbons and garlands and rosettes that he'd won at all the competitions. Kai entered Popcorn in all the competitions, too, but he wasn't a show jumper, so Silver Whisper always won. That was the rule. Izzy was the judge; Kai and Popcorn could only come in second. When Meghan wasn't looking, Kai whispered to Popcorn that the competitions were fixed.

Meghan looked up from Silver Whisper's withers. "What would we write?"

"We could tell her we like her."

"But do we?"

The answer was obvious. Kai began to braid Popcorn's long white mane. She eyed the purple fly hood—both of their favorite color, though it looked best on Popcorn.

"We could send it anonymously," Kai said, but Meghan had a better idea.

"I know!" She tossed down her brush and pushed Silver Whisper aside. "We'll write it in invisible ink."

"Invisible ink?"

"I saw it on TV. You make it with lemon juice. You write a message, let it dry, and then you can't see it."

"But if you can't see it what's the point?"

"You *can* see it! You hold the paper over a candle, and the message is revealed. C'mon, I'll show you."

They ran downstairs to the kitchen. There were lemons in the crisper. Meghan found a paring knife, paper, and a small brush; she fetched a candle from the dining room and matches from the junk drawer.

"Don't look," she said, dipping the brush into the lemon juice and shielding the page with her arm. When she finished, she blew on the letters and fanned the paper till it dried. She lit the candle and handed Kai the letter. "Not too close."

They watched as the words emerged, burned and brown, like old blood.

*Dear PP,*

*I'll be your friend even if you're pathetic and nobody likes you.*

*Love, Kai*

A huge heart dotted the *i* in *Kai.* Smoke threaded up from its center, and just as the heart caught fire and burst into flame, Cecily walked in. She shrieked, and Kai dropped the burning letter onto the counter.

"Jesus!" Cecily yanked open the fridge, grabbed a bottle of seltzer, and doused the flame. The fizzing water made scraps of ash skitter and dance. There was a black scar on the countertop. "Mom is so gonna kill you," she told Meghan, squinting at the page. "Who's PP?"

"No one," Meghan said.

"Patty Potts," Kai said.

Cecily stared. "Is this a *love letter*?"

"No."

"Are you crushing on Patty Potts?"

"No!"

"But you wrote it, so—"

"Meghan wrote it," Kai blurted.

Meghan glared at her.

"Oh my god," Cecily said. "I always knew you guys were lesbos."

"It was a joke," Meghan said.

"It's invisible ink," Kai added. "So Patty Potts can't read it."

"Wow," Cecily said. "That's *so* retarded. If she can't read it, what's the point?"

"We don't *want* her to read it," Meghan said. "We don't like Patty Potts. She's pathetic."

"*You're* pathetic." Cecily shook her head and dropped the sodden page in the sink. "Unbelievable. I'm telling Mom."

They watched her leave the kitchen, heard her go upstairs.

"My mom's gonna kill me," Meghan said.

"Your dad will stick up for you," Kai said.

"No," Meghan said, staring at the soggy letter. "He moved out."

• • •

Their assignment was due in two weeks.

"It doesn't matter *how* we do it," Meghan said. "We just have to do *something* so we can write the report."

"What if we just wrote her a regular note?" Kai said. "We don't have to sign it."

"We can use fake handwriting."

"We can say something really nice about her."

"Like what?"

They lapsed into silence, trying to think.

"We need to try harder to put ourselves in her shoes," Kai said.

It was their library period. They were stretched out on the carpet between the stacks, hidden from the librarian's desk, and eye level with Patty Potts's shoes under the table at the end of the aisle. The shoes were beige orthopedic sneakers with Velcro straps. Meghan took a sheet of ruled paper from her three-ring binder, chose a pen, and gripped it awkwardly in her left hand.

"Dear Patty Potts," she wrote. "You have hideous shoes." The left-handed letters were all cockeyed. She passed the note across the rug to Kai, who started to giggle.

"*Stop!*" Meghan hissed, snatching back the page and tearing it in half. "It's sad. It's not her fault. Her stepmother makes her wear them."

"She has a stepmother?"

"Yes. An *evil* stepmother." She took another sheet of paper, switched to green ink. "She's young and beautiful and despises Patty Potts. She wants Mr. Potts all to herself."

"Wait, what happened to her real mother?"

Meghan looked up, exasperated. "You mean Crazy Mother? She killed herself, remember?"

"I thought Patty found her in time."

"*You* said that. I wanted her to die so her father would be tormented by guilt for the rest of his life."

"Oh," Kai said. Meghan was in a weird mood. It was better not to say too much.

Meghan tore up the green note. She took out a third sheet and lowered her voice. "You know that room in the attic? That's where she did it. She hung herself from a beam."

*Hanged*, Kai thought, but this wasn't the time to correct Meghan's grammar.

"By the time Patty found her, she was already dead, so Patty has to live with her father and the stepmother."

"Oh."

Meghan switched to a pink pen. From Kai's angle she could read only "Dear Patty."

"That's why Patty Potts's shoes are so hideous," Meghan murmured. "Her stepmother makes her shop at Salvation Army. She buys her the ugliest things on purpose."

"She's a very evil stepmother," Kai said. Evil stepmothers were such a cliché.

"Yes. She makes Patty sleep in the basement and only feeds her egg sandwiches, even though Patty hates eggs."

"I guess Mr. Potts doesn't love Patty very much," Kai said. She felt a little mean saying it, like she was crossing a line she couldn't quite see.

"That's not true!" Meghan snapped. "Why did you even say that?"

Kai shrugged. "I just figured, if he lets his new wife treat her that way—"

"It's not his fault," Meghan cut in. "Mr. Potts doesn't know. He's never home. He's always away on some covert operation."

"Is he a surgeon?"

"Of course not, stupid. He's a spy, don't you know? He works for the CIA."

*Right*, Kai thought. She hated when Meghan called her stupid. "Good thing we never sent Patty that letter."

"Why?"

"Because if he's a spy, he knows all about invisible ink."

Meghan rolled her eyes. "Real spies don't use invisible ink." Just then, the bell rang, and Meghan tore up the pink note and stuffed the scraps into her binder. "And he wouldn't have seen it anyway. He's on a top-secret mission in Siberia. Or he's in a prison camp. Maybe both."

"Yeah," Kai said. "Probably both."

Meghan slammed the binder. "How would *you* know?"

• • •

The assignment was due in ten days, and they still hadn't done anything they could write about. Kai kept waiting for Meghan to come up with another plan, but Meghan was still being weird, and then she missed a week of school because she was sick, supposedly. After school, Kai walked downtown to the Psychology

Department and waited in the office until her dad finished teaching. It was okay, though. She liked being there. The secretary, an old lady named Evelyn, gave her stacks of recycled paper and let her type on the big IBM Selectric. Kai typed a letter to Patty Potts. Typing was better than fake handwriting. Better than stupid invisible ink.

Later, over dinner, when her father asked what she had been typing, she said homework, which was sort of true. Her mother asked whether she'd heard from Meghan and how she was feeling. Kai said fine, which might have been true, or not. Her parents did that look-across-the-table thing and dropped it—until later, when Kai overheard them. "Of course she's depressed," her mother was saying. "If you ran off with Evelyn, I'd be depressed too." Her father said something Kai couldn't catch, and her mother laughed. "Stop, it's not funny." Then, more soberly: "I'm not overly fond of Meghan, but I feel sorry for her. These things are always hardest on the kids."

But her mother was wrong, Kai thought. It *was* funny. The idea of her father running off with old Evelyn was hilarious.

• • •

Two days before Christmas break, Meghan slipped into homeroom just before the bell. She was pale, and her hair looked unwashed. In first-period English, she raised her hand: she had already written her report—could she turn it in early?

"I thought you and Kai were going to work together," the teacher said, surprised.

"No," Meghan said. "I decided to suffer alone."

She avoided Kai all day, and when school was out, she left without telling her. Kai hesitated—should she go to Meghan's as usual, or did this mean she was disinvited? She could walk to her father's office and wait there, but when she saw Patty Potts heading home she fell in behind her. At the end of the block, she heard someone running after her; she turned and it was Izzy.

"Meghan forgot me again," Izzy said, out of breath. "Can you walk me home?"

"No," Kai said. She didn't mind Izzy the way Meghan did, but being mean to Izzy was a habit. "Just kidding." The kid looked pathetic, all crooked and tangled up in her backpack. Kai bent down and tightened the straps. "There. Come on."

"Can I hold your hand?" Izzy asked, skipping to keep up.

"No." Patty Potts was nearly out of sight.

"Why are we always following that girl?"

"Shh! Keep your voice down."

"Is it a secret?"

"Yes. A top-secret mission." Meghan never let Izzy go on top-secret missions.

They tailed Patty Potts to the big Tudor house and watched her disappear behind the heavy wooden doors. Kai pulled out the letter she'd typed at her dad's office: she'd brought it to school to show Meghan, but now there was no point. She crouched and handed it to Izzy.

"Okay, this is your mission. See the mailbox by the door? Slide this letter into the slot. You have to be quick, and you can't make any noise. Take off your backpack."

Izzy wriggled free of the straps. "What is it?"

"A top-secret message. If you want to be a spy, you have to do this, okay?"

Wide-eyed, Izzy nodded, then she tiptoed down the walk, clutching the letter. The farther she went, the smaller she grew. The dark wooden door, banded with riveted metal, looked like it belonged to a castle—or a dungeon. By the time she reached it, she was tiny. She stood on her tiptoes but couldn't reach the slot. "*Jump*," Kai mouthed from behind the privet hedge. As if she'd heard, Izzy jumped, but the letter missed. It fell to the ground, and she bent to pick it up—just as the door swung open.

"*Gotcha!*" the woman said, snagging Izzy and holding her at arm's length like a scrap of dirty carpet. She was a large, dark-skinned woman in a maid's uniform. "I've been waiting for you. You the one sneaking around after Miss Patty?"

Izzy hid the letter behind her.

"Poor girl's got a hard enough time without you kids tormenting her. What you hiding there? Give it here." The woman reached for Izzy's other arm, but Izzy twisted free and bolted.

"Hey!" the woman shouted. "You come back here!"

Izzy kept running—flying down the walkway, scanning for

Kai crouched behind the hedge, and when she didn't see her, she took off down the street. The woman stood on the step, watching; when she finally went back inside and shut the door, Kai sprinted after Izzy.

She caught up with her at the intersection, just in time to grab her before she darted into traffic. For a moment Izzy struggled; then, realizing it was Kai, she buried her face in Kai's stomach, sobbing. Kai pried the letter from her clenched fist and shoved it in her pocket. Glancing up and down the sidewalk, she patted Izzy's shoulder.

"Don't cry," she said. A few pedestrians passed on the sidewalk, but none she recognized. "It was your first secret mission. You did good."

"But I got captured!" Izzy hiccupped.

Kai squatted and rubbed her back. "Sure, but you escaped, didn't you? And you didn't give away the mission—even after you were caught and tortured. You did great!"

"I did?" Izzy pulled away, eyes red and nose running.

"Sure," Kai said. "You're a really good spy—a super spy—and that's why you can't tell anyone. This is top-top-secret. We're the only ones who know. Don't even tell Meghan, okay?"

Izzy nodded. This was serious. She had never kept a secret with Kai that Meghan didn't know. She wiped her nose and shoved her snotty fingers into Kai's hand, and Kai didn't even pull away. They stood together on the corner, waiting for the light to change.

• • •

The teacher liked Meghan's personal essay, and the next day, when she handed it back, she asked if Meghan would read it aloud to the class. Meghan's face went very red, and she said she didn't want to, but Kai raised her hand.

"Come on, Meghan. Please! We want to hear it!"

The rest of the class chimed in. Meghan stared at the paper on her desk, and for a minute, it seemed like she might cry. Then she looked up and glared at Kai. "Fine," she said and walked to the front of the classroom.

The essay was about the bum in the city. Meghan wrote that the minute she saw him, she knew he would be the perfect person for her to be compassionate to, even though it was hard to put herself in his shoes because he smelled so bad. She held her breath, walked right up, and gave him a nickel, which was all the money she had. He looked at the coin, grabbed her hand, and began shaking it: *Bless you, thank you, kind young lady! Thank you for your generosity and compassion.* At first it felt good, but he kept saying it, over and over, like he was making fun of her, and she got scared. He squeezed so tight she couldn't escape, and it might have gone on forever, except her mother saw her and yanked her away, yelling that she shouldn't feel sorry for bums or give them money because it was never enough and only encouraged them to be lazy and beg for more.

That night her mom told her dad what had happened, and

they had a huge fight, and her dad said he was proud of her and gave her twenty dollars. Meghan was happy he had taken her side, and she put the bill in her piggy bank to buy something special. But then a couple days later, her dad decided to get a divorce, packed all his stuff, and moved out of their house. Meghan begged him not to go. He would be homeless! Where would he live? But he laughed and said he wasn't going to be a bum; he was getting married, and he and his new wife would have a new home, which would be Meghan's home, too, and wasn't she lucky to have two homes instead of one? But he was wrong, Meghan wrote, because in terms of her feelings, she had no home at all, and suddenly she understood what it was like to be homeless. So the next day, while her mother was at her psychotherapy appointment, she took the train into the city by herself, which was against the rules, but she didn't care. The bum was still standing on the same corner, and she gave him the twenty. The old guy looked surprised but didn't make a big deal of it or even try to shake her hand. He just thanked her and smiled, which, in the end, felt a lot better.

• • •

After she finished reading, the teacher invited questions, and Kai raised her hand. "Is that really true?"

Meghan looked her straight in the eye. "Yes," she said with great compassion. "It really felt better."

But in the hallway after class, Meghan turned on Kai. "Thanks a lot."

"For what?"

"For trying to get me in trouble."

"I wasn't," Kai said. "We were supposed to do the report together."

Meghan shrugged. "Yeah, well. I was busy. And writing stupid letters to Patty Potts was dumb. This was more interesting."

"So it really happened? You really did that?"

"Are you kidding?" Meghan laughed. "My mom would kill me if I went into the city by myself."

"So you made it up?"

"Of course," Meghan said, shrugging. "I mean, I *thought* about doing it." She was trying to be funny, but when Kai didn't laugh, Meghan suddenly looked tired. "Listen, it's a story, okay? Get over it."

Kai watched her friend walk away. Maybe it was more interesting than the stupid letters, she thought. But that still didn't make it fair.

• • •

This is the letter that Kai wrote to Patty Potts:

Dear Patty Potts,

You don't know me. I'm not in your grade or anything, but I see you at school at lunch and walking home by yourself, and, no offense, you seem pretty sad and pathetic a lot of the time, probably because you don't have any friends. I hope it's okay to say that. I'm not judging you or anything. I feel sad and pathetic a lot of the time, too, especially lately, so I think I feel a lot of empathy and compassion for you. My teacher says empathy is when you put yourself in someone else's shoes, and I think maybe you and I are wearing the same shoes in terms of our feelings. Some people think feelings aren't as important as being interesting and intelligent, but I don't agree. My teacher says feelings are necessary for compassion, and compassion is empathy in action, and that's actually why I'm writing to you, because I thought maybe you would feel better if you knew there's someone in the world who feels like you do. But now that I think about it, maybe you don't feel sad and pathetic at all! How would I know? I guess it's impossible to know what's really going on in another person's life, and what they're feeling and stuff, so no pressure, okay? We don't have to be friends or anything. And if you don't feel sad and pathetic, you can just ignore this letter or throw it away.

Kai reread the letter. It felt too short for the assignment and too flimsy to spin into a story. Nothing happened—she never delivered it, Patty Potts never read it, and Kai couldn't imagine what would have happened if she had. None of it counted. She threw the letter away, told her teacher she couldn't finish, and received an incomplete for the assignment.

The shame of that incomplete stayed with her—who gets an incomplete in compassion?—but time passed, and over the decades the details faded. Now she can't remember much of the letter she typed in her father's office, whether it was to Patty Potts (not her real name) or to Meghan (not hers either), or even if it was a letter at all. Once she stopped going to Meghan's house after school, she typed many things on that machine which she now only vaguely remembers—short stories, poems, even a play. (The typewriter was a 1964 IBM Model C Executive, electric, and state-of-the-art in its day.) She does remember the notes to Patty Potts that she and Meghan wrote by hand, but doesn't recall if they ever delivered them. She remembers Meghan's plush ponies, and Izzy's skinny, wet thumb. She thinks she remembers an angry housekeeper on the steps of the Tudor house, but she might have made that up. She remembers the invisible ink.

What she remembers most vividly about their Patty Potts phase are the feelings she and Meghan shared: the voluptuous delirium of making things up and then wallowing in their inventions; the pity that made them feel powerful and special; the bond those feelings forged between them. She remembers how confused and hurt she was when that bond broke. At the time she had no idea what was happening in her friend's family, no capacity to imagine what her friend was suffering. Her failure, she later realized, wasn't a failure of compassion so much as a failure of imagination, and this thought haunts her. Even now, whenever she types a story, she worries. She worries about this every time.

# ONE ART

This would never happen now, but in 1978 things were different. It could have, back then—and it did, at least as I remember.

When she walked into the classroom on that January morning, the first day of the new semester, we were curious. The course was Old English Language and Literature, and Professor L was a visiting scholar, hired to fill in for a lesser professor who was on sabbatical. An alumna of our college, L was rumored to be brilliant—a Rhodes Scholar with a doctorate from Oxford and a tenured post at a nearby Ivy. We were nervous and prepared to be awed, seated in a horseshoe with our backs to the walls. At the front stood the professor's desk. She strode to it, set down a stack of books, shrugged off her overcoat and draped it over the chair, then turned to face us. She walked slowly around to the front of the desk and leaned against it—posture languid, expression wry—letting her eyes travel around the room, taking us all in. There were eighteen, perhaps twenty, of us; we studied her too.

She was tall and slim, Eastern European, with dark, deep-set eyes, an aquiline nose, and straight, shoulder-length hair that fell like black wings on either side of her jaw. High forehead, high cheekbones. Elegantly hollow cheeks. She wore tan wool trousers, a dark wool blazer, a black turtleneck. She wore them well.

She briefly described the class, then asked us to introduce ourselves. I was near the end, and when I said my name, she repeated it thoughtfully. Her voice was like gravel and honey. She went to the blackboard and wrote my name in chalk, then added beneath it: "sorrow, repentance, regret."

"As in *rue*," she said. "From the Old Norse *hryggr*, meaning 'grieved.'"

My name was never the same after that. She held her left elbow when she spoke, tapping her chin with a long forefinger. She tilted her head and smiled at me, ruefully, and I fell in love.

• • •

Slowly, we became friends.

Is that true? Even as I write this sentence, I question its veracity; there was no phase of "becoming," and we were never friends. But if not friends, then what? Because we did become something—surely, if not slowly. I was twenty-two, and at that age I did nothing slowly. Looking back, I assume I engineered it somehow—I was good at falling in love and even better at consummation—but she must have played an equal part. Why am I so willing to shoulder all the blame?

In addition to Old English, I was taking the yearlong survey required for the major. The fall semester was a forced march through the early canon—from the Venerable Bede in the eighth century, through Chaucer and Sir Thomas Malory in the Middle Ages; then Spenser, Sidney, and Shakespeare in the sixteenth century; on to Donne, Marvell, and Milton in the seventeenth century; and finally Dryden, Defoe, Swift, Pope, Johnson, and Boswell in the eighteenth century and the Restoration. The format was a large lecture co-taught by members of the faculty, each of whom also led a small discussion seminar. I'd been assigned to Professor K's section, and we quickly developed an antipathy—mutual, I'm fairly sure. When Professor K went on sabbatical at the end of fall semester, I was delighted to learn that Professor L would take over our section in spring. We would start with the Romantics.

Since I now had Professor L for two classes, I had ample opportunity to study her: observing her as she lectured, noting how she handled questions, learning what pleased her. I probably didn't say much at first. I would have been wary, holding back even as I hung on her every syllable. She was teaching us about literature, after all—about *language*—our words and their histories, the essential objects that had made my world and shaped me into what I was: a body-and-mind primed to fall in love with her. Did I confuse her with her subject matter? Certainly. Listening to her long vowels, her diphthongs, her consonant clusters felt like being held in her arms and caressed, and I could hardly sit still on my hard wooden chair. The classroom smelled of chalk and the dark spice of her perfume. Did she notice me leaning forward, rapt, as she read *Beowulf* or Blake aloud? She must have. Professors notice these things and play to them. We find the attention pleasing.

At some point early on, I must have lingered after class—packing up slowly, watching from the corner of my eye as the other students said goodbye and filed out. Maybe she lingered too. Maybe she was watching me as she gathered her notes and slowly put on her coat, because our timing put us at the doorway simultaneously. I stepped aside, she said something, and I answered, so it was the most natural thing for us to leave together. We walked side by side down the long hallway and out onto campus. It was cold—January or February—and there may have been snow on the ground. Our breath came out in clouds as we talked about stress patterns, alliteration, and compound formations. Or not. Maybe she asked me about myself and, flattered by her curiosity, I told her stories of my travels: how I'd worked as a bar hostess in Kyoto, hiked in the Himalayas, traded blue jeans on the black market in Rangoon. I wanted her to see that I was different, not a run-of-the-mill undergraduate. I had taken time off to see the world because I wanted to be a writer. I wanted to enthrall her with my stories as she enthralled me, to make her laugh—her laugh was extraordinary, low and thrilling—and to make her fall in love with me, and so I kept on talking as we cut across campus to the stately old library that housed her office. I doubt I went upstairs that first time, but later I did. I visited her often in her office at first, before she gave me a key to her apartment.

I can't recall the particulars of those visits, but they're not hard to imagine. Office visits then were much as they are now. Chairs lined the hallway outside the professor's door—back then the doors stayed closed to protect the students' privacy; now they're left open for "transparency" to protect both parties against misconduct, real or imagined. There you'd sit and wait your turn, listening to the murmured voices seeping under the door, wondering which of your fellow students was in there and why on earth they were taking so long; impatient, because whatever your dim-witted classmate had come to see her about could not be as interesting as what you had to say—although, if pressed, you had nothing to say. You only wanted to be in her presence, so you invented something: a question, a theory, some glittering fragment you hoped might interest her. Cheeks flushed, blood in your ears, you tried to look nonchalant. Then the door opened. Your classmate emerged with stars in her eyes and little cartoon birds flying in drunken circles around her head—that was the effect she had on all of you. When the girl had staggered off, you waited a heartbeat so as not to seem too eager, then knocked softly.

"Yes, come in," she said. You did, and when she looked up from her desk and saw it was you, her lips twitched into an ironic smile. "Ah," she said, leaning back in her chair and raking her fingers through her hair. "*You.*" And the way she let that one small syllable fall made you feel as if you were the one she'd been expecting, and now that you'd arrived, she could relax. *You.*

• • •

I was living in a dorm then, engaged in an ongoing feud with the student next door. B was a well-known dealer on campus—nothing too heavy, just weed and the usual uppers and downers: white crosses, black beauties, quaaludes—the stuff we used for recreation and as study aids. I was never her customer. I was at war with her and didn't want to compromise the righteousness of my position, so I bought my drugs downtown. Our dispute was over noise. She hosted loud parties for friends and clients, getting high and cranking her stereo late at night, making it impossible for me to work. Mind you, I was no paragon of academic propriety myself; I spent many nights at a downtown bar scribbling short stories and drinking shots of whiskey, maintaining a facade of poetic dissipation. Beneath this studied indifference, though, I was a serious student with much to prove. I strove for sprezzatura: coming home late from the bar, popping speed, and toiling secretly through the night so my A's would look effortless. Her riotous partying wreaked havoc with my workflow. At first, we had an agreement—after midnight, if her music was too loud, I would rap on our shared wall with the phone receiver and she would turn it down. That held through the fall, but by spring she was failing most classes; as her grades slipped, the parties got wilder and she turned bellicose, ignoring my signals and jacking up the volume just to piss me off. One night, with a paper for L's class due the next day, I banged so hard I punched a hole in the wall with the receiver. Then I broke the phone. Another night, after repeated attempts, I went to her door and pounded with my fist. No answer. I tried again, harder, then took off my clog. The sound of the wooden sole cut through the music. Still no response. I drew back my arm to strike again just as she opened the door.

She was very stoned, so I can see why she was startled to find me standing there—furious, brandishing a clog—and this pleased me. I slid the clog back on and told her that unless she turned her music down, I would call campus police. I should have done that from the start, but I didn't want to get her busted for drugs. She turned the volume down, and I thought that was the end of it.

This war was running in the background during the first weeks of the semester while L and I were growing closer—a phrase too mild to describe what was happening, but not wrong. Did she feel it too? Our convergence seemed inevitable, and I know I worked like mad to impress her, writing papers for her classes, plying her with the poems and stories she had asked to see. My output was prodigious. Recently, sorting boxes in my basement, I found a thick manila folder from those years, filled with drafts typed on yellow legal paper that somehow survived the decades and the damp. Reading them, I can see how, in my besotted, clumsy way, I was using words to woo her. In those scraps, the desperation I felt while we were "becoming friends" and "growing closer" is clearly legible, but I find it hard to reconstruct the actual events crammed between the cracks of these tidy euphemisms. Something must have provoked the shift in our intimacy. I was visiting her during office hours, and then, suddenly, I had the key to her apartment and was spending the night. What happened?

As best as I can piece it together, it went like this: After the clog incident, a note arrived from the dean, summoning me to her office. I had no idea what it was about, and so I was surprised to walk in and find B already sitting there, looking hungover and cowed. The dean, stern and magisterial behind her desk, informed me that B had accused me of attempted assault with a clog.

"B tells me this pattern of intimidation with footwear has been going on all year. She says it's why she hasn't been able to do her homework and is falling behind in her classes. Do you have anything to say?"

I stood there, stunned by the absurd accusation and confused by the sudden shame of having to defend myself against a crime I hadn't committed. Haltingly, I described the noise and the nightly parties, explained the knocking, and denied the assault. Tempting though it was, I didn't mention the drugs. I hated dormitory living and had been lobbying to move off campus; at this point, I think I offered to do exactly that. At least this is my recollection of what happened, and I've told the story often enough that it feels true. But it's also possible that I was kicked off campus and ordered to move out.

I hadn't connected the clog incident to what was happening with L, but now I'm fairly sure it's what precipitated the shift in our relations. I would have been entertaining L with ongoing ironic dispatches from the front—embellishing the skirmishes, soliciting her concern, her sympathy, her indignation, making her laugh. It was the most typical undergraduate melodrama, the kind I've heard from my own students who come weeping to me for extensions with elaborate tales of distress. I doubt I used it as an excuse—I was too proud for that—but I would certainly have made the most of it.

So I can imagine my state when I left the dean's office: outraged, humming with righteous indignation. I couldn't return to the dorm where I was sure to run into B—afraid I might actually assault her this time—and with nowhere else to go, I went in search of L. She was in her office. I stumbled through the story. She listened, lips pursed, elbows braced on the arms of her chair, watching me over the peak of her long, steepled fingers. She'd never seen me angry. When I finished, she reached into her bag, pulled out her keys, unclipped one, and tossed it to me.

"That's a spare. You can stay until this gets worked out. Go get your books and whatever else you need. I'll be home later."

Clutching the key, I left her office, ran through the musty library stacks and out into the dim winter twilight. The cold air was thrilling. Thirty minutes earlier I had entered the library trembling with rage; now I was still trembling, but this time with elation—and terror at the sudden prospect of an intimacy I'd hungered for, which until now had been out of reach. As I hurried across campus, holding my hope like a living thing beneath my coat, the lanterns that lit the pathways flickered on, and the first stars glinted in the darkening sky. The thought hit me then: by giving me her key, L had *chosen* me. She had chosen *me*!

It was happening so quickly. Everything around me—the ivy-covered walls and clipped quadrangles of lawn; the clutches of students laden with books, hurrying from class—seemed to shimmer with promise. The word that comes to mind now is *imminence.* This impossible, unnameable thing was on the brink of becoming—and it would change everything. I raced back to the dorm and threw some clothes and books into a knapsack. A toothbrush too. B wasn't there; if she had been, I would have hugged her.

• • •

L was subletting an apartment from Professor K for the semester, a few blocks from campus in a rambling Victorian converted into condominiums. I climbed the front steps, used the key to let myself in, and wondered if anyone had seen me. Professor K's place was a small one-bedroom on the second floor. The front door opened into a living room that faced Oak Street; to the left, in back, was the kitchen; to the right, also on the street, was the bedroom—austere, furnished with a tall double bed, a dark wooden wardrobe, a dresser, and two straight-backed chairs. A pale blue chenille spread covered the bed, and a crucifix hung above it. Professor K was Catholic and single, and as I poked through her things, I understood why we hadn't gotten along. The lace runner covering the dresser was cluttered with tchotchkes and commemorative photos: a pair of porcelain French poodles, a small Virgin Mary, a musical jewelry box, a cluster of framed photographs from all the usual occasions. In the living room a long couch and a pair of overstuffed Victorian armchairs faced an empty fireplace. Next to it sat a stereo and a record cabinet. Reproductions of rustic still lifes—loaves, fruits, fishes—hung beside predictable landscapes by Constable and Turner. The books were mostly scholarly works and collections of Catholic poets: Dante, Thomas More, Edmund Campion, John Donne, Gerard Manley Hopkins. There was a shelf of Gothic novels and several Bibles too. More porcelain figurines dotted the shelves and mantelpiece: a flock of wide-eyed cherubim, a ballerina on her toes, a milkmaid, a shepherdess and her sheep. In the corner, with a view of the street, stood a large, solid desk with L's belongings—an Old English lexicon, an illuminated Blake, yellow legal pads covered in her indecipherable scrawl, a portable Olympia typewriter—a reassuring island of L in a frothy sea of K.

I was standing at the desk, studying a page of her class notes, when footsteps sounded on the stairs. I dropped the notepad on the stack, dug my *Norton Anthology of English Literature* from my backpack, and flopped hurriedly onto the couch, assuming an attitude I hoped would pass for indolence. That fall we had galloped through the first volume of the *Anthology*—twelve centuries in as many weeks—and now we were on to volume two. It was a brick of a book, containing over three thousand pages, but I balanced it on my chest and opened to Blake. My heart was beating so hard the *Songs of Innocence* rose and fell like a skiff on choppy waters. I stared at the words, listening for a key in the latch, but the footsteps receded down the hall. It wasn't her. I relaxed and let the book fall open on my chest, but my relief quickly curdled into panic. She would come, and when she did, how awkward it would be! What would I say to her? What would she say to me? Perhaps by now she regretted her impulsive offer and would ask me to leave. Or worse, she wouldn't, and then I would have to stay. I wanted to stay—of course I did—but until that moment, I hadn't thought through what staying entailed, and I wasn't prepared. How would we fill the long hours of the evening? She would arrive home and ask me how I was doing and if I was settling in and making myself comfortable, and I would say yes, even though I clearly wasn't. We would then need to make small talk until dinner, at which point there was the problem of food: a meal to prepare and eat, and dishes to wash, each step fraught with opportunities for me to drop things, break things, and embarrass myself, because I didn't know how to cook and I was clumsy in the kitchen. And even if I survived the dishes and the dishes survived me, there would be the long after-dinner hours, during which she would surely tire of me and realize she had made a terrible mistake because I was a fraud, clever enough to amuse her in office hours, not intelligent enough to sustain an evening of serious conversation before bed.

Bed?

I hadn't thought about bed! There was only one in the apartment. Surely she didn't intend us to share it—but what if she did? Would we make love? How would that even work? I'd kissed girls in high school, but I'd never slept with a woman. I had no idea what to do or where to begin, and it struck me then, lying there on her couch, how naïve I was, how ill-prepared. In all my feverish fantasies of L, I'd never imagined much beyond a stolen kiss or an urgent embrace behind her closed office door while other students waited impatiently in the hall. None of my fantasies involved a bed, much less the prosaic preliminaries: the donning or doffing of pajamas, the toothbrushing, the floss.

These thoughts juddered through me like voltage arcing through a body. When I again heard footsteps on the stairs, I froze; at the turn of her key in the latch, I clamped my eyes shut and pretended to sleep. A stupid ploy, childish and transparent, but it was the only one I could think of to forestall this disaster. I heard her enter the living room. She must have seen me right away—perhaps she'd even forgotten I was there—and, assuming I was asleep, she didn't greet me. She crossed the room and paused in front of the sofa, and I could feel her standing over me. Keeping my eyelids still and my breathing steady was an act of will. Did she know I was faking? Likely. It wasn't the first time I would pretend to be something I wasn't, nor would it be the last. After a moment she moved on, set her bag down on the desk, and went into the bedroom. I heard the toilet flush, drawers open and close, then she came back through into the kitchen and started opening and closing cabinets. Now I had a new problem: when, and how, to "wake." As I pondered this, she returned and sat down on the edge of the couch. The cushion sagged, then her fingers touched my knee.

"Hey," she said.

I blinked, opened my eyes, and her wry smile told me she had not been fooled. She was holding two stemmed glasses of red wine and offered me one. "Thought you could use a drink."

I blinked, sat up, and took the glass from her hand. "Oh," I said. "Yes. Thank you. How did you know?"

She just smiled and shrugged, as if the answer were obvious. "You're welcome. Cheers."

We touched the rims of our glasses and drank. The wine was delicious. She asked me if I was settling in; I said yes, and from there our conversation—about what, I can't recall—loosened and flowed naturally. If there were silences, they were not awkward. She sat at one end of the couch, and I sat at the other, hugging my knees to my chest, keenly aware that if I stretched my legs they would rest on her lap, so I didn't. Night had fallen.

When the glasses were empty, she said we should make dinner. I followed her and offered to help.

She told me I could start by putting on a record. My panic returned—it felt like another test, and one I would surely fail. I crouched in front of the record cabinet, scanning the thin spines of the LPs, pulling a few out to check the covers. There was the usual Bach and Handel, Mozart and Haydn, but most were recordings of orchestral works—masses and requiems—too grand and public for the small apartment. Then I spotted a recording of lute music from the Spanish Renaissance, which seemed just right. I slid it from its sleeve, wiped it with the dust cloth, and set it on the turntable. The soft, sad notes of the lute and the crumhorn filled the air.

"Good choice," L said when I came back into the kitchen.

"Are they yours?"

"The records?" she said. "A few of them. The one you chose is mine. Most of the others belong to K."

I hadn't failed the test after all.

• • •

She cooked pasta—Bolognese? Puttanesca?—something rich and red, with a simple green salad lightly dressed in olive oil and lemon. She poured more wine and said we deserved it. We ate at the small round table in the kitchen, and though I can't recall the particulars, we never ran out of things to say. After dinner, she washed and I dried—without breaking anything—then we went back into the living room to work. She sat at the desk while I lay on the couch and pretended to read, studying her over the top of my book, trying to learn by heart how she bent to the typewriter, thin shoulders hunched as her fingers flew across the keys—the clatter of her keystrokes was mesmerizing. From time to time she paused to think, lifted her head, checked her notes, or consulted a reference book; I remember the way she slipped off her reading glasses to pinch the bridge of her nose, the black wing of hair falling across her cheek like a shadow. There was something vampiric about her. We sat like that for hours—her typing, me watching—until she pushed back her chair and got up to make tea. Chamomile, I think; I remember she liked chamomile.

"So?" she said, handing me a steaming mug and taking the book from my lap. I drew up my feet and she sat at the end of the couch. "How's it going?"

I was pretending to read *Beowulf*, a text for her class; we were to parse and translate a passage. "Not great," I confessed. "It's hard to concentrate."

She took the book from me and began to read:

> Hwæt we gardena ingear dagum,
> þeod cyninga þrym ge frunon
> huða æþelingas ellen fremedon . . .

Rapt, I listened to the guttural Old English rise from her throat and trill at the tip of her tongue. From time to time, I recognized a word or a phrase, enough to identify the passage: *Lo! We Spear-Danes in days gone / have heard the power of the hero-kings / and how princes did great deeds of valour* . . . Her voice was resonant and rich; the rhythmic cadence made dark music. After a few pages she closed the book.

"No," I protested, sitting up. "Don't stop!" I sounded like a child at bedtime.

She laughed and patted my foot. "That's enough for tonight."

I sank back against the cushion. "The words come to life when you read them. I could listen to you forever."

"It's a school night, dear girl, and you need sleep. As do I." She fetched bedding. I slept on the couch. In the morning, she made me breakfast. The coffee she brewed was strong, and she drank it black. I learned to do the same, to love the bitterness and the bite. We settled into a domestic routine that felt inevitable and eternal, but in truth could only have lasted a few weeks. I must have known from the start it couldn't last; that's why I watched her so intently, memorizing her before I lost her.

• • •

Now, as I try to recall her here on the page, I see how my plausible sentences paper over what I don't remember—the gaps and elisions where the real story hides—because while I say I slept on the couch, that isn't quite true; I doubt I slept a wink that night. Lying there in the dark, every molecule in my body was alive, attuned to the smallest shift of sound and light. Most of the furniture was in shadow, but a streetlamp cast a narrow shaft across her desk, illuminating the edges of her slumbering things—stacks of books, the lamp, the silhouette of her typewriter—and even in the dark I could feel her presence emanating from everything she touched. The light traveled from the desk to the cut-glass knob of her closed bedroom door. A band of light leaked from beneath the door, and I watched her shadow move; I heard soft footsteps, water splashing, the brushing of teeth, a drawer opening and closing. The bedsprings creaked as she climbed in. In the silence that followed, the blood beating from my heart to my ears was so loud I was sure she must hear it. She had closed the door after saying good night; did she always sleep that way, or was that for my benefit—to keep me out?

She must have known how I felt, how much I wanted her. How could she not? And at times I was certain she wanted me too—when she poured wine into my glass and our eyes met, or when our fingers touched as she handed me a plate to dry—but then I scolded myself for indulging in clichés. Yet when she patted my foot and said, "That's enough for tonight," surely this implied there would be other nights when there would be more? After I brushed my teeth and returned to the couch, she tucked a blanket around me and let her hand rest lightly on my forehead, hesitating. She looked down as if she were about to say something, then smiled and shook her head.

"Sleep," she said, brushing back my hair and straightening.

As if. The pillow, which she had taken from her bed, smelled of her, and after she closed the door I buried my face in its softness, replaying our small exchanges again and again, wild with hope one minute and despair the next, trying desperately to understand. Desire isn't simple. I didn't just want her—I wanted to *be* her.

There was this one afternoon, in her office, when I was chattering with great excitement about something I was working on—by then she had asked to see my poems and stories—when a strange expression crossed her face, something between pain and bemusement.

"What?" I asked.

The expression vanished, and she laughed, rueful, shaking her head. "Nothing. You just reminded me of someone."

"Who?" I demanded, already jealous.

She didn't answer right away. And then she said, "Myself. When I was your age."

It dawned on me then that the mirroring went both ways. Perhaps I flattered myself, but from then on I fancied us as two parts of one body—one mind, one heart—born out of time, with only time between us. Once I saw her hurrying across campus, clutching a stack of books to her chest, and I stopped and stared as if at a vision: L at my age, a student like me, late, rushing to class. Time seemed to spiral, my knees buckled, and I felt certain that my desire could collapse the decades that divided us. I hurried to catch up with her. I was always hurrying to catch up with her.

• • •

With each day my desire grew, and each night, when she stood by the couch to say good night, it was all I could do not to grab her wrist and pull her to me, to confess. But I waited, hoping that one night the bedroom door would be left ajar.

Then one morning she left early, and I woke to find a note on the kitchen table asking me to come to her office that afternoon. When I arrived, she said she wanted to walk. It was freezing outside. The thawing snow had refrozen into glassy sheets, and the paths were slick. We walked side by side in silence; I waited for her to say something, but we were muffled in hats and scarves, which made conversation awkward. As we passed the botanic gardens, a cutting wind blew up from the lake, and she suggested we go inside.

The Plant House was a Victorian conservatory, built in the late 1800s, with ornate glass panes and paths that led through the separate greenhouses, each with a different habitat to accommodate all manner of flora. We entered the Succulent House, dry and hot and silent. I followed her past euphorbias, prickly cacti, and other aridland plants, braced for the correction I was sure was coming—that she'd made a mistake and I needed to find someplace else to stay. Instead, she told me about the woman she lived with.

Her name was E. They had met when L was in graduate school. E was twenty years older and had been her professor. They fell in love in a seminar, then moved in together after L finished her degree, living and working side by side, writing books and collaborating on scholarship. Their lives, L said, were entwined, inextricably so, and she was not looking for extrication. She was committed to their relationship.

I followed her in silence from the aridland into a long, humid corridor, brushing past orchids and bromeliads that left traces of moisture on the sleeves of our heavy winter coats. Why was she telling me this? I was desperate for her to stop, but the tropical sweetness and my own humiliation choked me. In the Fern House, among the ancient cycads and early gymnosperms, it finally hit me: she knew very well how I felt about her. Of course she did. I hadn't been subtle, mooning around, and now she was letting me down gently. Her gentleness was unbearable.

We came to the Palm House—a rotunda with a vaulted glass ceiling and a pond in the middle, surrounded by tall palms and epiphytes. She sat on a stone bench and motioned for me to join her. I did, but I couldn't face her, so I looked away. The tall glass paneled walls were white with steam, streaked with condensation.

"You're wondering why I'm telling you this," she said. It was a statement. I nodded, studying a frond.

"I'm telling you because I want you to know that I know how

you feel," she said, and when I didn't answer, she put her hand on my forearm. "You must believe me."

"Why?" I said. "How would you know?"

She sighed and withdrew her hand. "I know because I feel it too."

"Felt it, you mean," I said, bitter at the mention of her precious E. "When you met her."

She shook her head. "No. You misunderstand." She turned away, and when she spoke again, her voice was low. "I mean now. I feel it for you."

• • •

This was my memory of what happened, one I held close for decades. Sometimes I wondered if I was misremembering. Did it really happen this way, or did I embellish it over time? Embellishment is a novelist's trade, to be sure, but this was never meant to be a fiction. And then there's the question of credibility and taste. The critic in me winces at the pathetic fallacy—mawkish, even: a torrid confession in a steamy greenhouse—why would I choose this setting unless it were real?

I know that my memory plays tricks on me, which is just a nice way of admitting that I'm beginning to have some memory loss, but that's not what is happening here. In the basement folder, I found a draft of a poem I wrote to L soon after that walk. Here's the relevant passage:

You walked slowly ahead
past masses of tropical flowers—
bright birds of paradise, bleeding hearts—
trailing your confession like a thin
green tendril
around fat leaves of palm
that came snapping back after you,
slapping me as I tried to understand.

It's called "First Walk," typed on her Olympia on a sheet from her yellow legal pad. Holding the brittle paper in my hand, running my fingertip over the impressions of letters those keys left behind, I am transported by the undeniable physical presence of this particular page, and there's no doubt in my mind that what I wrote and what I remember are both real. Whether anyone believes me is not the point, because what I'm writing here isn't for anyone but me. My memory is going; I am trying to remember her one last time before I forget.

• • •

You might imagine we went back to her apartment and tumbled into bed, but it wasn't like that. Our relationship had shifted—the intimacy had deepened—but we didn't act upon it; I kept living at her place, and the bedroom door stayed shut. Midterms loomed, which helped. She held fast to the importance of work, and by example taught me to channel my unruly energy into my research and writing. On campus, we were careful. I rarely spoke in class anymore, afraid I might blurt out something inappropriate, and from time to time, as if to bait me, she would call on me and watch me stumble through an answer—head cocked, eyebrow arched, forefinger pressed against her chin, all seriousness save for the faint glimmer in her eye. After class, I would berate her; she would laugh, pat my cheek, tell me I'd done well.

Dusk was the time of day I loved best, when we would come home, drink wine, and make dinner together. She taught me about poetry, and German film, and how to use the tines of a fork to extract the juice from a lemon. After dinner we worked, and when we were done she would read to me—*Beowulf*, Blake, Chaucer, and contemporary women poets too: Bishop, Sexton, Rich. Sometimes she made me read my own poems and stories to her, the ones I'd written. I didn't want to, but she insisted, and if I mumbled, she made me start again. "Never undermine what you've written," she once said. "Treat your words with respect, even the wrong ones." This was a gift I've never forgotten.

There were other gifts, too: a bottle of French perfume, a pair of burgundy leather driving gloves. She took me to the local art-house theater to see Fassbinder's *The Bitter Tears of Petra von Kant*, and over dinner afterward we talked about choreography, camera angles, Anti-Theater, stagecraft. (This memory, too, seems suspect: Was it really *Petra von Kant*—a lesbian chamber drama about an older woman who falls obsessively in love with a manipulative younger woman whom she invites to move in, and who then breaks her heart? It's too on the nose! A good fiction writer would choose a different film, one less obvious.)

I grew bolder. The first time we sat together on the couch, I kept my body to myself—knees hugged to my chest, feet tucked carefully in—so I wouldn't inadvertently brush against her. As the weeks passed, I was less careful and more calculating: I let my foot graze her leg and linger, slid my cold toes beneath her thigh, and surrendered my stockinged feet to her hands as she set them on her lap. Soon we were reclining at opposite ends, legs loosely piled then casually entwined; then my head was in her lap as she read, her fingers stroking my hair while I looked up at her, delirious.

Like writers throughout literature, I struggle to find the right words to describe how much I wanted her. My desire was ecstatic, the way desire is when you're young, and if anyone had asked me then, I would have sworn that I had never been happier, or more anguished, but my grief was ecstatic too. The years that separated us were a torment, and this was my fault: I had been born too late. If I had been born earlier, we would have been classmates; E would never have entered the story because I would have claimed L first. Time, not E, was the enemy, and I would never catch up.

One night, when we were talking with my head resting in her lap, she leaned over me, and I watched the weight and tug of gravity disfiguring her forty-year-old face—bloating those fine contours, pulling skin from bone. I confess I was horrified, and in my confusion, I reached up and touched her cheek; it felt soft and puffy, like an old mushroom. In that moment, I hated time for what it was doing to her, and as if to retaliate, I pulled her down and kissed her. It was a clumsy kiss, a desperate, futile attempt to delete, as if by magic, the years between us. And perhaps she sensed my intent and understood that if the magic had any hope of working, she would need to kiss me back, and so she did. When we broke apart and caught our breath, we looked at each other and laughed because, for a moment at least, it seemed we had succeeded. From then on, this became part of what we did at night: we finished our work and then lay on the couch, entangled, forestalling time and practicing this magic. I wanted more—of course I did—and it seemed she did, too, though her desire was more conflicted. When I touched her breast, she didn't stop me, and yet the bedroom door remained closed.

• • •

How long ago this all was! Is it unseemly for a woman my age to write about sexual desire? Male writers do it. *Th'expense of spirit in a waste of shame / Is lust in action*—only it wasn't merely lust that drove me. Lust is urgent, but it comes and goes. What I felt was more enduring. How is it that even now, all these years later, thinking of her makes me cry? (There's no answer to that question, so let it hang . . .)

The snow was starting to melt, and the days were growing warmer. We had been living in a small bubble of suspended time, but spring break was approaching, and L was going home to E. Somehow, I knew that when she returned, what we had would be over. Each day I grew more desperate—but for what? For her to open the door, invite me in, and make love to me? Yes, but it was more than that. The consummation I wanted was the total collapse of everything that stood between us, a merging of our separation into one. Which, of course, was impossible.

*Farewell: thou art too dear for my possessing . . .*

• • •

She said I could stay in the apartment, but we agreed not to speak while she was away. In the folder in the basement, I still have pages of unsent letters, typed on her Olympia on those yellow sheets of legal paper. I must have been writing them day and night.

L.

It's daytime now and it's still bad. I don't know if I can stand this anymore. I keep seeing you walking up the front steps. We come upstairs and lie down, and we are grief-stricken. You cry and I comfort you, or maybe it's the other way around, and we are happy. It's so simple! And it's not. Nothing makes sense anymore, because then I see you and E, doing ordinary things together, and you look so happy. I hope you are happy. I hope you are well. I need to see you as soon as you get back. Or, I don't ever want to see you again.

Last night I kept saying your name until it sounded to my ears like you were lying here on the couch next to me, and so I talked to you as if you were, but you never said anything back, and I fell asleep talking. I'm crazed and exhausted. This is not a letter, and anyway I will never send it, and you will never see it, and I don't know why I'm writing at all, except that it is all I can do. Only sit here and type madly to no one, because just knowing that your fingers have battered these same keys helps. Your fingers. These keys. I cannot bear this. No, there is no help at all.

One of the pages in the folder is a transcript of a phone call, again typed on her Olympia, about a poem. I must have been alone in the apartment, pulling books from the shelves and reading, when I found it. I don't remember which of us broke our promise and made the call. I don't think I would have phoned her at home, for fear E would pick up, so I think she must have called me. The poem was "Spring and Fall, to a young child," by Gerard Manley Hopkins.

"I found a poem. It's very sad. I've been thinking about it all day. I can't work for thinking about it. I dreamed about it. It won't go away."

"Don't be sad. What's the poem. Tell it to me."

"It's by Hopkins. It's about Margaret. Do you know . . ."

"Margaret. I know that. Of course. I found that poem a long time ago. Someone showed it to me. I can't remember . . ."

"'Margaret,' it goes, 'Margaret, are you grieving, Over Goldengrove unleaving . . .' It has all the accents so I can't say it right. It's so sad. I don't know what it means, but the sounds are so sad."

"Don't worry. Just get up and stop thinking about Margaret. Do your work. Over the weekend when I get back, we'll read Margaret and find out why it's so sad. Don't worry. We'll take it apart and analyze the sounds. There's a reason, you know. Why the sounds sound sad. We'll find out why."

"Oh, L. I'm so sleepy and sad. I just want to see you. I love your voice. Don't hang up. Just talk to me. Tell me a story."

"Love, I can't. I have to work. You have to work. Get up, my darling. Forget about me. Forget about Margaret. Get up and work. Don't let me do this to you. I can't bear it."

It's a beautiful poem.

I must have typed our conversation after she hung up. In those days, long before cell phones, telephone calls were tactile and intimate. The telephones themselves were robust, with plastic receivers hefty enough to punch holes in dormitory walls. On one end was the mouthpiece you spoke into; if you spoke long enough, the plastic would grow wet from the condensation of your breath. On the other end was an earpiece that grew hot where you pressed it to your head. Reading that transcript now, I can almost feel the moisture and the heat and the ache in my ear, and hear her voice—low, urgent, despairing—whispering to me.

I wish I could say I moved out before she came back, to spare her, but I did not have the strength. Instead, I was waiting when she came home, and as soon as she walked through the door, I knew. She poured me a glass of water, sat me down, and began to talk. She said she had told E about us—about what she felt for me and what I felt for her, about what had happened between us. E had listened, and when L finished, E had asked her to please end it. L promised she would. And that was that. I moved out shortly after. I don't remember where I went.

The semester wasn't over. We still had four weeks of classes, and she and I still met and walked—always outdoors. The snow was gone. Spring was on the brink, about to burst upon us the way it does in New England, in one great eruption of furious fecundity. In my folder, I found another poem called "Last Walk," which I must have written then.

```
In the dark, raw earth,
Made wet with the furious emotion of early spring,
Red shoots spear the ground from underneath,
As dark and sharp as anger or as loss.
You bent your knee to stroke the point,
Poked it gently with your forefinger,
Murmured, "the ensanguined earth."
```

I don't know why she said that.

• • •

The last time we met was in her office. I had written two heroic term papers for her, pouring everything I had into a last, futile attempt to prove I was worthy. One of these survives in my folder: an analytical paper about William Blake, typed on that crisp, almost brittle "corrasable" bond—a portmanteau, I think, of "correct" and "erasable." The typeface isn't L's Olympia, so I must have borrowed another machine.

The title of the paper is "From Satire to Prophecy: The Development of Irony and Satire in Blake's *Songs of Innocence and Experience* and *The Marriage of Heaven and Hell.*" I wonder why I chose this topic; I suspect I was projecting my own unresolved struggle between ironic distance and prophetic fervor onto his work. Most of L's margin notes are now indecipherable, except for one: "The paper badly needs a bibliographical apparatus—that is its only flaw. With one, it would be an A by anybody's standards."

Fair enough. As if to compensate for the paucity of scholarly end matter, the paper opens with not one but two epigraphs from "Proverbs of Hell":

"The road of excess leads to the palace of wisdom"
or
"The busy bee has no time for sorrow."

• • •

I was her last meeting; she had arranged it that way. She had already moved out of Professor K's apartment and was leaving campus for good that afternoon. She sat behind the desk in her office, and I sat across from her. She had packed up her books, and the room was empty except for a large manila envelope that lay between us. With nothing familiar left to anchor us, we were awkwardly formal. She asked how I was, and I said I was okay. I was far from okay, and she knew it. I can almost hear her sigh as she slid the envelope across the desk. "Open it later," she said. "After I'm gone."

This was the first of the last two gifts she left me. Later, at home, I opened the envelope and found a limited-edition letterpress of the Elizabeth Bishop poem, "One Art," which she had read aloud to me one evening and which I loved. *The art of losing isn't hard to master . . .*

The second gift was a prophecy. I walked her to the street where her car was parked in front of the apartment. For a moment we just stood there. The car was packed, and she was going to get in and drive away.

"You will be fine," she said, taking my face in her hands and wiping my tears with her thumbs. "You are going to be a writer. You will write novels about all your adventures, traveling and growing up between two cultures. You mustn't think about me, or call, or write to me. Forget me, my darling. Please. Just live your life and write your novels. You will be fine."

I did my best to obey her. Years passed. I traveled, married, divorced, and then married again. I had a child and wrote the novel L said I would write. When it was published, I wanted to send it to her so she would know her prophecy had come true, but I refrained—the book wasn't good enough, and I had promised not to contact her. I wrote another and didn't send that one either. I thought of her often. I was catching up to the age she had been when we met, and as I aged, my memories changed, or at least my understanding of them did. One afternoon, when I was in my early forties, I was outside playing catch with my daughter—she was ten or eleven and just getting into softball—and a speck of dirt or something painful got lodged in my eye and wouldn't come out. Inside, I found a hand mirror and placed it on the bathroom counter. As I leaned over to inspect my eye, I saw my face reflected up at me. I'd never seen myself from this angle before, and I was horrified at what gravity and time had done to me, bloating the contours of my cheeks, pulling skin from bone. How could this be? I wasn't so old. And then it hit me: she hadn't been so old either.

When the internet arrived and took over our lives, finding her was easy. I learned her email, her physical address, even her phone number, but I still didn't call or write, though it felt reassuring to know where she was. More years passed. My parents grew old and died. My daughter grew up. When it was time for her to go to college, I drove her there and helped her move into the dormitory. We hugged goodbye, and for a fleeting moment I saw my face in hers. Who would break her heart? I hugged her tighter before letting her go. She waved as I drove away—she looked so brave, so young. I had never been that young.

After my daughter left, I took a job teaching at my alma mater. Teaching shifted my perspective once again, and I found myself remembering L differently; she felt more like a colleague now. My first office was in the same stately old library building (since demolished) where hers had been. Soon I was talking to her in my mind as I walked the dusty stacks or sat at my desk during office hours. See? I would say as I propped my door open. See how careful I am? Students fall in love with me sometimes, but I am never tempted—though none have pursued me with the same conviction I had when I pursued you. Mores have changed, but even so I've watched other professors succumb and fall. I suppose it is a good thing that young people are so well-protected by statutes and laws these days, and I should be glad. Yes, of course I am glad. I'm a mother, after all. But I'm also glad we weren't living under the constant threat of denunciation and censure back then. There might have been repercussions had anyone known, but no one did know. You trusted me enough to make yourself vulnerable. You trusted me not to turn on you and tell.

Only now do I see the risk you took, and I am grateful. Your confession showed me I was desirable and worthy of your love. Had you not spoken, I would never have known this; I would have been ashamed of my feelings and castigated myself for being a fool. Instead you trusted me to know and still be strong for you—*with* you—to suffer together and survive.

At the time, of course, I didn't understand any of this. I couldn't fathom how you could love me and still keep your bedroom door shut. To confess your desire and then forbid us to act—it felt like a bait and switch. Now I see it differently. That closed door taught me how it's possible for a person to love and not act; how we can transmute pain and pleasure into something else: Words. Work. Language. Lifeblood.

When I published my third novel, I decided it was time to break my promise and write. I googled you to confirm the address and found your obituary instead. You had died three weeks earlier.

I was too late. Again.

Your obituary said you were survived by E, your "longtime friend." I felt a sharp pang of grief for her, knowing her grief must be unbearable; it crossed my mind to reach out to her—a terrible idea that I quickly discarded. There was a link to a memorial page filled with tributes from your former students: "She was a brilliant teacher, tough and exacting, and her class was magical." "She was passionate about my sentences." "She changed the world. She changed my life." And it went on and on like this: "She saw something in me that I didn't know I had." "I am a writer now because of her." "I will never forget her." Reading between their lines, I could tell they were in love with you, too, and for a moment I was fiercely jealous of them, as only a twenty-two-year-old can be.

In your office that last day, you told me that what had happened between us—our feelings, the intimacy—had never happened to you as a teacher before, and you would never let it happen again. Hearing that, the crushing weight on my heart eased slightly. I don't think you said it to flatter me, or make me feel special (I felt flattered and special), or to excuse yourself. Rather, I think you were making a vow. Reading those tributes, I wondered if you kept it. I suspect you did. You were nothing if not faithful.

And now there's one last thing I want to tell you before I forget. That phone conversation I transcribed ends with your plea: "Don't let me do this to you. I can't bear it." When I read that now, so many years later, I hear the desperation in it. At the time, though, I suspect I took a grim and childish satisfaction in knowing that my suffering was hurting you too. Maybe I even tried to make you suffer more. If so, I am sorry. And I want you to know that while I didn't forget you, as you requested, I did survive you, and I went on to have other loves—full, requited, and long-lasting. But you were the first, the one who opened chambers in my heart I had not known existed, and once opened, they stayed available for other loves to fill.

That spring I fell in love with you, I also fell in love with my work—with writing, with language—and ever since, those feelings have been fused. Opening my heart to you opened me to the latent potency of work, and even now when I write—when I find just the right word, or a sentence snaps into place, when I'm racing toward the ending of a novel—the ecstatic love I felt for you comes back to me. Not always, but sometimes. And when it does, there is nothing in the world like it.

Of all your gifts, this is the one I most treasure. The leather driving gloves are gone. I lost my taste for the perfume too—it didn't smell the same on me as it did on you, and I stopped wearing it. For years the bottle migrated from shelf to shelf in the various medicine cabinets of apartments and houses where I've lived, until, during one move, I finally threw it away. Somehow I managed to hang on to the box with the folder from that semester. I found it when I was cleaning out the basement—"death cleaning," they call it. We were downsizing and getting ready to sell the house, and I didn't want to leave all this detritus for my daughter to deal with. The box was buried under other boxes, most of which I've since thrown away. But when I lifted the lid and saw the folder—those poems and stories I wrote during that ensanguined spring—I decided to keep it. My memory is going, and I am forgetting you now, not because you asked me to but because I have no choice. Still, I have the box. When I want to remember, I open it. The paperclips and staples are rusted; the pages have gone brittle. Silverfish have been at them, feeding on the paper, and the bottom of the box is sprinkled with their frass, like grains of sand. The letterpress edition of the Elizabeth Bishop poem you gave me, "One Art," is in here too. The thick, creamy stock it was printed on must have tasted especially delicious, because the silverfish have nibbled away at it until it now resembles a fine piece of lace, filigreed with gaps and holes. Many of the words have been eaten, which seems appropriate, yet much of the poem remains, including most of the final stanza:

> —Even losing you (th_ joking voice, a gest_r_
> I love) I shan't _ave lied. It's evident
> the art _f losing's not too hard to master
> tho_gh it may look like (*Write* it!) like di_____

The last word—the one that's mostly missing—is disaster.

# DEAD BEAT POET

You have to understand, I was fairly happy until *he* showed up. I'd landed a job in New York City, in a field I supposedly loved. I had my own room in an apartment I shared with three roommates I didn't hate. I was paying down my student loans. I'd found people to hook up with once in a while. A couple of exes were starting to do the marriage-baby thing, which made me anxious about securing my place on the space-time continuum, but I was learning to transcend all that. I meditated. I did yoga. I had prospects.

The first time he appeared to me was during a Hot Titles meeting on a Monday morning in Midtown—this was before the pandemic, when we still did things in airless rooms together. The publisher sat at the head of the long conference table, flanked by her editors in descending order of rank. Crammed along the walls were the editorial assistants, seated in spare desk chairs behind the editors we served. I was dozing because the air conditioner was broken, the room was hot, and somebody else's assistant was being yelled at, not me. This was before people talked about triggers and traumas at work. The phrase "toxic workplace" was a tautology, public humiliation was part of the job, and an assistant's only recourse was snark. I remember one guy blaming the publisher's mood on PMS, which he defined as "perimenopausal syndrome," and we all laughed while privately clocking him as a sexist moron—or maybe that was just me. Personally, I liked working in an office where the higher-ups were women, even if it meant more screamers. Those ladies were serious about their careers. They knew how to lean in.

Even before the pandemic, the House was toxic—a cocktail of power, page mold, and printer cartridge toner, trapped by windows that were hermetically sealed so the junior editors couldn't jump out. There were *emanations*—not the woo-woo kind, but real pharmaceutical off-gassing of Zoloft, Prozac, and Ritalin—sweated out of the aluminum-chloride-coated armpits and furrowed brows during a Hot Titles meeting, which then evaporated into the air we *breathed*.

Did I say furrowed brows? Wrong. No self-respecting brow over thirty still furrows.

Of course, before he showed up, I never saw things quite this way. I was happily complacent—enjoying my nap, the sound of somebody else's humiliation, and the relative dryness of my own well-sealed armpits—leaning out before out was cool. Maybe that's why he chose me.

He arrived in that third-eye place, midbrow, where Botox is injected, and where, in the old, pre-psychopharmaceutical days, they drilled holes to aerate the brain. The procedure was called trepanation, the precursor to the frontal lobotomy. Archaeologists have found ventilated skulls from 3000 BC, and there are still advocacy groups who defend your right to take a drill bit to your head. They say it drains brain water, increasing blood flow to the cerebellum. Sort of the opposite of Botox.

He chuckled when he told me that.

Him: You don't believe me? Look it up: www.trepan.com. See for yourself.

Me: Who are you?

He hovered there—a skinny guy with a big nose, a balding pate fringed with wild curly hair, and thick black-rimmed glasses—enveloped in a faint aura of pulsing white light. He was dressed in worn brown corduroys, a black turtleneck, and an old tweed jacket. His legs were folded neatly into full lotus. When I opened my eyes, he vanished.

I blinked. The meeting churned on. A new Hot Title, someone else in the crosshairs, so I closed my eyes again. He was still seated, now rubbing his nose and casing the room.

Him: So this is what goes on in these meetings. I always wondered what you people did all day.

Me: Excuse me?

Him: Fascinating business, publishing. Whatever happened to Jack? He was my editor here. Nice guy. Gave me this jacket.

He lifted a sleeve, admiring the ratty tweed.

Him: He'd give you the shirt off his back, he would. A real enlightened being, Jack.

Me: You've got the wrong house. There aren't any enlightened beings here.

He had become preoccupied with picking off a crusty bit of food from his cuff, and he wasn't listening. I watched him. There was something familiar about the full lips, the stringy black hair, the stare.

Me: Are you a poet?

Him: [*looking up, fixing me with a piercing, poetical gaze*] How can you work here and even ask that question?

Me: Well, we don't really publish poetry . . .

Him: [*jaw drops*] You don't? You used to. What on earth do you people publish?

Me: Books. Novels. Memoirs. Nonfiction.

Him: [*disappointed*] Oh. Commercial stuff.

Me: [*defensive*] What do you expect? There isn't exactly a huge market for poems, you know.

Him: [*sharply*] Did you say *market*?

Me: Yes.

Him: You think poems are a *commodity*—something to peddle in a *marketplace*?

Me: [*shrugging*] It's a business. If you expect—

Him: I'll tell you what I expect: I expect poems *not* to make money. I expect poems to transcend finance. That's why they need to be published—to give people something higher to aspire to!

Me: Great. I'll be sure to let our publisher know.

• • •

It's not like I disagreed with him. I studied poetry in college. I majored in English while the sensible kids were doing computer science or econ or gov. Poetry only gets you so far in this world, and dactyls don't pay the rent, but still—I wasn't in the mood for a lecture about the commodification of the literary arts at ten o'clock on a Monday morning in the middle of a Hot Titles meeting. Even so, when he pumped his fist and shouted, "More poems!" I heard myself echoing him, oddly excited.

Him: More poems!

Me: More poems!

• • •

When I opened my eyes, everyone at the table was staring at me—except our publisher, who had turned her attention inward, apparently contemplating the tip of her nose.

My editor leaned back and turned slightly—only as far as her stiffened spine would permit—so I could see her profile. "Uh, Caitlin . . . ?"

My fist was still in the air, a prime use case for aluminum-chloride if ever there was one.

Her expression attempted a frown, only it was more conceptual, more frown-adjacent. "Did you have something you wanted to say?"

Her tone made it very clear that I did not. I let my arm drop, and just then his deep, sonorous voice punched through my forebrain and burst from my mouth.

Us: *I saw the best minds of my generation destroyed by madness* . . .

• • •

He was still reciting when the meeting broke up. The other editorial assistants watched with fascination and horror as I followed my editor down the long cubicle-lined corridor to her office.

Him: *She's a one-eyed shrew who does nothing but sit on her ass and snip the intellectual golden threads of the craftsman's loom* . . . or something like that. I can't remember.

Me: Fuck. Fuck. Fuck.

• • •

When we reached her office, she went inside and closed the door behind her. I ducked into my cube and briefly entertained the wild hope that maybe nothing had happened—that in a fleeting fit of lunacy I'd imagined the whole thing—or, better yet, that she might actually find it funny, and we'd have a good laugh. She had a decent sense of humor. Mostly we got along. It wasn't impossible. I hunkered down in my swivel chair and started shuffling through manuscripts like they mattered. My cube sits sentry outside her office, and like Cerberus, part of my job entails keeping a vigilant eye on any unauthorized attempts to gain access. She is a big deal, my editor, a power player in the publishing world, and there are lots of crazed wannabe authors out there who are dying for a contract, including the one currently squatting in my brain.

Him: Me? Dying for a contract? You gotta be kidding. You think I'd sell you a strophe for an American buck? Besides, I'm already dead.

Me: Shhh! Go away. I'm busy.

Him: *Unscrew the locks from the doors! Unscrew the doors themselves from their jambs!*

My phone rang. It was her. "Come on in," she said. "Let's get this over with."

• • •

We walked home down St. Mark's Place through the East Village where no one notices a girl muttering to herself or to her imaginary friends.

"Now what do I do?" I asked, somewhat rhetorically.

"No sense crying over spilled milk." He chuckled. "It's an old Zen koan . . ."

"I can't believe she fired me."

"Of course you can. You agreed with her. You're an underperformer with a poor values fit. Whatever that means. She did you a huge favor."

"How's that?"

"Saw straight through you. 'You'll never be happy here, Caitlin. You want to write books, not publish them.' She's right. Admit it."

"What I *want* is to pay my rent, which I could do if you hadn't hacked into my brain—"

"You should thank me. '*You—*'"

"Me?"

"'. . . *who were burned alive in innocent flannel suits on Madison Avenue amid blasts of leaden verse* . . . '"

"Oh, please."

"'. . . *& the tanked-up clatter of the iron regiments of fashion & the nitroglycerine shrieks of the fairies of advertising & the mustard gas of sinister intelligent editors* . . . '"

I was listening in spite of myself. "Okay," I conceded. "That's pretty good. Did you write it?"

"Nah. Allen did. Ginsberg. Good buddy of mine. He's dead now too. Another dead Beat poet. He lived near here. A lot of us did."

It was early evening, and St. Mark's Place was waking up.

Shiny-faced NYU students were eating Szechuan noodles and soup dumplings. Tech bros were downing fatty slabs of tuna belly in pop-up sushi bars. Punks in graffitied overcoats walked dogs on chains. No dead Beat poets, though, as far as I could see.

"Are there still a lot of you around?" I asked.

"Over here? Tons. Back on your end of the space-time continuum? A few. Returnees whose poetic karma binds them—happily—to your grindingly mundane and beautiful world."

"Returnees?"

"Sure. And I'm not talking about the genre hacks stuck in the bardo, writing upbeat affirmations and self-help slogans, doomed to loop back over and over in nauseating spirals. There are plenty of those. You should know. You publish them. I'm talking about the ones who return by choice—the bodhisattvas of poetry who come back to rescue the noble art of *poesie* from the greeting-card companies. I'm contemplating making the trip myself. Call this a location scout."

We crossed Avenue A into Tompkins Square Park. He eyed the gated playground, the fenced mounds of lawn, the elliptical paths. He shook his head.

"Man, this place sure has changed."

"They renovated it."

"Crowd control," he said, disgusted. "The hegemonic powers of the police state manifest in urban design. The usurpation of the commons."

"I guess they had a riot here once."

"Fucking right, we did."

We cut through the park, pausing at the small dog run so he could watch a French bulldog hump a tiny male chihuahua. He joined a Rasta for a round of tai chi. We exited at Seventh and B, across from a new interior design store. He glared at a teak chaise in the window; I coveted an "ethnic" pillow.

At the German brewhouse on the corner of Avenue C, he ogled junior stockbrokers sitting at sidewalk tables with ties loosened and frosty steins of Weissbier in hand. It was happy hour, and a suckling pig was roasting on a spit. The dudes pinched hot chunks of meat between their fingers and laughed as the fat dripped down their shirtfronts.

He shook his head. "Man, there goes the fucking neighborhood."

We reached my building between C and D. I fished my utility bills from the mailbox and tossed them straight into the recycling on the curb.

"No way I can pay these. Not now."

"Cheer up," he said. "You've got a good six months before they start shutting things off."

We sat on the stoop and watched a large Dominican family walk to evening service at the Baptist church down the block. The little girls wore lacy dresses and patent-leather shoes; the little boys wore suits. They chased one another up and down the street, jumping over cracks in the sidewalk. The adults carried prayer books. I leaned forward, cupping my chin in my hands.

"I wish I believed in something."

He closed his eyes. "Believe in everything. Believe in nothing. The world is beautiful, and the world is a disaster. Accept it."

I looked up. "Why me? Why *my* head?"

He opened one eye. "You got a poetry portal up there in your cerebellum, babe. A little hole where truth slips through. A profound ability to suffer."

"That's just what I need to hear."

"You should be happy. Most cats in this country get their mind-holes sealed by the time they enter grade school. Only their assholes are left. It's a national catastrophe."

"I'm not talking about cats. I'm talking about me."

"Cheer up. You're built to take it."

An elderly Chinese lady pushed a wire shopping cart down the street, filled with plastic bottles and cans. She stopped at our curb and sorted through the recycling. I could end up like her—or worse. I wanted to cry.

He sighed. "Listen. Let me tell you something that'll save you a lot of unnecessary grief in the long run."

"Oh, great. What."

"I'm serious. You ready?" He narrowed his eyes, studying my face for signs of karmic readiness. "I don't think you're ready . . ."

"For fuck's sake, just tell me!"

"Okay, here goes . . ." He drew a breath. "It's okay to be unhappy."

"That's it?"

"That's it."

"Wow," I told him. "Thanks a lot."

"It's true," he said. "You're fine. You're human. There's nothing wrong with you."

I lost it, then. "That's such bullshit! I *was* fine until you came along. I was happy. I had a job. I was paying off my student loans. Now look at me!"

The Chinese lady looked at me. She was wearing pink rubber gloves, an empty Diet Coke bottle in her hand.

He shook his head. "You're so American. Happy-happy. Gotta-be-happy. All-the-time happy . . ."

"Oh, shut up."

"It's not your fault. It's in your Bill of Rights. If you're not happy, you've failed yourself and your country. You're a defective American."

"Well, so are you."

"No way. I'm dead, remember? There's no America in heaven, babe. No barbed wire on the pearly gates, no Homeland Security, no immigration police with truncheons and Tasers and mirrored sunglasses, no X-ray machines, or great sniffing triple-headed dogs with meticulously trained noses . . ."

"Whatever."

The Chinese lady finished and moved on. The wheels of her cart rattled on the sidewalk. A homeless guy passed her going the other way. He nodded, but she snubbed him. Competition.

He cocked his head. "I sense you're not finding solace in my words . . ."

"I feel like shit."

"Well, you don't have to feel shitty about feeling shitty. You don't have to feel meta-shitty." He chuckled and rubbed his nose. "Meta-shitty. That's good, huh?"

When I didn't laugh, he got serious. "Look," he said. "Answer me truthfully. How happy were you, really? If you can honestly tell me you were happy working at that factory, I'll turn back the clock, pop you back into your cubicle, and you can forget this ever happened."

"You can do that?"

"Just answer the question."

I thought about my cubicle. I thought about my editor and my space-time continuum.

"Well? Were you happy or not?"

"Of course I was—" I started, then stopped. The homeless guy was going through our recycling, looking for a newspaper. He slept under a tarp in the vacant lot beside our building. He read the *Times* but preferred the *Wall Street Journal*. I knew that because he told me.

"Okay fine," I said. "You were right. It's like my editor said. I got into publishing because I love books. I even thought I wanted to write one, but I had student loans and stuff."

"I knew it!" he cried. "So what are you waiting for? Write! This is your chance!"

"And wind up like him?" I nodded at the homeless guy who was flipping through a Pottery Barn catalog one of my roommates had tossed.

"You wanna go back? Just say the word . . ." He raised his arms.

"No, wait . . ."

He let his arms drop. "Whew."

"What?"

"I was just kind of winging it there."

"You mean you can't turn back the clock?"

"Sweetheart, I've got no idea." He took off his glasses, cleaned them on his sweater, then put them on again. He looked at me, sternly. "So what are you waiting for? Grab a pen. Steal a typewriter. Hunker down in the corner of a smoke-filled bar and—"

"We don't use typewriters anymore. And there are no smoke-filled bars New York."

"What, no typewriters? No smoke-filled bars?" He blinked, sighed in disbelief, flickered gently. "Okay, forget that instruction. It doesn't matter how or where . . ." From the neck down, he was starting to dissipate, turning transparent. "The point is you gotta *start*. Come on! There's no time to lose . . . !"

But I was losing him. He was breaking up, moving from signal to noise.

"Wait! Where are you going?"

He was disembodied now, a faint staticky glow, and when he

spoke his words were barely audible. "Quickly," he said. "*Before it closes . . .*"

And just like that he was gone.

"*Wait!*" I shouted. The homeless guy was walking down the block. He turned and waved at me, or maybe he just flapped his hand in annoyance. I couldn't tell. I waved back anyway, and he nodded and gave me a thumbs-up. I stood to go inside. My head was aching and I needed to think. I unlocked the door, and the lines he'd quoted came back to me.

*Unscrew the locks from the doors! Unscrew the doors themselves from their jambs!*

Right, I thought. Like it's ever that easy—and yet. I rubbed my forehead. He was gone, but in his place something started to shimmer.

# WHERE AMBITION GOES TO DIE

*(A Ghost Story)*

"I saw yours today."

"Oh?" you said. "Where was she?" Your tone was nonchalant, but I knew you were pretending. I'm your husband. I can tell.

"On the side of the road by the Gorge. Near the big Douglas fir."

That part of the road curves around the fir, cutting so close that the cars drive right over its roots. Back when the road was still dirt and not well-traveled, the tree was fine; then the car ferry arrived in the '60s, and the road got paved, and the fir began to die. A pity. It was a magnificent tree—old-growth and girthy. The old-timers came to rue the ferry. They rued all of us newcomers who crossed into Canada and drifted up the coast: first the hippies and draft dodgers, then the New Age seekers and utopianists, then the Silicon Valley doomsteaders, dropouts, and the pandemic refugees. We came with our big cars and big dreams. Our architects and our American dollars. Our fancy ambitions.

"What was she doing?"

"Hitchhiking. Toward the ferry."

The ferry is the only way off the island. Sooner or later, all our ambitions try to leave—when they wake up and realize we've betrayed them, when they understand what staying means.

"How did she look?"

"Not great. Pretty wan. Transparent, even. It won't be long before she—"

You cut me off. "Yeah," you said. "Well, it's probably better."

"I suppose."

What I didn't tell you was how young she still looked, with her long black hair and furious face, even in her frailty. She was so beautiful once: strong and full of life, lithe in her struggle, vivid in her suffering. I remember how she animated you, glaring at me from behind your eyes during those first long winters of rain. The storms caged her; the island imprisoned her; she clawed at you like a wild animal, and I could feel her writhing when I held you in my arms. From time to time, you would fling the door open and stride out into the squall, throw your head back, and let her howl. I watched through the kitchen window as you turned your face to the sky. Her howl tore from your throat, but from inside the house I could barely hear it. Just a thin vibration of sound, swallowed by the pelting rain and the mossy forest, by wind lashing the cedars and the thick fog. We are so insignificant in this landscape, and she hated that. She was still trying to write that novel back then. I mean, you were.

"Did she see you?" you asked.

"Yeah. She gave me the finger. I saw her in the rearview mirror as I passed."

You smiled. "She's got some life in her yet."

"She still blames me for bringing you here."

"You didn't bring me," you said, tucking back your long, graying hair. "I came of my own accord."

Dripping, you would come inside, face wet with rain, and I never knew if you were crying—or if she was.

• • •

"I'm not unhappy," you informed me. As if I, your husband of nearly three decades, wouldn't know.

"I know."

"In many ways I'm happier without her," you said. "She was never satisfied. Always complaining . . ."

"Yeah, she was a total pain in the ass," I said. You looked wounded, so I added, "But she was awfully cute." You frowned. "I mean, *you* were cute." You glared. "I mean, you still are."

You made a face, then relented. "And those insanely grandiose plans of hers! One damn thing after another. Endless!"

"Remember the bakery? The cob oven that almost set the forest on fire?"

"Well," you said, smiling. "We ate some nice bread for a while." You paused. "Sorry about your tooth."

I'd cracked a tooth on one of her sourdoughs. Hard as a rock. "Do you remember when she got into ayahuasca and apprenticed with that shaman?"

You shuddered. "Her shamanic phase was the worst."

"No," I said. "The worst was the polyamory."

You didn't answer—or maybe you did by changing the subject. "And the Institute—her plan for an international field station for mycologists and fungi researchers and canopy biologists."

"That was my idea."

"Oh," you said. "Right."

"I had my dreams, too, you know."

"I know. I forgot."

• • •

The polyamory phase nearly ended our marriage, but you don't like to talk about it. I think you're still embarrassed, even after all these years. I don't blame you, though. I blame her—the way she fell for that charismatic New Age Prophet who came to the island to teach energy healing. She convinced you to take the workshop, insisting it was "research" for the novel: a slightly futuristic back-to-the-land tale, peopled by neo-hippies, earth muffins, meat punks, and New Age refugees, set on a remote Pacific Northwest island in Desolation Sound. You once described it as a fictional meditation on failed utopias, which I thought sounded fascinating, but I never got to read it. I think there's still a draft in a box in the basement, moldering away, being eaten by silverfish. You never finished—because she abandoned you. You couldn't finish a novel without her.

Failed utopias. Failed novels. Failed marriages. Desolation Sound abounds in these.

One night, during the weeklong workshop, the Prophet was slated to give a public talk for the islanders. The subject was Sylphs. Needless to say I didn't want to go, but she insisted. We argued. She won. By the time we arrived, the big yurt was mostly full, but we found seats on the floor in front. When the Prophet stepped to the mic, I was startled. I had expected a tall, willowy man with flowing gray hair, pulled back in a ponytail. Maybe an ethnically embroidered skullcap over his bald spot, prayer beads, a caftan. But I was wrong. This Prophet had an expensive haircut and a suit. He had the body of a man who works out with a trainer. Sitting at his feet, I listened as he laughingly shared the story of his tremendous success: the fortune he'd made in new battery technologies, the Awakening that led him to sell his company and retire at the age of thirty-five. He explained how the Sylphs, with their ætheric bodies, transmute the toxic chemtrails pumped into the sky by government geoengineers, multinational corporations, and U.S. Army biological weapons programs. Without the heroic intervention of the Sylphs and other intra-cosmic beings, he said, we would all die of bioengineered pandemics.

Of course I assumed he was being ironic. At some point, I nudged you, but you didn't turn or seem to notice. When I looked back, he was speaking directly to you, and she was gazing back at him, transfixed by his pale blue eyes. After the talk he glided over, captured both your hands, and clasped them. I glanced at you and saw her blush. When you introduced us, he pressed his palms to his heart chakra and gave a slight namaste bow. I bowed, too—awkwardly—and as I straightened, he smiled and winked at me. Later, at home, she said I'd imagined it, but I swear that wink happened. I went online and found his website offering exclusive workshops, consulting, and a full line of high-end orgone generators, tower busters, and power wands. When I showed you, we both scoffed, while she stayed silent. When I made a harmless joke about the spelling of "profit," she left the room. I sensed her attraction to him then, but you denied it, and I let it go.

Like so many prophets and gurus and shamans and healers before him, he fell under the island's spell. Soon we heard that he had purchased a prime stretch of waterfront on the desirable south end, where he was building a Longhouse designed to deflect microwaves, electromagnetic rays, and cell phone signals. This was not surprising. What surprised me was when you said he'd invited us to move onto his land, into his Longhouse, to join his polyamorous Family. I knew she was behind it—she had a weakness for men in power, an itch to climb the ladder of discipleship and bask in his esteem—but what truly surprised me was that you wanted us to try.

"Wife swapping?" I remember asking. The island has a long history of that sort of thing, dating back to the proto-hippies in the '60s. "Free love?"

You glared at me—or maybe it was her. "I'm not a commodity you get to trade," she said. (Or maybe that was both of you.)

The Longhouse, with its cubit coils and crystal shields, was not what protected us from the pandemic. We had left by then—it had become clear that the Prophet, too, was driven by ambition, which dwindled the longer he stayed. Ambition fueled his sexual charisma; without it he paled. His hair grew long and lank. He stopped working out and developed a paunch. She came to her senses then, and so did you. Once he started wearing tie-dye, we moved out and put the Longhouse behind us. Our marriage survived, though the episode left a mark. You began to distrust your judgment, and as for your ambition, she never quite recovered.

I've always fancied I had a slight edge in judgment, but my ambition was never a match for yours, so I had less to lose. My ambition never troubled me the way yours did, and when I stopped hearing from him I assumed he was dead. Given my relative contentment during the pandemic, it was a reasonable assumption. People say this is the island where ambition comes to die. I figured mine had passed away quietly in the night, and I didn't really miss him.

• • •

When the pandemic hit, the island shut its doors. The ferry still ran on a reduced schedule, but only islanders and essential businesses were allowed passage; tourists and nonresidents were turned away. The wealthy Americans with homes here, fearing long months of isolation and deprivation, cut their vacations short and left before the border closed. They have big lives and big needs—primary residences in big American cities serviced by Amazon Prime and concierge medical care—so we weren't terribly worried about them. The rest of us hunkered down and counted ourselves lucky.

We had public health care through our little clinic. Food was available. With the tourist trade suspended, even the young earth-muffins had year-round housing. People kept small gardens, and local farms stepped up production. The food co-op brought in bulk flour, rice, and pasta. We collected oysters, dug clams, grew garlic, and traded it for butter. Certain things—like toilet paper—were scarce, but that was true everywhere. Cash drifted out of use as people bartered and shared. The population has always been sparse, so social distancing was easy. Folks drawn to a remote island in Desolation Sound tend to be social isolates. We prefer it this way. We had enough, and we were content.

During the lockdown, everyone's ambitions were equally thwarted, and even the most unbridled offered little resistance. The island's equilibrium depended on keeping their overweening appetites in check, and the way we came together seemed proof we had succeeded. Indeed, by year two, we thought they might be gone for good, casualties of the pandemic.

But then, when restrictions eased and the world began to recover, something odd started happening. There were reports of sightings. Shadowy ambitions—like the ghosts of skittish children—were spotted hiding behind tree trunks, fences, and outhouses, quietly watching as we went about our business. We'd spy them while chatting with a masked neighbor at the post office or walking after dinner. Sometimes, we'd feel eyes on us as we weeded or chopped wood, look up, and there they would be, observing from a socially appropriate distance.

Figuring yours would be among the first to reappear, I was on the lookout for her, but instead someone told me they'd seen mine. I was at the food co-op when a neighbor said they'd spotted him, alive and running through the forest. I was surprised, first that he was alive, and second that he was running. I've always been a runner—you know this—but never an ambitious one. Other people clock their pace and mileage, run marathons, set goals, post milestones, but not me. I run for the pleasure of moving through the trees along narrow trails, skirting old growth, jumping roots, ducking under dripping moss, feeling the spongy ground underfoot. Sometimes I stop to eat huckleberries, photograph a slime mold, or stare at an owl. I run for the smells of cedar and fir, for sweat and the clean ache after. Ambition has never been part of it.

So when this neighbor said they'd seen him running through the forest, I pressed for more details. Did he look ill? Was something chasing him? Was he running away? No, they said: he looked fit, jogging at a moderate clip up one of the steeper trails that the mountain bikers sometimes use, not even breaking a sweat. So yes, I was surprised, and, if I'm being honest, a little proud.

I didn't mention that when I told you about the sighting; I only said I found it worrisome, which was true as well. And I wasn't alone. Had our ambitions survived? Were they in training? Making a comeback? What did they want? The period after the pandemic was unsettling, and their reemergence unnerved us. We didn't know what to think. For a while we stayed vigilant, but as the months passed we relaxed our guard, and in the absence of wild leaping or vaulting antics, we allowed them to drift closer. Maybe the thwarting had done them some good. Maybe they'd learned moderation. Maybe they had acclimated to island life. We dared to hope because apparently we missed them after all.

You remained wary, though. Once, when you were gathering oyster mushrooms in the alder grove, you glimpsed yours flitting from tree to tree in the dappled light.

"I think she was looking for mushrooms too," you told me later. "I think she was trying to help me."

"That's sweet . . ."

"No, it's not sweet. It's terrifying! I don't want her help! She'll try to monetize the mushrooms—turn them into a business."

"Don't be so hard on her. She's helped you in the past . . ."

You grimaced. "Listen. You don't know her. You don't know what it's like to live with her."

I placed my hands on your shoulders. "Well," I said, kissing the frown line on your forehead, "actually, I do."

• • •

In the end, you didn't have to worry. Lately, you've even started to write again. Not novels—nothing big or ambitious—just a draft of a short story now and then, or a poem, scribbled on the back of a recycled envelope and read aloud to us by the fire. I say "us" because the four of us are often on the couch together: me, with my arm around you as you read; her, listening quietly, leaning into mine. We're all older now. The stories are short. We listen and nod, maybe ask a question or two. She is careful never to offer feedback unless asked, and you rarely ask these days. What's the point? Like my running, you now write for your pleasure—and for ours.

The Native people once called this the island of the dead, for surely it is full of ghosts. After you read to us, I dampen down the fire, and we all say good night, and then we go to bed. When we sleep, we dream unhaunted.

# THE PROBLEM OF THE BODY

## *1.*

My granddaughter just turned seventeen. She does not get along with her father and his new wife, so when Covid started, she came to live with me. This is not our first time living under the same roof. Her mother—my daughter—died shortly after she was born; her father, Francis, is an idiot who was incapable of caring for an infant, so my husband and I took her in and raised her until Francis decided he wanted her back. She was already two by then. We were reluctant to let her go, but he was her father. I never liked him. Never understood what my daughter saw in him.

My granddaughter's name is Madison, but I call her Maddie—Mad for short—and she calls me Moony, or Moon. The name Madison is from Francis's side; Moony is a name she invented. When she was a baby, I read *Goodnight Moon* to her every night. The first night Francis had her back, she sobbed inconsolably, wailing "*Moon! Moon!*" when he tried to put her to bed, so he panicked and phoned me. I reminded him about the book and the clear instructions I'd given him to read it to her at bedtime. "Oh, right," he said. He'd forgotten. Apparently he tried, and after the poor child finally cried herself to sleep, he called me back. "Didn't work," he said. He sounded pleased. This went on for months. Tears every night. Never occurred to him that what she wanted was me.

During Covid, we had to quarantine, and because I'm old, Maddie promised to be careful and to always wear a mask when she went out, and mostly she did. "I would die if you got Covid and it was my fault," she said, with those big, fat tears in her eyes that look just like my daughter's when she was that age. "If I killed my Moony, I would have to die immediately." I told her that was unacceptable. Girls that age are so dramatic.

We live in a rickety New England multifamily house, a boxy, inelegant thing from the nineteenth century, built for multigenerational immigrant working-class families from Italy and Ireland living stacked on top of one another. The house, like me, is tired. It has faded gray clapboard siding and bones that sag. The floors slant and nothing is level. Doors refuse to latch, books slide off shelves, office chairs roll of their own accord—you can wind up across the room from your keyboard if you're not careful.

Mad lives in the mother-in-law suite, which my husband once used as his office when he still saw patients. It's a fine arrangement and gives her some privacy. She turned his waiting room into her bedroom, and she shares the bathroom with his turtles and what remains of his little fungi farm—mostly oyster mushrooms these days, which are easier than the psilocybin. She loved her opa and always remembers to mist his shrooms and is careful not to step on the turtles in the dark. Not that they would mind. They're box turtles. They have hard shells.

The male turtle's name is Ebeneezer. The female is Eleanor. Ebeneezer is very old, and Eleanor, his second wife, is much younger.

"Like She-Whose-Name," Mad says. She-Whose-Name is Maddie's stepmother, Joia, who is twenty years younger than Francis. "Only Eleanor is sweet and not evil."

Maddie sits on the closed toilet seat, holding a long pair of forceps with a fat nightcrawler dangling from the tips while I watch from the doorway. Eleanor sees the worm, cocks her head, and looks up expectantly. When Maddie drops the worm, Eleanor bites it clean in two.

"And she's a good little eater," I add—the comparison, once again, being Joia, who is anorexic. The front half of the worm writhes in Eleanor's beak while the rear half flails on the white bathroom tiles—or maybe it's the other way around. Hard to tell a head from a tail on an earthworm.

"Joia says I'm getting fat," Maddie says, fishing another worm from the cottage cheese container. "Do you think I'm fat?"

"Of course not," I say evenly, pressing my spine against the sharp edge of the doorjamb, as if contact with the house will keep me from driving over to Francis's condo and strangling his wife for body-shaming my radiantly healthy, well-adjusted granddaughter. It works. I don't.

Maddie digs around in the plastic container for another nightcrawler. We're getting low, and I make a mental note to buy more at the bait shop—though I know perfectly well I'll forget. She finds one, fishes it out, and dangles it in front of Ebeneezer, who is basking under his heat lamp. The old turtle blinks up at her and then closes his eye.

"He won't eat," she says, frustrated. "Why won't he eat?"

"He's very old," I tell her.

"How old?"

"He must be almost seventy by now."

She holds the worm to his nose, trying to get his attention. "He's older than my dad, even."

"Much."

"But not older than you."

"No. Nobody is older than me."

"Even Opa?" she asks, though she knows the answer. She loves to talk about Stefan, and I'm grateful to her for speaking of him in the present, as if he were still alive.

"Even Opa. I married a *younger* man."

The innuendo makes no sense to her; she cannot imagine someone as old as her opa being younger than anyone. At our age, words like "younger" no longer apply. Maddie wiggles the worm to make it more alluring. It's alive, but barely. "How old was Opa when he got Ebeneezer?" she asks. She knows this answer, too, but she also understands that stories are alive, that they change and grow, and the world of adults is mysterious.

"When he was six," I say. "He was just a little boy." I watch her face as she ponders the unimaginable, and so, to be helpful, I add something new. "He sent away for him from the back of a comic book."

I explain how, in the olden days, there were advertisements at the back of comic books for Sea-Monkeys and Amazing X-Ray Specs and Disappearing Ink, and for the Charles Atlas's Dynamic-Tension workout routine—guaranteed to give even a ninety-pound weakling a He-Man physique. Bullies would no longer kick sand in your face, I tell her. Busty girls in bikinis would cling to your biceps.

She listens, then says, "I don't know what you're talking about." She pokes the worm to see if it's still alive and looks up at me, frowning. She frowns at me a lot, but not meanly; she's trying to understand. So I explain how you could buy dried-up, dead-seeming Sea-Monkeys and put them in a glass of water and they would come back to life.

"They were supposed to be merpeople—mermaids and mermen and merbabies, with tiny webbed mer-fingers and mer-toes and mer-crowns on their mer-heads—but they were really just dried-up shrimps."

"But did they come back to life?"

"Briefly. Then they died. It was always a disappointment."

"What a rip-off."

"Total rip-off," I agree.

"But Ebeneezer didn't die," she says. "He's still alive."

"Yes. Ebeneezer was not a disappointment." Which isn't entirely true. Despite having had two wives—whom he wooed enthusiastically—Ebeneezer failed to sire offspring, a bitter disappointment to Stefan, who had been hoping for a clutch of Neezer-babies for over sixty years.

"I don't want him to die," Maddie said, anxious. "Why won't he eat?"

• • •

Maddie likes learning about the world from before she was born. She's really into details, and after I tell her things, she looks them up on her phone and soon she's the expert.

"Did you know that the guy who invented the X-Ray Specs and the Sea-Monkeys was a Nazi?" she asks the next morning, over breakfast.

"No, I didn't."

"Well, he was. A neo-Nazi. But he was Jewish." She holds up her phone to show me a natty man with a slick side part, dressed in a white plaid suit with wide lapels and an absurdly wide tie, staring out of the photo with a mesmerizing gaze.

"His name was Harold Nathan Braunhut," she says, stumbling over the pronunciation. "But he added *von* to make it sound more German."

"Von Braun*hoot*," I say. "'Brown hat.' Harold Nathan of the Brown Hat."

She reads on. "It says he bought guns for the Ku Klux Klan. He thought Hitler wasn't a bad guy—he just got bad press."

"I did not know that."

"'So eager to please, they can even be trained! Surprise your guests! Teach them to obey your commands like a pack of friendly trained seals!'"

"Who?" I ask, thinking she is still talking about neo-Nazis or the Ku Klux Klan.

"Sea-Monkeys." She looks at me and shakes her head. "How could you guys have been so gullible?"

"Well," I say. "People are gullible. And those were different times. But I don't think your opa bought Ebeneezer from a neo-Nazi."

"Did you ever buy any Sea-Monkeys?"

"No. But I did get some Disappearing Ink once."

"Cool! Did it work? What did you write?"

"I don't remember."

## 2.

"The problem is the body," Maddie muses. "Nobody's gonna believe it unless we can show them a body."

"True," I say. "The body is such a bother."

She's determined to solve this. She's a smart girl—and practical too. "That means the usual things are out. You can't die in a car accident. You can't catch a disease or fall off a roof."

"I could be abducted . . ."

She shakes her head, emphatic. "Not believable."

"Are you saying no one would want to abduct me? That I'm unabductable? I'm famous, you know."

She looks skeptical. In her world, fame requires social media followers. I have none.

"Okay, not super famous," I concede. "A little bit famous."

"Maybe, but you're not rich. Nobody's gonna abduct you unless you're rich."

She has a point.

She chews the edge of her thumb, thinking. "I know! You can drown!"

Now I'm the skeptic. I'm a strong swimmer, and Maddie knows this, and there's still the problem of the body.

"No, listen," she says. "You can drown in the Connecticut River. People do it all the time. They jump off the Coolidge Bridge or fall out of boats. Their bodies get carried downriver by the current. They snag on tree roots. They decompose before they're ever found."

I don't want to jump off the Coolidge Bridge. Coolidge was an unremarkable president, but that's not why. "I'm not killing myself. It would be bad for sales."

By "sales" I mean the new book that's coming out in the spring.

Maddie is helping me fake my own death so I won't have to go on tour. She's funny that way: all weepy about my demise one minute, and eager to help kill me off the next.

"I'm not saying suicide," she says, rolling her eyes in the way only teenagers can. "Suicide is such a cliché."

"Whew," I say. "Thank you."

Covid all but killed the ritual of the book tour, and I'd hoped to do the publicity for the new book on Zoom. But I was too slow, and the world reopened.

"Ice fishing," Maddie declares. "Just listen: You take up ice fishing now. We get you a fishing rod and an ice saw and one of those little tents. You can use Ebeneezer and Eleanor's night-crawlers for bait. You start going out on the river at night, and—"

"It's too cold. And I don't like fishing even in the summer."

"You don't have to go a lot. Just once—no, twice—to establish a plausible narrative."

I taught her about plausible narratives. I taught her the Rule of Threes.

"Then, the third time, you cut a hole big enough to fall through and—boom!" She claps her hands.

"Boom?"

"Boom," she repeats, but she's not finished with me yet. "Probably best to lose the pole in the water, but leave the worms and tackle. Also a half-empty flask of whiskey, so it looks like you were a little drunk. And maybe one frozen mitten, clutching the edge of the ice hole, like you were trying to pull yourself out and it came off. Red would be good. Do you have red mittens? I could knit you some . . ."

She really does have an eye for detail, I think proudly. Takes after me. She'll be a writer someday.

"You'll need a separate getaway car, parked nearby," she muses.

"Can't I just call an Uber?"

She rolls her eyes. "No! You have to leave your phone behind or throw it in the water. You can't go making calls to Uber after you're drowned and frozen and drifting downstream." She sighs. "I'd better come pick you up."

She finally got her license—delayed by Covid—and she's very pleased with herself.

Together we work out the rest of the plan. She'll take her opa's car and drive me to the airport. The name on my passport is not the pen name I publish under, so no one will recognize it on the flight manifest. I will fly to the coast of Spain and live in the private villa that I will buy with the massive royalties from the new book, which will instantly become a bestseller after the publishing house announces my tragic and frigid death by ice fishing. In Spain, I will continue to write. Every three or four years, with mounting fanfare, my publisher will "discover" another unpublished manuscript. My editor will love it—living authors are a pain in the ass. Dead and undistracted, I'll be far more prolific. Maddie can visit in summer; she's in her last year of high school, taking Spanish, and thrilled at the prospect of practicing with actual Spaniards. "I'll be fluent in no time!"

What could possibly go wrong?

I text my friend KJ, who writes murder mysteries, and ask what she thinks of Maddie's plan.

KJ writes back:

> No. Occam's razor—you die of Covid. You will need to die at home, but someone (Maddie?) will remove your virus-ridden body to one of those refrigerator trucks. The paperwork is rushed and spotty, then the body goes missing. Our best guess is that you were mislabeled and then cremated. A tragic end to a tragic tale. Meanwhile, a cousin who looks much like you, only blond and possibly a smoker, inherits your car and is last seen speeding north to Canada . . .

It's a liberatory image. I read it to Maddie, who doesn't know what Occam's razor is, but vetoes the Covid plot. "Too late," she says. "They're not losing bodies anymore."

She is right, of course. "I like the blond smoker," I tell her. "I've been dying for a cigarette."

"Smoking is bad for you," she says sternly.

"If I'm already dead, what harm could it do?"

## 3.

My husband missed the pandemic. Always a considerate man, he died peacefully a month before anyone had even heard of Covid, and in retrospect I am grateful. He wouldn't have wanted to burden an overtaxed hospital system, and it would have pained him to leave me to face quarantine alone. Francis solved that for me: Faced with the prospect of locking down with Maddie and Joia at each other's throats, my son-in-law phoned and, in a show of concern for my recent bereavement, suggested it might comfort me to have my granddaughter come live here. For once, he was right about something.

Maddie attended school remotely, which meant most days were spent on the couch in front of her laptop. She didn't move much, and I worried, but my own days looked much the same, so I had little moral authority when I told her to go outside and run around. Sometimes I lured her into a walk by pretending I was afraid of slipping on the ice. I still do this. We put on our parkas and hats and matching Ugg boots and mittens. She grips my hand as I step gingerly onto the sidewalk. Mostly it's an act. I could stride if I wanted to, but it's good for young people to feel a sense of purpose—and, in truth, I find her presence reassuring. She's a strong, sturdy girl. Sometimes, when she pads around in her underpants or I catch sight of her naked coming out of the shower, I remember when my body looked like that: smooth skin, long, lean muscles. I remember never being happy with mine, just as she is never happy with hers—forever finding faults—and living with Joia doesn't help. She worries her breasts are too small. She twists around in front of the mirror, hunting for cellulite on her bottom. There isn't any, I tell her. She won't believe me when I tell her she is beautiful.

She's going to college next year, which means she'll be moving out in the fall, but I have her for the rest of this school year and the summer. I worry about her going away. They say the pandemic and quarantine have stunted the psychological development of kids her age, and I fear there's truth in that; she strikes me as emotionally young. As far as I know she's never had a crush—on a boy or a girl—never shown any interest in sex, and I doubt she knows much about the mechanics, though she can tell you everything about the mating habits of octopuses and jellyfish. She loves undersea creatures. Stefan was a psychotherapist, and although he specialized in treating people at the ends of their lives, he knew plenty about beginnings. He would have had a better sense of Mad's development than I have. He would have observed and assessed. I miss him especially at times like these. I confer with him constantly, but it isn't the same.

During the pandemic, Maddie spent every spare moment on her phone, scrolling feeds and messaging friends. I finally set limits—no phone at meals—which, thankfully, got her reading again. I've never been especially worried about what she looks at online, but lately she's grown squirrelly with the phone, which makes me wonder. When I walk into the living room, she looks up quickly from the couch, and when I get close she turns the phone facedown.

*Should I?* I ask Stefan in my mind.

Do it, he says.

I nudge her knee with mine. "Hey," I say. "Shove over."

She does, and when I put my arm out, she curls into me, folding her long body into a smallish packet that still fits neatly under my armpit. It's like a magic trick—the Incredible Shrinking Girl—though she stands taller than I do when we get up.

"What are you doing?" I ask into the crown of her head. Her scalp smells faintly feral; her hair tickles my lips.

"Nothing. Just looking at some stuff."

"Can I see?"

She shakes her head.

"Please . . . ?"

She hesitates, phone in hand. When she doesn't answer, I take her wrist and gently turn it over. On the screen is a picture of a boy. It takes me a minute to understand.

"Is that a dating app?" I've never seen one before.

She squirms a little. "I know, I know. But I'm almost eighteen."

This is untrue, but I let it pass. "Oh," I say. "Is there an age limit?" In my day, we didn't need dating apps. We were already having sex at her age—a fact I will not be sharing. She swipes the boy away and another appears.

"How did you get a . . . whatever. Subscription? Membership?"

"A profile." She grins. "I lied. Don't tell Dad, okay?"

"Can I see?"

She pauses long enough for me to glimpse the boy. He looks very nice.

"Ick," she says, and swipes left—gone.

"Hey, slow down. I wanted to see."

"Too late."

Another picture appears, and she swipes him away, and then another, like she's dealing out poker cards from an endless deck.

"You don't like any of them?" I ask.

"Not my type."

This is news to me. I didn't know she had a type. "How can you tell?"

"I just know. They're all losers."

"*All* of them?"

She nods, vehemently, and I marvel at her certainty. The only time I felt certain about my first husband was when I filed for divorce; with Stefan it took me months even to agree to a drink.

A boy in a red baseball cap grins up at us.

"What about him?"

"Big teeth. Definitive ick." Swipe.

Big Teeth vanishes, and a handsome, clean-cut kid in a crew-neck sweater—a look we would have called preppy in my day—takes his place. I don't know what they call it now.

"He's cute," I offer.

"Bot," she says. "Total AI."

She flicks him away, and he's replaced by a glowering bad boy in a bomber jacket. Maddie hesitates, index finger hovering over his face, and I dislike him instantly. He's slouched against a brick wall in a trash-strewn alley that looks like a movie poster or an album cover. A cowlick falls over his forehead. Smoldering eyes. Please no, I beg silently, though to be fair, I can see the appeal. I open my mouth to say something derisive—just as I do, her finger moves.

"Wait," I say, and her finger freezes. "Don't you think he's kind of hot?" I'm fishing now, trying to discern the type of boy she might like.

She swivels her head in my armpit and looks up. "Ew, Moony, *seriously*?" There's a new pimple on her nose.

"Well . . ." I'm thinking, a little wistfully, of James Dean, a reference lost on her. She pulls away to study me, eyes wide, as if seeing me for the first time.

"*Wait*," she gasps. "Is he *your* type, Moony?"

It's sweet that she uses the present tense; it makes me feel viable. "It's that vintage-leather-jacket energy," I admit, and she nods somewhat skeptically—and then her face lights up.

"Oh my god, Moony! We have to set you up!" She bounces on the sofa, already scheming. "With a profile and—" But then she breaks off, remembering her opa. Her eyes go all tragic, and she shrinks back into me again like a mollusk. "Oh, Moony, I'm so sorry," she says, muffled, into my chest. "I'm so stupid!"

I pat her head, tell her it's fine, tell her not to be silly.

• • •

That night, I download the app, create an account, and pick a name—sticking with the Avenues, I go with Lexington. I make Lexy the same age as Maddie and upload a few generic photos of attractive, athletic, intelligent-looking eighteen-year-olds. I know my granddaughter pretty well, so it should be easy to create a profile for a girl like her. I'm a novelist, after all. I make up people for a living. How hard could it be?

But I underestimate the challenge. Dumbfounded by the idiocy of the prompts, I open Reddit for tips and then microdose, hoping *Psilocybe stefanensis* will help. Unsurprisingly, it only makes the inanity more inane. *How would you survive a zombie apocalypse?* Why on earth would a prospective mate need to know this? What difference would it make? *What's your secret talent?* How would this predict compatibility, and would you really want to know in advance? Stefan had many secret talents, but I didn't learn about them until *after* we started sleeping together—that was the fun of it. *The hill you'd die on?* Stefan's was universal health care, but that wasn't why I dated him. *Most spontaneous act?* Asking me to marry him. *Villain origin story?* We never discussed it, but I suspect he would have said all decent villains get their start in the anal phase of psychosexual development. It never occurred to me to inquire which dead person he would invite to dinner. Hannah Arendt? Walter Benjamin? In the nearly half century we were married, the subject just never came up, and now it's too late. I apologize to my dead husband. There was so much we didn't know about each other. I should have asked.

None of this helps with eighteen-year-old Lexy. I need to stop overthinking and decide. She will feed the zombies her pandemic sourdough, which will kill even the walking dead. Her favorite animal will be an octopus because they have three hearts. When asked to choose between dogs or cats, she picks box turtles. Favorite person: her grandmother, of course.

I upload the profile and wait. That night I dream of Stefan. He's speaking German with a small bespectacled man and a mannish woman in a suit, smoking a cigarette. They drink red wine and peer down at me through a luminous portal in the clouds. They look amused, if a little baffled. He seems happy.

## 4.

When Maddie was an infant, I loved the heat of her small body, and I missed it terribly when she was gone. She was barely three months old when she and her mother moved in with us. Emmy had stopped breastfeeding to start chemo, which had been deferred during the pregnancy, but the cancer didn't respond. It spread from her breast to her liver and lungs, yet she kept her baby clasped to her chest, even when the infant's weight felt crushing. She held on as long as she could for Maddie's sake; then she had to concentrate on dying. Stefan helped her do that. He was her stepfather, devoted to her from the start, and the long journey toward death bound them even closer. After she died, Stefan and I carried that baby everywhere—strapped to our bellies and backs, perched on our hips, and later straddling our shoulders—to help her form the necessary bonds and attachments. We were trying to mitigate the trauma of losing her mother. We were grieving the loss of our daughter.

Maddie was two when Francis remarried and announced he was ready to be a father. Stefan, muttering darkly, did the packing. For such a tiny person, Maddie had a startling amount of stuff. He loaded the crib, high chair, potty seat, and little desk into the car, then made piles of books and toys and clothes in the living room and began boxing them. Maddie, excited to see her whole kingdom gathered in one place, careened from box to box, flinging her treasures into the air and shrieking when they fell.

I was in the kitchen making lunch but came out to see what all the commotion was about. Stefan sat on the floor beside a megapak of diapers, draped in rainbow leggings with a pink onesie on his head. Maddie had been decorating him. A stuffed turtle sailed past, and he caught it.

"Maddie," I said. "You're slowing Opa down. Let him finish."

"It's fine," Stefan said, delighted. He'd missed Emmy's toddler years and was making up for them now. He tossed the turtle back. Maddie tried to catch it with both hands and missed. She clapped and threw it again.

"Francis is waiting," I said.

"Good," Stefan said, putting the turtle on Maddie's head. "Let him wait." He pointed to the diapers. Maddie had started toilet training herself at eighteen months and hadn't worn one since her second birthday. "What about those?"

"Pack them up," I said, heading back to the kitchen. "Let Joia deal with it."

Francis lived two towns over and taught marketing management at the state university. Joia had been his student. I suspected the affair began while my daughter was pregnant and continued through the cancer and the chemo. I think Emmy knew. She never said so to me or to Stefan, but that explains why she insisted we take Maddie. Emmy and I got along pretty well, considering, but she adored Stefan. She was six when he and I got together, and he took over much of her care so I could write.

To be honest, I was not a very good mother. Writers often aren't. I'm a much better grandmother.

• • •

We delivered Maddie to her father's house. Joia watched Francis and Stefan unload the car, then Stefan went back for another load. The living room was already crowded with bright kiddie gear that clashed with Joia's monochrome décor. Stefan brought in a bright blue Jolly Jumper and looked for a place to put it.

"Don't leave it here!" Joia said, pressing her fingers to her forehead. "Take it up to her bedroom!"

Stefan set the Jolly Jumper in the middle of the marble coffee table.

"Jump!" Maddie said.

"Francis!" Joia cried.

I studied Joia from the sofa. Maddie sat in my lap, eating apple slices from a plastic bag. Francis had waited a decorous interval after Emmy's death before remarrying, but of course Joia had still been an undergraduate then; once she graduated, they wasted no time. Before the wedding, I had watched Joia pour it on, fawning over her future stepdaughter. Now that moving day was upon them, the veneer was wearing thin; she was beginning to grasp the impact a two-year-old has on a life.

Maddie tried to feed me an apple slice, then changed her mind and ate it herself. "I fear the bloom is off the rose," I whispered into her hair. The soft fuzz tickled my lips.

Francis came in carrying a pink wheeled pig and a Radio Flyer Retro Ride-On Rocket we'd found at an antique store.

"What's that?" Joia said.

"Pig," Maddie said, pointing with her apple slice. "Wocket."

"See?" Francis said. "My daughter knows a pig when she sees one."

"*Our* daughter," Joia said, placing a hand on his arm.

I winced. A chunk of apple fell to the floor. Maddie looked down, then up at me to gauge my reaction. I kissed her nose; she laughed and dropped another.

They walked us out to the car. Francis towered over Maddie, his hand on her head as if to hold her in place. She had stayed with them before, of course, but this time she was uneasy. As Stefan backed down the driveway, she broke free and darted after us. Francis grabbed her arm, and she started to cry. It took everything I had not to leap out and run back for her.

As we drove away, I twisted in my seat and watched her grow smaller and smaller—my incredible shrinking girl—until we turned the corner and she disappeared.

## 5.

"Oh, Maddie, dear," I say offhandedly. "Remember that app you were using? The dating one?"

We're having dinner, and I'm trying to sound as if the thought has just occurred to me, though I've been waiting all day to ask her.

Maddie looks up from her fantasy novel, mouth full of lettuce. "What about it?"

"Well, I was wondering what happens after you find someone you like."

"What do you mean?"

"You know. Someone you think you might get along with. Do you call each other?"

"You mean like on the phone?"

"Well, yes, a phone call or . . ." I should know better. She has trained me to text and never call unless it's an emergency.

"No," she says, incredulous—like, who does that?

"Okay, so what's the next step? Do you text? Do you make a date to meet somewhere?"

She shrugs, and I infer, much to my relief, that she's never gotten that far. I reframe my question to let her off the hook. "I mean, not you, necessarily. What would someone do?"

"I dunno. If you match and you like the person, I guess you could meet up. I mean, that's the point, right? But you have to match first . . ."

This is precisely what I wanted to know. It means she's browsing and has never even liked anyone back.

"I don't wanna match," she says. "Because then they want to chat, and that's just boring."

I already know this, because I have matched and chatted with a dozen boys—I mean, Lexy has—while in the background I consult Reddit to decode acronyms and master the digital vernacular. At first it was fascinating, the way an ethnographic study is fascinating, but now I'm bored. A couple of the boys have asked to meet, and I've said no and ghosted them, but why not take it to the next level, as they say? It's a chance to observe them up close, in their natural habitat. They'll never guess that the old lady sitting alone in the corner, nursing a latte, engrossed in her book, is the girl they're looking for. Perhaps it's cruel to get their hopes up, but the data I collect could be useful down the road, once Maddie actually starts dating.

"And where might such a meeting take place?" I ask. "A coffee shop? The public library?"

At the word "library," she gives me that look again. "Um, public is good—but like Starbucks."

"Right," I say. "Of course."

I realize she's studying me now. "You don't have to worry," she says, carrying her plate to the sink. "I'm not planning to hook up with some random guy. I think I might like girls better anyway."

"That's good," I say. "Smart."

My granddaughter is a sensible girl, and I trust her to make wise choices. I'm less certain I can say the same about myself.

• • •

I take Maddie's advice and schedule the first meetup at a Starbucks in the next town over. I don't want to risk bumping into someone from the university—not that it would matter, since I've been retired for years. From our chats, Boy #1—let's call him Billy—seems harmless enough: guileless, goofy, not terribly bright. Unremarkable. Not the type to get his feelings hurt, which is why I chose him. I arrive early, claim a corner table with a sightline to the door, and order a grande latte that is big enough to sip for a while. I've brought a book too: *Great Expectations*. The title would have made Stefan laugh.

Don't judge me, I tell him. It's research. But I call everything research—most writers do—so even as I think this, I know how questionable it sounds. I picture Stefan's bushy eyebrows rising. Okay, fine, I tell him. But it's not like I'm catfishing. And it is research, only not for me. For Maddie.

Billy is late, which doesn't surprise me. I spot him immediately by the ball cap and skateboard and have to stop myself from calling his name when he pushes through the door. He's shorter than I expected. He checks his phone—refreshing his memory of Lexy's face, no doubt—then scans the room. As he looks my way, I glance down at my book, but his gaze slides right over me. I have never felt so unseen or so safe.

I'm not *famous*-famous, as Maddie often reminds me, especially among her generation, but it isn't unusual to be recognized in coffee shops near the university, where I still have readers. I needn't have worried. This Billy boy is clearly not one of my readers—or anyone else's. And I needn't have worried about his feelings or his self-esteem; after a second glance at his phone and another once-over of the room, he shrugs, plugs in his earbuds, and skates away, leaving me with my grande latte barely touched and my great expectations nicely deflated.

Boy #2—let's call him Dylan—I meet a week later. He's marginally more interesting than Billy, though that may be because I microdose before leaving the house. From his profile, I have gleaned that he plays the guitar, is into acoustic bands I've never heard of, and wants to be a musician or a poet—probably both. If Boy #1 was a himbo/NPC, Boy #2 is a try-hard, pick-me softboy type, who might, I worry, be more to Maddie's taste. I order a flat white, secure my seat, and have barely opened my book when Dylan slouches in. He's early, which I suppose is a point in his favor. He orders a tall cold brew and, to my surprise, sits at the table beside me. This worries me. My book is *An Anthology of*

*Beat Poets*, which I chose to amuse Stefan; when I pulled it from the shelf, he'd chuckled approvingly. Now I'm concerned that young Dylan might notice the title and try to start a conversation when Lexy doesn't show. What should I do? My plan was never to interact with these boys. Only to observe.

Once again, I needn't have worried. Dylan is not interested in dead Beat poets. Dylan is preoccupied with Dylan, with his here and now. He keeps checking his phone, and as soon as Lexy is a few minutes late, he starts firing off messages. This causes me a moment of real panic, because his messages are triggering my phone notifications, but I manage to silence them before he notices the odd synchronicity between his texts and the pings emanating from the pocket of the old woman beside him. My pocket is now buzzing, and I am dying to know what he's saying. When I can no longer resist, I peek.

2:03 PM
hey! i'm here:) window seat, between the weird plant and the old lady lol

2:14 PM
not worried or anything. just me and my overpriced cold brew and a vague sense of yearning lol

2:27 PM
starting to feel like maybe this is less a date and more an exercise in radical unknowing?

2:41 PM
i just watched a barista steam milk with the intensity of a man seeking god. time is becoming conceptual

2:57 PM
are you performance art? is this a bit? bc if so i'm into it but . . .

3:12 PM
leaving now. this has been a beautifully humiliating chapter in my memoir. working title: ghosted under the green mermaid's gaze

"Bitch," he mutters as he gets up.

Asshole, I think.

I sit there fuming, debating whether to send a scathing message from Lexy but decide to block him instead. I finish my flat white and scroll through the endless stream of boys flooding my phone, on and on, day and night. If you were serious about finding love, how could you possibly choose from this infinitude? How would you know you'd picked the right one? Wouldn't you always worry there was someone better if only you'd kept swiping?

Don't worry so much, Stefan whispers.

## 6.

I said earlier that it took me months to agree to a drink with Stefan, and that is true, but not because I didn't like him. Quite the opposite, but I was recovering from a failed marriage; my ex decamped to Costa Rica the minute the divorce was filed, and I wasn't sure I would ever trust anyone again.

We met at a local conference of Jungian psychoanalysts. I was attending because I was interested in Jung's notion of the Shadow and its connection to creative expression and the workings of dreams. Stefan was presenting a paper called "Dancing with the Shadow: Imagination, Creativity, and the Alchemy of Death," a title that caught my eye, though I confess I remember little of the paper itself. During the Q&A, someone asked about psychotropic visions as a route to the Self. Stefan said that Jung considered chemically induced ecstatic experiences to be a "foretaste" of such encounters with the Self—useful perhaps, but ultimately illegitimate and unearned, leading to ego inflation and failure of integration. He paused, then added, "But maybe a foretaste is better than no taste."

The audience responded to the quip with laughter—unearned, I felt—and he left it at that. He wasn't wrong, but the question of what counts as a "legitimate encounter" genuinely interested me, and I was disappointed that he had dealt with it so glibly. Perhaps I was already attracted to him, because afterward I went up to the podium, thanked him—somewhat archly—for the "foretaste," and suggested there was a lot more to say on the subject.

He perked right up, and the glint in his eye told me I'd read him right. He loved a challenge, so we exchanged numbers and agreed to have a drink and discuss the matter further. Over the next few weeks, I kept finding reasons to put him off—not intentionally. I was teaching; Emmy was six and had a complicated schedule of school, playdates, and babysitters who canceled at the last minute, all of which I explained over the phone. Then one afternoon he simply showed up at my office at the college, which was kind of stalkerish, but the wine he brought was excellent, as was the gorgeously illustrated book of Grimms' *Fairy Tales* he'd found for Emmy. I was on my way to pick her up, so I invited him along. When she clambered into the back seat, he handed her the book and she was overjoyed, flipping pages all the way home; by the time I came out with the wine they were already on the couch, heads together, reading. The living room was a mess, the couch covered in unfolded laundry, but he didn't seem to notice. Somehow the conversation turned to animals; he told Emmy about his turtles, how he'd had them since he was her age. He described their habits and their personalities and drew pictures of them for her. She was enchanted. When she ran over to show me the drawings, I saw the look in her eye and knew what was coming.

"Mommy, I think it would be really good for me to have a box turtle."

"I'm sure you really do think that," I said, trying to be affirming. "It's a big commitment."

"It will teach me to be responsible, right?" This last appeal was directed to Stefan, who nodded. "See! Can I get one, *pleeeease*???"

"I promise I'll think about it," I said, glaring at Stefan, who managed to look both pleased and sheepish. It made me laugh, and he laughed, and Emmy laughed too; and the three of us sat there, laughing amid the heaps of laundry. The problem of acquiring box turtles solved itself when Stefan moved in. The house somehow stayed a lot tidier after that.

Ebeneezer's first wife was Genevieve, older even than he was. She died of natural causes several months after the move. At first we couldn't tell she was dead; she had withdrawn into her shell, closed her hinged plastron, and looked like she was sleeping, but when she hadn't moved for a few days, it became clear. Stefan was devastated, and so was Emmy. It was her first encounter with death. Ebeneezer lost his joie de vivre, retreated into a corner, and refused to eat. A cloud settled over the household as my new boyfriend and my daughter tried to cheer each other—and the widowed turtle—up. I think that was when they truly bonded.

They spent hours trying to coax Ebeneezer out of his shell, plying him with mealyworms and blueberries. Finally, Emmy proposed a solution: the old turtle needed a new girlfriend. Stefan located a reptile store that sold captive-bred animals, and off they went, returning with an elegant young ornate box turtle whom Emmy named Eleanor. As soon as Ebeneezer spotted her, his spirits lifted, his appetite returned, and the two of them have lived together, more or less in harmony, for the last thirty years.

I've told Maddie this story about her mother over and over, from the time she was very little. I wanted her to know the turtles are part of a lineage she shares with Emmy, and I know I succeeded because I used to hear her explain it to her friends: "Eleanor is my mommy's turtle. Ebeneezer is my opa's. And if me and Opa take really, really good care of them, someday they'll be my turtles too. Then, after that, my kids' turtles, and their kids' turtles, and their kids' kids' turtles . . ."

It's turtles all the way down.

Maddie has no memory of Emmy, but she always understood that her mommy grew up with Eleanor and Ebeneezer, loved them, cared for them, and that it's her turn to do what her mommy once did. Now that both her mommy and her opa are gone, feeding the turtles reassures her. Sometimes, watching her talk to them, I feel she is communing with the dead. This, too, seems to run in the family.

## *7.*

Fine, I tell my dear dead husband. You're right. I'll delete the app. It's creepy. Unkind. Stalkerish. A waste of everyone's time, okay?

But when I log in to cancel my account, I can't resist one last peek, and that's when I see Boy #3. At first glance, he's like all the others, but something makes me pause before swiping him into the void. He's a nice-looking Asian boy, understated rather than flashy. His posture and attitude seem relaxed, normal, nothing special—which is exactly what makes him special. I study the photo: straight black hair, clear, dark eyes, a self-deprecating smile. He seems intelligent, an impression strengthened by his profile. The quickest way to his heart is to ask what he's reading, but only if you really want to know. He would survive a zombie apocalypse by unionizing the undead. His favorite useless fact is that there's a species of jellyfish that is biologically immortal. He judges people by their bookmarks and marginalia.

Later, at dinner, I ask Maddie, "Did you know there's a species of jellyfish that is biologically immortal?"

"Really?" She looks up from her book and reaches for her phone. And then, "Oh my god, you're right!" She reads aloud: "'*Turritopsis dohrnii.* A small, biologically immortal jellyfish found worldwide in temperate to tropical waters.' How did I not know this?"

Maddie loves jellyfish. She prides herself on knowing everything about the things she loves, and this omission annoys her. She reads on in silence.

"Are you going to enlighten me?"

"It's complicated," she says. "Basically, it can revert its adult cells to a younger polyp stage when it's threatened or gets old—so it starts life over again, indefinitely."

"Useful trick."

"But even though technically they're immortal, they can still get sick or be eaten. They just don't die of old age."

"Still," I say. "I wish I could do that."

She looks up and frowns. "You're just not trying hard enough."

• • •

I can't decide what book to bring, and Stefan is no help—he feels distant today, probably because he disapproves of what I'm doing. I'm tempted to give up and ghost the boy, but a small cap of psilocybin gets me out the door. I'm late. When I reach Starbucks, Boy #3 is already there—sitting at my usual corner table by the weird plant as if he's waiting for me. He looks up when I come in; I turn quickly away. All the other tables are taken by young people on their devices, so I stand there looking like a befuddled old lady—which, at this moment, is exactly what I am. Soon, though, this starts to seem silly, so I stride to the counter and order a drink. "To stay," I tell the cashier, out of habit, and by the time I realize this is a mistake she's already serving the next person. I retreat to the end of the counter to wait for my order. My latte arrives in a hot ceramic mug that requires two hands to hold, and now I'm stuck, because I can't just walk out with it. I consider asking for a to-go cup, but the mushroom has made me bold, so I carry the mug to the nearest unoccupied chair—at my table—where Boy #3 is seated, reading a book.

"Excuse me," I say. "Would you mind if I sit here? There aren't any empty tables."

"Actually," he says, "I'm waiting for someone."

"Oh, never mind then."

But by now he's registered my presence, and because he's a well-brought-up boy who's been taught to respect his elders, he rises halfway, reaches across the table, and pushes out the chair. "No, I'm sorry. Please."

"But your friend," I say.

"It's fine. I don't think she's coming, and if she does . . ." He leaves the sentence hanging.

She won't, I think. I demur, but he insists, so I thank him and sit. This is not at all what I expected, but still. I sip my coffee and open my bag. The book I brought is a collection of stories by the wonderful Scottish writer Janice Galloway, whom I met at a literary festival in Edinburgh. I love her work, but I chose this one entirely for its cover: a plain brown background with translucent, seaweed-like fronds hanging from the top and, in bold red letters, *Jellyfish.* Now, facing Boy #3, the choice feels a little on the nose, but I can't just sit there empty-handed, so I open it quickly before he can see the title.

He's gone back to his own reading. Every time the door opens he looks up, and it's like watching unsettled weather: his face brightens briefly like the sun before clouding over when he sees it's not Lexy. I remember his profile then: his so-called secret talent was an inability to lie (not a secret at all, he'd written, because his face turns bright red when he tries). He checks the time on his phone, notices me watching, and gives me a small, rueful smile.

"Guess I've been ghosted," he says.

"Maybe your friend is just running late?" I offer.

"She's not really a friend. I was hoping she would be, but . . ."

"I'm sorry," I say.

"It happens."

"You're very philosophical about it."

"Ghosts," he says. "You know."

"I do." And then, in my most sincere voice, as if I truly care, I ask what he's reading; and sure enough he brightens again and shows me his book, which is, of all things, a battered copy of Chekhov stories. I ask if he's studying literature at the university; he says no—he's premed, but he audits lit classes when he can—and now he's studying me.

"You look familiar," he says. "Do you teach at the university?"

"No." It's not a lie, since I've been retired for years. And even if it were, he would never know. I'm a good liar. It's my job.

"Huh. I know I've seen you someplace. I've got a good memory for faces." His gaze circles the room as if searching for a clue and lands on my book. "What are you reading?"

Because he, too, sounds like he genuinely wants to know, I show him the cover.

"Jellyfish?" he says. "That's so random! I'm really into jellyfish. Did you know there's a species that's biologically immortal?"

"*Turritopsis dohrnii*?" I ask, hoping I've remembered the Latin.

He leans back, impressed. "Wow."

"My granddaughter," I say. "You'd like her. She knows everything about jellyfish. I pick it up by osmosis."

"Is that book about jellyfish?" he asks.

I slide it across the table to him. "Not exactly. It's a collection of short fiction. 'Jellyfish' is the title of one story."

"Is the story about jellyfish?"

"Not really. There are jellyfish in it. Dead ones, on a beach."

"Oh." He's already studying my extensive marginalia. I do that—have long conversations with the author and the characters, ask questions, lodge complaints, share whatever notions arise in my mind as I read. Sometimes I cram so many words into the margins that the ink is darker and denser there than on the printed part of the page, sentences twining around the edges like serpents, so you have to rotate the book to follow them around.

He is doing just that when he realizes, mid-spin, that reading a stranger's marginalia without consent might be a boundary violation. "I'm sorry," he says, sliding the book back to me.

"It's okay," I say.

"It's cool that you do that," he says, pointing at the margins.

"I think of books as conversations," I say, aware that I'm quoting myself. "With readers. With other books. Taking place across vast expanses of space and time." That's from the lecture I used to give to my creative writing students in the first class of a new semester.

He looks intrigued, which is all the encouragement I need.

"Books are like a rhizomatic network—a vast, subconscious

fungal mat that spreads beneath human consciousness, knitting the world of thought together . . ."

Or something like that.

I stop myself. The microdose was perhaps not as micro as I had thought.

"You sound like a professor," he says accusingly, or perhaps that is my paranoia kicking in.

"I was," I confess, and he nods.

"That's cool. I've never thought about books that way."

He's pondering what I've said, and I watch him. I like this Boy #3. He's thoughtful. Smart. A bit too old for Maddie, but maybe in a few years? A book-loving doctor would be a fine addition to the family. And Chekhov, no less.

"Do you like fungi?" he asks. "I do. Did you know there's a zombie fungus that colonizes ants and takes over their minds?"

"It sounds familiar. My granddaughter may have mentioned it. There's a TV show based on it, right?"

"A video game, too, but the real-life fungus is way cooler. It colonizes the ant's body, then it makes the ant march around until it finds a location where the conditions are perfect for fungal spore growth. It's super precise. When it finds the right spot, it makes the ant climb up a plant and bite down on a leaf. The fungus controls the ant's mandibles, so it can't let go. The ant just hangs there until it dies, and then the fungus explodes from its head."

"Why on earth . . . ?"

"Sporulation," he says, savoring the word. "The fungus sends up this weird stemlike thing called a fruiting body from the top of the ant's head and releases its spores. It's sick." He sits back and smiles.

"It's horrifying," I say.

"It's life."

He's right, of course, but still. "Are you studying fungi?"

"Plant chemistry," he says. "There's a lot of interest in fungi these days. *O. unilateralis* has some cool medicinal properties for immunotherapy. Antibacterial and anticancer agents. Stuff like that."

My impression of Boy #3 is changing rapidly, and a terrible thought crosses my mind. "Wait, are you saying books are like zombie fungus colonizing people's minds?"

"Maybe," he grins. "Or writers are." He lowers his voice to a sinister whisper. "*The fungus among us . . .*"

It's a writer's worst nightmare, and the mushroom in me is not helping, amplifying my paranoia and making my head throb. He catches my expression, and his face softens with concern.

"I'm just kidding," he says. "Are you okay?" I nod and swallow. Then his eyes widen. "Hey, I know who you are!"

The edges of things start to dissolve. I need to get out fast. I shove *Jellyfish* into my bag and reach for my coat.

He leans forward across the table. "You're that writer, aren't you?"

"No," I say, pushing back my chair to stand. "You must be thinking of someone else."

"I'm sure it's you!" he says. "I read that novel you wrote—the one about the kid who hears things and talks to books? My roommate gave it to me. I really liked it!"

Looking down at his bright, sunny face, I take a deep breath and my paranoia recedes, dispelled by the warmth of his praise. A soft nimbus of light gathers around him, and as I watch, a slender fruiting body sprouts from the top of his head, only it's made up of words—a long, sinuous sentence twining into all the white space of the margins. I can't make out what it says, but it's profound and beautiful. Isn't it? *Yes*, Stefan says. *But this is not the time or place. You have to behave like an adult.*

Okay, I tell him, and we watch the words disperse. I smile at the boy. "Yes, you're right. I am. And thank you."

"Are you writing any new books?" he asks, as if writers could sporulate like fungi.

"No," I say. My new book is a collection of short fiction called *Dancing with the Shadows*. I don't want to talk about it.

"My roommate's not going to believe this," he says. "You're like his favorite writer."

I ask him to give the roommate my regards and then tell him I have to run. "Thanks for sharing your table," I add. "I'm sorry your friend never came."

"Whatever!" he says. "This is way better. Hey, can I take your picture?"

He's already got his phone out. "It's for my roommate," he explains.

I feel guilty, but I hate having my picture taken, so I raise a hand to block my face. "I'm really sorry, Matt," I say, trying to make a joke of it and moving toward the exit. "There's no point. I don't show up in photographs."

He looks confused, then disappointed, then confused again, and I realize what I've just let slip. "Hey, wait," he calls. "How did you know my—"

The closing door cuts off his question, so I don't have to answer.

## 8.

The cancer that colonized my daughter's body first showed itself as a tumor in her left breast. The initial diagnosis was delayed because of the pregnancy and the normal physiological changes in the breast tissue. Emmy had always had small breasts and was pleased to see them growing larger. Francis liked them, too, she confessed shyly one day, when we were shopping for maternity clothes. I wish she hadn't told me. Afterward I couldn't stop picturing him "liking" her breasts. I've never forgiven him for that.

Radiation and chemotherapy were ruled out because of the danger they posed to the fetus. The oncologist urged an immediate double mastectomy—the left essential, the right prophylactic—but there was no sign of disease in the second breast and she wanted to keep it so she could nurse. Perhaps that was a mistake. Perhaps waiting to start chemotherapy until after the delivery was a mistake. Or perhaps there were no mistakes at all; micrometastases had already started colonizing her liver and lungs.

Her labor was long and brutal, and after more than twenty hours she delivered my granddaughter flawlessly. I'll never forget the sight of that tiny body lying naked across her mother's fresh pink scar.

I was in the room when the baby latched for the first time. "She's doing it, Mom," Emmy gasped. "Look! We're doing it!" Those big, fat tears of hers rolled down her cheeks. One landed on the soft crown of Maddie's head. Emmy bent and licked it away and laughed. I never saw her happier.

She nursed from that remaining breast for a little over a month, until her milk dwindled and the coughing began. Imaging confirmed the spread; she consented to chemo, but her health deteriorated rapidly after that. She was in so much pain. Francis couldn't manage a newborn and a dying wife, so we brought Emmy and Maddie home and set them up in the downstairs spare bedroom so she wouldn't have to contend with the stairs. We rented a hospital bed; Maddie's crib stood beside it. It was like old times, only now there were four of us. I don't remember Francis being there much, though Stefan assured me he came most days. Perhaps that's true, and I've just edited him out of my memory.

That was when Stefan began growing psilocybin. He'd long been interested in psychotropic medicine and had been reading the Johns Hopkins studies with terminal cancer patients—carefully guided trips that helped the dying come to terms with mortality, whatever that might mean. Emmy, newly postpartum, was in agony about her imminent death, grief-stricken and sunk in guilt about abandoning her baby. She blamed herself.

I was horrified when Stefan told me what he had in mind. I remember hissing at him—quietly, so as not to wake Emmy and the baby—that I would not let him use my daughter as a guinea pig in some Mengelean experiment. Harsh, I know, but I was distraught. Emmy took matters into her own hands. She told me I was infantilizing her and being unfair to Stefan, who knew what he was doing. She trusted him completely and, by then, needed him more than she needed me. I cannot pretend that did not hurt. She and Stefan conferred at length—how and when and where to conduct the sessions—and, once I had calmed down, they let me help. She wanted to be upstairs in her childhood bedroom. She wanted Maddie there, so I bought a bedside bassinet and set it beside the little twin bed. She chose the music; I made the playlist. I brought flowers, a cooler, a changing table, a tower of diapers. I washed the sheets and curtains and scrubbed that room on my hands and knees with organic, nontoxic, scent-free cleaners.

There were three sessions, each lasting six or seven hours. I helped them get settled and then dimmed the lights and stepped out, positioning myself in the hallway on the tiny wooden chair Emmy used as a child. I wanted to be ready to take the baby if she cried—she never did, and Stefan handled the feeding and changing. There was nothing for me to do but sit there and listen to the murmur of their voices: my husband's low and steady; my daughter's tense, angry, spiraling up the octaves until it broke into sobs—then, gradually, long silences, punctuated by sighs and sometimes even laughter.

I don't think I've ever felt so alone. Sometimes I drifted off. I paced the hallway to keep the blood from pooling in my legs. But I never left my post, as if being there, guarding the closed door, might hold off the worst. Then, about five hours into the third and final session, I was dozing in that hard little chair when the bedroom door opened. I woke with a start. Stefan stood in the doorway looking down at me.

"What's wrong?" I gasped, sitting up in a panic. He shook his head and smiled and held out his hand.

"She wants you," he whispered, and he pulled me to my feet and led me back to my daughter.

• • •

Francis was not told about any of this until the sessions were over, and by then the change in Emmy was obvious to everyone but him. She was still grieving, but somewhere deep in her body she had accepted that death was real and really happening; she was able to let go and relax into every precious moment she had left. She was more like her old self, calm and loving. Her sense of humor returned.

Francis assumed she was high, of course. He called us criminally irresponsible—drugged-out hippies—and threatened to call the police, have us arrested, and have Stefan's license revoked. I was not surprised, only disappointed by his lack of vision. I'd expected more from someone who teaches at a business school, and I told him so. Surely he could see the value proposition here: psilocybin as an end-of-life therapeutic, a monetization opportunity with enormous growth potential and an ever-renewing customer base; untapped end-of-life verticals awaiting brand activation; a beyond-the-horizon market in the truest sense—I was on a roll. Francis didn't think this was funny, but Emmy thought it was hilarious. She laughed until she cried; Francis, as usual, did nothing.

## 9.

I walk quickly away from the Starbucks in case the boy—Matt—decides to follow. There is no way to explain how I knew his name, and I'm furious with myself for the slip. In the car, breathing hard, I'm exhilarated to have escaped but also ashamed. Matt was a good kid. A sweet kid. A reader. I liked him. He shared Maddie's interest in jellyfish and had a mind full of random interesting facts. Would that make him a reliable provider? Of course not, and yet there I was, like a pimp, sizing up a john. What was I thinking? I check the app—no messages. I feel terrible about ghosting him—first as Lexy, then as me—and I wonder if he'll figure out what happened. I delete Lexy's profile and cancel the account. I hope he's not upset.

I need to leave, but I'm feeling unsteady and wonder if it's wise for me to drive. It crosses my mind that a fatal crash will solve the book tour problem, but I can't do that to Maddie, who has lost enough already. I can't abandon her until she's through college—possibly grad school—has settled down with someone decent and established herself in a stable career with excellent health insurance and retirement benefits. Naïve, yes, in this calamitous world, but still: I have to stick around to keep her company. My hands are shaking, but I start the car and head toward home. At the Coolidge Bridge I pull into the parking lot that overlooks the Connecticut River.

I sit a long while above the dark river, thinking about everything my granddaughter has lost and reliving Emmy's death in my mind. Maddie doesn't know the particulars, of course. She knows her mom died of cancer—nothing more—though she was there during every hour of those final days, asleep in her bassinet or cradled weakly in Emmy's stick-thin arms. She was there during the sessions, too, in that darkened room with the flowers and music, listening while Stefan walked her mother through the shadow of death toward an imperfect but adequate acceptance. Emmy was grateful; so was I. She had nearly three peaceful months before she went. Then years passed. Stefan and I never spoke about the details in front of Maddie—not to hide them, but because we both knew that there is a time and place for every story. We'd tell her if and when she asked.

I don't know why I'm thinking all this now. Maybe it's the mushroom. After Stefan died I started microdosing when I was lonely; it made him feel nearer. He grew the mushrooms, after all, tended them, loved them, so perhaps they absorbed some part of him—the careful, caring part. *Psilocybe stefanensis.* After Emmy died, he branched out into lion's mane and oyster mushrooms that we used for cooking, but every so often he would raise a small batch of the hallucinogens. Not a lot, but enough so we could take them once or twice a year on special occasions, like a spring afternoon when the cherry trees were in bloom or a scintillating fall day when the leaves were turning color, before they fell. We would set our two folding chairs on the little upstairs deck and sit there, side by side, holding hands for hours. Sometimes we talked, but mostly we just watched the golden leaves trembling in the wind and the migrating birds flying south across the bright blue sky. The cul-de-sac below was usually empty; when someone did pass, we fell silent. Hidden up there, we could see everything, and the smallest thing felt miraculous. I tried to keep his fungi farm going after he was gone, but I never had the knack for it, and when Maddie moved in, I let the psilocybin die. The cap I took today was the last of them. For the first time it hits me—really hits me—that Stefan is gone.

My forehead is pressed against the top of the steering wheel, and I realize I'm crying. The realization only makes me cry harder. I'm not much of a crier. I didn't cry when Stefan died, or at Emmy's funeral, and I felt guilty both times. The last time I remember was during that final session in Emmy's darkened bedroom, but we were all crying then. While infant Maddie made happy cooing noises in her bassinet, the three of us held each other and wept.

After a while I sit up, wipe my face, and look out past the bridge to the river. From here the dark water hardly seems to be moving. The trees along the riverbank look dead, though if I squint there's the faintest haze of green, which may just be from my tears. This is where I would have left the car the night I went ice fishing, before falling through the neat round hole into the frigid water. I picture the red mitten Maddie offered to knit, frozen fast to the ice.

I roll down the window. The air is softening now, and the ice is starting to melt. Maddie taught herself to knit during the pandemic and got quite good at mittens. She's a smart, kind, competent girl, and given my somewhat agitated state I should probably consider calling her to come get me and drive me home. But I don't call. I'm already feeling steadier, and I've always insisted on being the strong one. Aside from those winter walks when I pretend to be afraid of slipping on the ice, I've never asked her to do more than small household chores—she washes the dishes and folds the laundry and feeds the turtles and sometimes picks up groceries. She enjoys helping, and it occurs to me that maybe I should let her help with the larger things, too, especially now that Stefan is gone. She likes being the strong one, after all. Why deprive her of that?

Suddenly, I am overwhelmed with gratitude at how lucky I am to have a granddaughter like her. Yes, I worry about her future, but I'm also confident that she will manage whatever life throws her way, and I need to tell her so before the feeling passes. I dial her number, forgetting our phone protocol—calls are only for emergencies. She answers before I can hang up.

"Moony, what's wrong? Where are you? Are you okay?"

"I'm fine," I say. "Nothing's wrong."

"Then why are you calling me?"

"No reason. I just wanted to hear your voice. I'm sorry if I scared you."

"Don't do that!" she says, scolding. "Are you sure you're all right? Where are you?"

"By the bridge. Looking at the river. The ice is breaking up."

There's a pause while she remembers the ice-fishing story, remembers the problem of the body. Then: "Do you want me to come get you? Do you need a lift to the airport?"

I understand I'm forgiven and laugh. "I'm fine," I say again. "I'm sorry, darling. I'll be home soon."

"Drive safely," she says. "Oh—and can you stop at the bait shop? We're almost out of worms."

I pull back onto the road, then onto the highway. As I accelerate, a gust of warm air from the open window buffets my face, and I remember the two endings to our ice-fishing story: I can either be the dead author holed up in a Spanish villa, churning out "posthumous" novels, or the mysterious blond cousin smoking a cigarette as she speeds north to Canada. Maddie, who likes fantasy, would choose the villa, but I'm more of a realist, and the mysterious cousin is more appealing to me. Easier to imagine. Gloriously untethered.

# Acknowledgments

First, my thanks to the authors, artists, editors, and friends who invited me to write the stories that seeded this collection: Jessica Hagedorn for "Ships in the Night"; Chandra Prasad for "The Anthropologist's Kid"; Marina Zurkow for "Immortal"; Susan Squier for "The Death of the Last White Male"; and Hanya Yanagihara and Thessaly La Force for "Where Ambition Goes to Die." These stories were prompted by a vision you had. Thanks to you, they made their way into the world, and now they're coming home to roost under one roof with their new flock.

Thanks to my generous friends and early readers: Heather Abel, Miles Bond, Liz Gaudet, and Katie Young—your keen eyes, quick minds, and big hearts improve my writing and enrich my life. Thanks to Adrienne Brodeur and Carole DeSanti, my stalwart shipmates, who have stood watch beside me whilst storm-tossed or becalmed. And particular thanks to Karen Joy

Fowler for Occam's razor, our long friendship, and your liberatory vision.

Thanks to my students, whose hard work and talent rekindled my love for the short story form. They say the best way to learn something is to try to teach it; teaching you was my excuse, my occasion, and my joy.

Thanks to my amazing agents and dear friends at Family Friedrich: Molly Friedrich and Lucy Carson, Marin Takikawa, Heather Carr, and Alex Greulich. Your invaluable feedback, support, and wise counsel throughout the evolution of this collection have helped it grow and find its way. Thanks to Caspian Dennis at Abner Stein for your friendship and tireless advocacy abroad. Thanks to my assistant Molly Zakoor for keeping me on track and unerringly finding the best of the best.

At Viking US, I am unbelievably lucky to have Ibrahim Ahmad as my editor. Thank you, Ibrahim, for the care, precision, and poetry you bring to the editorial process—what a joy it is to work with you. My thanks to Brian Tart, Kate Stark, Andrea Schulz, Tricia Conley, Matt Giarratano, and Patrick Nolan for the warmth and ongoing support of my books that has made me a "lifer." It's inconceivable how much work goes into bringing a book into the world, and I am grateful to all who make this happen: Carolyn Coleburn and Yuleza Negron in publicity; Anna Brill in marketing; Bridget Gilleran in subsidiary rights; Jason Ramirez in art; Alexis Sulaimani in design; Lavina Lee in production editorial; production manager Katelyn MacKenzie; and assistant editor Elizabeth Pham Janowski. Thank you to Diane McKiernan for producing my audiobooks, and to Maureen Monterubio for your inspiring direction.

At Viking Canada, my heartfelt thanks to executive editor Deborah Sun de la Cruz, Curtis Samuel in publicity, managing editor Alanna McMullen, and production manager Brittany Larkin.

At Canongate in the UK, I am so grateful to work with the incomparable Jamie Byng and Jenny Fry; thank you for the boundless energy, creativity, and goodwill that you bring to the publishing adventure. Thank you to Rosamund Hutchison in publicity; Jamie Norman in marketing; managing editor Louise Tyler; Rebecca Bonallie in production, and editorial assistant Claire Ion. Thank you (and congratulations!) to Anna Frame. And very special thanks to the brilliant Gill Heeley, whose cover designs capture and convey the heart of my books.

And, Oliver. Always and forever, my love and thanks to you for sharing this precious human life.

Grateful acknowledgment is made for permission to reprint the following:

"One Art" from *Poems* by Elizabeth Bishop. Copyright © 2011 by The Alice H. Methfessel Trust. Publisher's Note and compilation copyright © 2011 by Farrar, Straus and Giroux. Reprinted by permission of Farrar, Straus and Giroux. All rights reserved.

Excerpts from "Howl" from *Collected Poems: 1947–1980* by Allen Ginsberg. Copyright © 1984 by Allen Ginsberg. Used by permission of HarperCollins Publishers.

The following stories have been published previously, some in slightly different form:

"The Anthropologist's Kid" (as "The Anthropologists' Kids") was first published in *Mixed: An Anthology of Short Fiction on the Multiracial Experience*, edited by Chandra Prasad, W. W. Norton, 2006.

"Immortal" was first published *in Petroleum Manga: A Project* by Marina Zurkow, punctum books, 2014.

"Death of the Last White Male" was first published in *Configurations: A Journal of Literature, Science, and Technology*, volume 14, number 1–2, Winter–Spring 2006.

"Ships in the Night" by Ruth Ozeki Lounsbury, copyright © 2004 by Ruth Ozeki Lounsbury first published in *Charlie Chan Is Dead 2: At Home in the World (An Anthology of Contemporary Asian American Fiction—Revised and Updated)*, edited by Jessica Hagedorn. Used by permission of Penguin Books, an imprint of Penguin Publishing Group, a division of Penguin Random House LLC. All rights reserved.

"Where Ambition Goes to Die" (as "The Spirits of Abandoned Ambitions") was first published in *T: The New York Times Style Magazine*, 2020. Copyright © 2025 by Ruth Ozeki and The New York Times Company.